WINTER
OMENS

WINTER
OMENS

TRISHA LEIGH

*For Grandpa Martin, who made me feel as though
being me was a pretty special thing*

1.

I guess when we travel on our own we don't magically wake up tucked into our beds in clean pajamas. Instead, my filthy shoes grind Danbury dirt into the carpet of my Des Moines bedroom. The same wet, dirty clothes I've worn all day—or yesterday, whenever—cling to my clammy skin. The pride and novelty I felt at finally having control over hopping seasons fills me for a moment, and then vanish quickly as I remember the new note in my locket:

> Althea—
> Lucas is safe. We will help in any way we
> can. You need to run.
> —Cadi

Desperation over losing Lucas rushes over me as the memory of his dimpled smile, careless blond curls, and protective arms threatens to undo me. I shove it all into my center; giving up is the one way to ensure I'll never see him again.

Cadi says to run, but if I can't stay here with the Clarks, where can I go?

It doesn't matter. She and Ko have never led me astray.

The bag I packed to run away with Lucas is nowhere to be seen, so I fill a new one with the warmest clothes in the closet. Winter is settling in and this is Iowa; it must be freezing outside. Once that's done, I sneak across the beige carpet and crack open the bedroom door, greeted by a silent blackness. The door to the linen closet in the hallway creaks slightly, causing me to wince and freeze. Nothing stirs; not a sound comes from the Clarks' room downstairs. My winter family is asleep, like normal humans after midnight.

I grab three blankets, resisting the urge to take the whole stack, and reposition the rest so a glance won't show that some are missing. The longer no one realizes anything is amiss the better. It won't take them long. The Others are smart and there are only so many places to look.

Back in my room, I assess my options. I take a deep breath as my mother's disembodied voice bursts into my mind, pushing aside my own thoughts.

Run, Althea.

It urges haste, and after the events of the past months I'm not inclined to argue with her.

The blankets barely fit in the bag with the clothes, and after I add some toothpaste, a toothbrush, shampoo, and deodorant to the pile I have to sit on it to tug the zipper shut. Down in the kitchen, I prowl through the pantry and grab as much nonperishable food as I can find in the dark. My fingers race along the shelves, filching cans of vegetables, soup, and a couple bags of pasta. I dump the lot into a second bag and add six bottles of water to the top.

I slip through the empty living room, past photographs of me huddled with the Clarks on Outings to the local skating pond. I'm trussed up like a marshmallow in most of them, head and hands covered with thick woolen garments. They never provide enough warmth. Nothing does. Even though fire simmers inside me, and last autumn I even began to control it a little, I'm always cold. It's as though my center attracts the heat, sucking it inward and leaving my extremities constantly on ice.

My heavy winter coat hangs in the front closet as if I'd left it there after Cell, even though I haven't been back to Iowa for months. I slip it on, finding my hat and mittens in the pockets. My mother's voice grows impatient with my stalling, pressing harder and harder against my mind. The idea of stepping out of the warm house and into the bitter wind, not knowing when I'll find shelter again, fills me with dread.

I have to go, though. I know it deep in my bones. If I can find a place to hide outside the boundary before morning I might even have a chance. Not to escape forever—that's impossible—but to live another day. Maybe even get back to Lucas.

A blast of cold air nearly knocks me over as I crack open the door and my lungs constrict, trying to reject the frigid oxygen. Icy fingers squeeze my chest as I force myself to breathe deep through my nose. Pools of light from the streetlamps don't quite reach the rows of houses, leaving the porch bathed in darkness. The sidewalks are barren as I hustle down the quickest path to the park. Thoughts of Lucas bombard me, pushing tears down my cheeks where they freeze around my mouth and chin. The park reminds me of him, of what happened last night when we almost escaped together. The note says he's safe, but even if he were safe when it was written it doesn't mean he still is. He's going to be running, like me. Hunted. Alone.

The park is full of ominous shadows cast by the bare branches as they sway in the bitter wind. The frozen ground muffles my footsteps as I make my way to the boundary. I've got to get out of the city, but don't know how to accomplish the feat. There's not time to explore every inch of the fence the way Lucas and I did, hoping to find a gap in the electricity. We were able to

10

climb over a dead section of the woven metal, but I found that spot by accident.

I study the electrified ten-foot boundary, at a loss.

Run, Althea. Now! My mother's voice shouts in my mind.

Shut up. I'm thinking. Better yet, go away.

Before last autumn, when I learned that my mother is Fire—an Element, one of the four most powerful Others—the encouraging voice in my mind soothed me. But the idea that she has access to my brain clangs warning bells through me despite the pull toward wanting to know her. Right now, getting out of Des Moines takes precedence over the confliction I feel about my dubious parentage. She's distracting me, and my frozen forehead crinkles as I try to focus on the problem at hand. The fences that border our cities are made of metal, so in theory it could melt, I guess. The high-temperature heat that flows through my body would be more than enough to set a pile of leaves on fire, or even one of my precious blankets. If it burned hot enough under the boundary it could soften a hole big enough to crawl through.

It would leave such an obvious trail, though, that I discard the idea. Damaging the fence isn't an option if I want my fraction of a head start to remain intact.

A memory pummels me, unbidden, accompanied by Lucas's heart-stopping smile:

"... *I saw you wandering by yourself near the boundary every day last week.*"

"*You saw me? How?*"

"*From the trees. You never look up, you know.*"

That's it.

Saying silent thanks and wishing he could hear me, I turn my eyes upward and peruse the tree line. Maybe a hundred yards away an ancient oak stands near the electric fence, its thick, leafless branches hovering over freedom, however temporary. I grimace at its height. I've never climbed a tree. In my sixteen-plus years on Earth I've never even *wanted* to climb a tree. But there's no time like the present to figure it out.

I stand underneath it and make an effort to calm the butterflies flapping in my belly. They're nowhere near as uncomfortable as the flock that attacks with Lucas's kisses, but they're annoying all the same. A deep breath helps. The guts to do this are in there. I injured an Other last night. I hid from the Wardens and saved Lucas from the Prime's son, the one they call Chief. I can climb a stupid tree.

A strong toss sends my bags sailing up and over the fence; they land with a dull thud on the opposite side. I turn back and face my new nemesis, stowing my mittens back in my pockets. Oak tree, meet Althea, daughter of Fire. I shall conquer you.

I swipe my red hair out of my face and pull myself up on some low-hanging branches. There are plenty of strong ones within reach, but even though the climb isn't difficult, my limbs shake violently, making it harder than it has to be. Still, the only major problem arises after I crawl out on a long branch to make my escape . . . when I look down.

The ground spins as my fingers clutch the tree, pointed pieces of bark jabbing the tender skin under my nails. I close my eyes and count to ten. When I open them, the world has stopped moving. My knees move inch by inch and, after what feels like hours, I reach the end. The boundary passed under me five feet back. I gauge the distance to the ground. At least twenty feet.

Maybe I didn't quite think this through.

Voices filter through the still night and freeze me in place. Men. Several, by the sound of it. I can't see their perfect faces or feel the stabbing pain that accompanies the sight of them, but their tones are melodious and sweet, oozing across my eardrums like globs of maple syrup.

Others.

Probably Wardens. A quick peek over my shoulder reveals weak flashlight beams penetrating the inkiness.

Their appearance makes up my mind, and I jump.

2.

Cold wind whistles past my cheeks as the ground rushes up to meet me. I force my limbs to go limp before smashing into the ground. Pain shoots up my right leg. A flash of light bursts behind my eyes and a whimper escapes no matter how hard I bite my lip in an attempt for silence. Tears course down my numb cheeks.

The flashlight beams probe the night; the men's voices get clearer. "I don't think they'll be in the park. It's too cold."

The Others don't know Lucas and I are separated. Which means they're not sure where we are, or in which of our four home bases we've landed.

It's a small comfort at the moment, but I'll take it.

"How do you know, Gagej? Can you read crazy, half-breed minds now?"

"No. I'm just saying. We would have seen them already. And it's freezing out here."

I don't wait to hear the rest of the conversation, sensing the need to get out of flashlight range and hide myself among the dense trees. Snowflakes start to drift down, not sticking to the ground yet but darkening my mood. I rise from the matted brown grass, putting weight on my sore leg little by little. I taste blood before I realize I'm still biting my lip to hold back the screams. Lightning bolts of pain grind into my leg muscles like shards of glass. Not good.

Have to move. No choice.

At least my footprints can't be seen in the hard earth. They won't be so easy to hide, though, if the snow keeps coming. The wind howls, racing around me and through the forest ahead, tugging me forward and making it impossible to hear any more of the Wardens' chatter. I don't look back, just focus on my destination. The tree line sits a mere thirty feet away, but with the pain in my leg it seems much farther. The bags, heavier than they felt twenty minutes ago, embed a throbbing ache in my shoulder and back. Black spots dance in front of my eyes and nausea bubbles up from my stomach, but I make it to cover, grabbing on to the nearest tree trunk and using it to hide my body.

I resist the urge to collapse, worried that getting upright again will prove an insurmountable task. The tree braces my weight as I peer around it, resting my cheek on its rough bark. The Wardens' flashlights shine toward the woods, light from the beams thinning out ten feet short of the trees. I hold my breath, wishing with all my might for them to stay on their side of the fence.

"You think we should check the forest?"

A deeper voice answers the first. "No. They said to check the boundary for signs of a breach, that's all."

"They won't survive long in this weather. Chief's got Apa whipping up a blizzard, I hear."

Apa is the name of the Other I've always known as Water. He's Lucas's father, and together with my mother, along with Pamant and Vant—Earth and Air— they are the four Elements that the humans believe rule this planet. Last season, though, Lucas and I learned the Elements are imprisoned, trapped and controlled as much as every human on Earth, by the Prime Other. The true leader.

The weak beams swing away from me and the Wardens' voices disappear into nothingness. Relief at their departure is replaced by an immediate fear.

I've left the city boundary. Now what?

As the adrenaline from my close call fades, the pain settling in my ankle and foot resurfaces with throbbing intensity. I ignore it as best as I can and struggle deeper into the Wilds. I don't have a specific idea what I'm looking for, all I know is I haven't found it yet. Some kind of shelter.

Stupid Water. Lucas's father is going to cause me a mess of trouble with a blizzard. It was probably all Deshi's idea.

No, he's not Deshi. The boy who tried to capture us is the Prime's son, that's all I know. He never told us his real name once he dropped the disguise. The Others call him Chief. It turns my stomach to think of him right now, dredging up the memory of last night, when he tortured Lucas, then tried to kill us both to prevent our escape.

The absence of Lucas, the only real friend I've ever had, brings fresh tears and a new awareness of the black, writhing loneliness settled in my gut. I want more than ever to give in, to sit and cry, but I can't. I drop the bags from my shoulder when the ache in my muscles becomes unbearable, tugging them along the forest floor behind me. They leave a slight trail in the dusting of snow crusting the frozen blades of grass.

The night starts to lighten, tones of gray smudging out the black while more snowflakes join the two or so inches now gathered at my feet. My eyes have been fixed on the ground for so long I almost miss the clapboard structure when it rises out of the early morning. It's small and brown, the wooden exterior sagging in all the wrong places. The building looks like I feel—defeated and frozen. Still, the roof is intact. No

18

door at the front, but a ginger step over the threshold offers immediate relief from the wind. It reminds me of the nook in the tree in Connecticut, the one that hid me the night I saved Lucas from— I push the memory away with renewed ferocity. *Not yet.*

The place is as small as it looks from the outside, just one boxed-shaped room I could cross in either direction in less than ten steps. It looks forgotten, making me feel better about staying here. If the Others ever knew it existed, it's no longer on their radar. And why would it be? No one leaves town. Humans don't cross the boundary.

No furniture clutters the room; it's bare except for empty shelves and a barren rack of some sort lining the walls. Two dirt-caked windows, one cracked and the other missing about half the glass, sit in the same wall as the door. A strange black metal box rests under the half-empty window, a thick, round pipe running from the top of it through the roof. Some of the floorboards are rotted through and the wet, packed dirt underneath pushes into the room.

I dump the bags on the ground and glance at my leg. My jeans are stretched abnormally tight from my knee down to my ankle but I'm not ready to face the sight of my injury just yet. Shivers clatter my teeth as I unzip my duffel bag and yank out a couple of blankets.

I throw one on the floor and wrap the other tight around my shoulders.

Good sense hits before I sit to inspect my leg. I should build a fire. These blankets aren't going to be enough warmth, not with a blizzard blowing up to the nonexistent door of my newfound shelter. I've never started a fire with the express purpose of warming myself, but I've also never been trapped alone in a drafty building in the middle of an Iowa snowstorm.

I glance over at the rotted place in the floor and chew on my finger. If I line it with rocks and clear a big enough hole, maybe I won't burn the whole place down.

I really don't want to burn the whole place down.

The floor is weak in the corner by the hole, and it doesn't take more than a few minutes to pry up several boards until the hole grows to about three feet long and wide. Satisfied, I wander outside, wincing with every step. On the back side of the building is a small clearing leading to a stream. I'd take time to appreciate the crisp smell in the air, or enjoy the babble of flowing water over rocks, but the snow falls harder every minute. The earth huddles under an endless white blanket. Soon, the water will freeze.

The obscured sun climbs higher as I haul enough good-sized stones from the bank of the creek to line my fire pit. My eyes cloud over from the pain and fatigue at least once a trip and I have to stop to keep from toppling to the ground. I venture deeper into the trees to gather sticks, making three more trips in and out as the sun rises above the horizon. I don't know how long the snow is going to keep up, so I should be prepared to hunker down for a few days. Unless the Wardens show up first.

A stoic pair of eyes—one blue, one brown—meets mine as I straighten up from gathering one final load, nearly killing me with shock.

A wolf blocks my path, its thick black-and-white coat hardly visible in the snowdrift. This is the first time I've seen one in person, of course, but it looks exactly like the textbook photographs.

Breathe.

I stand frozen in place, not wanting to alarm it. The memory of the deer in the forest outside Danbury, how our presence frightened it, does little to comfort me. After all, deer are herbivores and wolves are cold-blooded killers. Even though animals are not allowed within city boundaries, we learn enough about them to know *that*. Although I suspect now that we're taught the worst possible aspects of wildlife in order to reinforce our contentment under the Others' control.

As I watch, the wolf loses interest in me and wanders into the trees.

Even if I could run, there's nowhere to go. No time to find another place to shelter during the storm. Instead I limp a few feet at a time, holding one of the longer sticks out in front of me. I know it's no protection against the wolf's fangs, but I feel better brandishing a weapon. Every time I stop I hold my breath and look around, blinking away the snowflakes alighting on my eyelashes. The wolf doesn't reappear, and I make it into the house without being eaten alive. The open door frame worries me, but there's nothing I can do except keep an eye out. I knew coming out here that animals lurk in the woods. That I am an intruder in their world.

It doesn't mean I have to like it, or be a willing meal.

I circle the fire pit so the door stays in my line of vision, arranging a neat pile of sticks in the center of the stones. In spite of everything, fatigue has me in its clutches and the fuel stares at me, taunting my confidence. There isn't much energy lurking inside me, and the worry reappears that I won't be able to do it.

The memory of the Prime's son on fire, the security cameras melted at Cell, and the burning skin of the Warden in the Administrative Center parade behind my closed eyes. I *can* do it. The thought of the power running through my blood, of the terrible things I am capable of, makes me not *want* to, though.

Don't be such a baby, Althea. It's time to grow up.

I snarl at the insistent voice in my head, tired to death of being pushed. I'll do it. My bum leg makes it hard to squat, but eventually my palms rest atop the pile of wood. With my eyes closed, I push my emotions—worry over the wolf, agony at losing Lucas, terror of being hunted by the Wardens—deep inside me where they simmer and gather strength. After a minute, all those mixed-up feelings spurt into my chest, down my arms, and finally out my palms. Within seconds the sticks crackle, and the first tendrils of heat fan my face. Flames, small but growing, meet my eyes.

It doesn't take long to realize I should have considered the smoke. Maybe having made a fire isn't that smart—the smoke could lead the Others right to my door—but the alternative of freezing to death doesn't leave me an option. At least the door provides good ventilation. Plus, the storm should hold them up even as it traps me, and by the sound of it they're unsure whether I'm in Iowa at all. There aren't that many Others in the city, let alone on the planet. It will take them days to search the Wilds outside all four of the cities Lucas and I each travel to.

Cadi called this place America when she told Lucas and I the story of our parents and our births, but I have no idea how big it might be. It feels very small in the cities where I've spent my almost seventeen years, but out here, in the Wilds, it stretches to infinity. It could take the Others a long time to search every square inch. Or it might not. There's no way to know for sure, but at the moment staying alive and unfrozen is enough worry.

With the last of my strength I cross to the door and peer toward the spot where the wolf disappeared into the trees. A jolt of terror slices through me when its cool gaze emerges between the snowflakes. Lying on its belly, it watches me from the tree line. Not any closer, but clearly without plans to go away, either. A sigh slips past my lips as I tear my eyes away from the killer's. I can't make it go away. If it's going to eat me, who's going to stop it?

With the flames between me and the door, I fashion a makeshift bed and pillow out of blankets and clothes. The fire is warm, and I did an okay job not building it too big. I watch it with a critical eye for a few minutes, but don't see any indication it will try to escape its stone boundary while I sleep.

Finally, curled up beneath a scratchy blanket, I give in to the darkness.

3.

I don't know how long I slept, but when I wake the fire has died to glowing embers and my entire body shakes with cold. The sky outside is black, opaque even. Wind howls and fat, wet snowflakes swirl like tornadoes through the night. Still shivering, I sit up and pull the blanket tight around me, then watch as more sticks catch fire under my hands. I huddle close until the blaze throws off enough heat to temper my shudders. There must be a way to draw the fire out of my middle and let it warm my limbs without losing control, but I've yet to discover it. And it's not exactly the kind of thing I want to play at. All I know is that I get cold so easily, and Lucas often felt too hot. I still have so many questions.

The pain in my leg has ebbed, now a dull throb instead of the stabbing, debilitating pain I'd experienced while gathering stones and wood. Staying off of it has helped, I guess. I glance outside. I'm not going anywhere, even if I want to. Extending my right leg out in front of me, I lean over and start to roll up my jeans. My fingertips brush the puffy, tender skin at my ankle and make me wince. I stop, breathing in slowly through my nose until the pain recedes, and it takes several more pauses before my jeans clear my knee.

Deep reds and purples decorate the enormous, swollen flesh around my foot and ankle. I gather the shreds of my courage and perform a closer inspection, grimacing with each gentle prod of my fingers. It hurts to move it back and forth, but my foot responds to the commands. Not broken. I don't think.

I leave my pant leg rolled up in case my foot swells more while I let the nausea abate. When it leaves my insides hollow again, I drag my reluctant body to the bag stuffed with food. Back beside my fire, I dig through the pilfered goods and choose a pull tab can of chicken soup and some crackers. It's not good cold, but I've eaten half the can before I remember my hands could heat it up. After sucking down my food, fatigue attacks again and I burrow back under the blankets, trying desperately to ignore the throbbing in my leg. It takes longer for sleep to come and steal away my discomfort, but as always, it does.

***

I wake up fast, full of a panicky feeling reminiscent of my morning-after-travel episodes. Every time I go to sleep in one place and wake up in another, a crushing black nothingness lingers, making me sure I've disappeared for good. It would be nice to never feel that again, and if Lucas and I are right about being able to control our traveling, we could stop, in theory. The idea of never having to wonder if I've slipped out of existence sits like a present in my open palm, one I want to open so badly but can't without scissors to snip the string.

There must be scissors somewhere—the answer to how to gain control of our lives has to be out there.

The mixture of the cold and smoky air helps clear my head. It might even have calmed me, except for the appearance of company lounging in the open doorway.

The wolf lays lengthwise in front of the door, his fur-covered body blocking the opening and then some. His head rests on his mostly white front paws, and he's angled his long snout and penetrating gaze in my direction. Closer now, I can see his mismatched eyes clearly. He looks sleepy, or maybe as if he's enjoying the fading warmth from my fire.

I glare at him, stopping to wonder for a moment if it's even a *him*. It doesn't matter. "Hey! Get out of here!" I shriek at the animal from my spot in the far corner. He doesn't look impressed, but raises his head off his paws and regards me with a wounded look.

I shake off the certainty that I hurt his wolf feelings and try again. "I said, go on!"

His gaze, which still looks reproachful, doesn't leave mine while he lumbers to his feet, stretches lazily, and turns from the door. Satisfaction steals through my blood at the meager victory as his fat tail disappears into the snowy gloom. I rub the heel of my hand where I smacked the wall to frighten him. *Ow.* At least the wolf and my hand took my mind off my pity party for five minutes. Who does that wolf think he is, anyway, enjoying my fire?

I study my creation, adding a few larger sticks and waiting for them to catch. It's pretty, in its own way. Scary, too. Powerful. Like my mother.

Maybe like me.

I lie back down and study the ceiling, ignoring the tears winding out of my eyes and down my warmed cheeks. After two days of pushing thoughts of Lucas and our parentage aside I invite them in, let them batter my heart and mind. I wonder where he is, if he's safe, if he's cold. That thought makes me smile. Lucas is never cold—he's winter.

The worst part is that I have no idea what I'm supposed to do now.

A few weeks ago Cadi told us the Others will leave Earth irreparably damaged when they use up whatever resource they need and move on to their next unsuspecting planet. She and Ko saved Lucas and I, along with two mysterious counterparts, because they believed we could make a difference for the humans, that we could somehow help them survive the Others' habitation. The four of us can control the same elements as our parents—we each have one human parent and one Element parent—but to what extent can we really help? The idea that we can save a planet is ludicrous. We can barely save ourselves. All Lucas and I managed to do is get separated, confirm for the Prime and his Wardens that we are, in fact, who they have been searching for, and let them know exactly what powers we possess. Not the smartest getaway plan ever.

The memory of the safe, protective circle of Lucas's arms leaves me feeling cold and barren. I roll over on my side, pulling the blanket with me, and try to fall asleep. With a bum ankle, a snowstorm, and no plan, it's not like I'm going anywhere. Tonight, I'll feel sorry for myself. Tomorrow, I'll try and figure out what to do.

First on my list—find a way to get back to Lucas.

***

The next two weeks leave me mostly healed and going banana balls from the captivity. Most of the swelling in my ankle disappeared four or five days ago—I've been marking days with small sticks in the corner—and though it is still tender, the only visible remnants of my injury are deep purple and black deposits along the base of my foot and over my ankle.

Moving around gets easier every day, but since it's barely stopped snowing and the drifts outside my little refuge climb past my knees, there's nowhere to go. The wolf has never disappeared for more than a few hours at a time: sometimes watching me from the trees, other days growing bold and lounging just outside my door again. I stopped yelling at him after about a week, growing more confident myself, and also fueled by loneliness and curiosity. I've started talking to him, too. He never answers but he does listen, tipping his head one way and then the other while he tries to figure me out.

Another visitor, a strange, golden bird with eyes that look purple in the sun, sweeps by occasionally. It seems to enjoy sitting in my windowsill and watching my movements, but I'm not fond of the thing. Twice when I went out to gather wood it has left waste on me. Once in my hair. So gross.

A bigger problem bears down, though, one that will have to be solved sooner or later. Apa needs to quit with the winter weather, because my stack of provisions is dwindling toward pathetic. Only a few cans of vegetables clatter around in the bag, and I've starved myself for the past three days to save that much.

Today the wolf has been absent for longer than ever before, so the sight of him in the doorway startles me. I'd been planning to go out; the pile of firewood is low, and though gathering more is a miserable process, it must be done. At least the chore freezes me so thoroughly that my foot doesn't ache for at least an hour afterward. The wolf stares in my direction, his uneven eyes thick with a question. He looks a lot like he's asking permission to come inside.

I shake my head. "No, Wolf. I think it's nice you haven't eaten me yet, especially with the weather, but I'm not ready to cuddle."

Something brown and furry between his powerful jaws catches my eye. As I watch, he drops it gingerly in the doorway, its form recognizable now. It's a rabbit, small and unmoving, its neck lying at an unnatural angle. There's no doubt he killed it.

For me?

The wolf flops into the snow, watching me with keen expectation. In order to gather his offering I'll have to come far closer to him than I've dared. What if it's a trick?

I laugh quietly. *Right, Althea. The wolf is smart enough to play tricks on you.*

My stomach rumbles, the empty ache gnawing as it has for the last two days. The mere thought of meat makes my mouth water. I ran out of protein in the first week. But I haven't the slightest clue how to make a rabbit edible, even if I can get past my fear of immediately infesting myself with all kinds of diseases by touching it. I've never eaten meat that isn't sanitized and prepared in a factory before it's delivered. Inside the boundary, the Others provide animal proteins every morning and night. It's not always tasty, but it is safe.

The wolf and I engage in a staring match while the wheels turn in my brain. I'm out here now, on my own. That fact isn't likely to change anytime soon. Eating sanitized meat is probably a luxury of the past, so I may as well figure out how to cook a fresh animal. Despite my worries, I feel a warm tingle of gratefulness swim through me and land in my chest. The wolf brought me food. He looks skinny to be sharing.

Pushing aside the fear of him attacking me, I sidle to the door and snatch the rabbit up by his ears. Cute, sort of, except for the dead part. No bugs. That I can see.

It's obvious the little guy needs to lose his fur and skin first. Ordinarily such a thought would bother me, and my brain takes a moment to register how much I've changed in a couple short months. Part of me still loathes the idea of cutting the rabbit open. The rest of me, the rational part, understands on some deep level that this is the natural way of the world.

I hobble back to my corner of provisions and dig through discarded cans. I've gathered the metal lids to the soup, beans, and tuna in a neat pile; stacking my emptied provisions into towers has entertained me in my bored hours.

There have been lots of them.

I cut my finger on a lid just yesterday, drawing blood. The rabbit's skin is bound to be thicker than mine, but maybe with enough determination I can get through it.

Armed with a sturdy lid, I carry the animal to the corner farthest from my makeshift bed. The wolf's gaze remains trained on my every move. He looks like he's laughing.

"What are you staring at, fur face? You think you're gonna see a show?"

"You're probably right," I mutter under my breath.

Crouching down, I hold the small mammal firmly around the neck and twist until its back faces up. I bunch skin and fur together at the base of its skull, remind myself to breathe through my mouth, and start sawing.

The skin separates more easily than I expected, blood seeping onto my hands. Bile rises into my throat but I swallow it, determined not to give up. After widening the initial opening I put down the lid and tear its skin the rest of the way off with my bare hands. I leave the head and legs, because my flimsy tin lid isn't strong enough to cut through bone.

A glance over my shoulder reveals the wolf still standing guard. This part makes me nervous. I want to go outside to dump the skin and wash the meaty layer in the snow, but talking to a wolf from across the room and waving a bloody carcass under its nose from inches away are two different things.

As though he read my mind, the wolf gets to his feet and wanders away, stopping halfway between the cabin and the stream. Unexpected tears fill my eyes at the animal's grace. He's been a better friend to me than any human my entire life, save Lucas. And Cadi—but then again, neither of them fall strictly into the human category.

I hurry out the door and toss the gory remnants into a drift. Bending down, I scrub the exposed layer with snow until the space in front of me is stained pink with the rabbit's life. Now that I'm finished, my concentration on the task broken, the condition of my clothes registers and I gag at the blood spotting my hands, arms, pants, and shirt. Once inside I strip them off and replace them with clean ones, sorry to have ruined one of my three pairs of jeans.

The meat obviously needs to be cooked, and the only method of accomplishing that is using the fire. It takes several minutes of staring before an idea hits.

Using another lid to scrape the bark off the end of a stick, I fashion a very ugly but workable point. My nervous energy coaxes the flames higher and I secure the rabbit carcass on the stick. It probably would have been better to slice him open and scoop out his organs or something, but getting rid of the fur is enough for one day. Touching insides will have to wait.

The transformation of the rabbit's glistening muscles and tendons from red to brown is mesmerizing, and soon the enticing smell of cooked meat wafts about the cabin. The wolf smells it, too, and reclaims his spot inside the doorway. I smile at him. "Thanks, Wolf."

My eyes grow wide and the rabbit almost catches fire when a low sound rumbles from his throat. Not a bark or a howl, which Lucas and I heard on adventures outside the boundary in Connecticut. Not a growl, either. Not a warning. This noise is almost playful, answering.

Like he understood me.

I avoid his gaze while my dinner continues to cook. When pieces start to turn black and emit a charred scent, I pull the rabbit out of the fire and inspect my handiwork. The flesh looks overcooked, with some pieces near his legs falling off the bone. I shrug.

"Better safe than sorry, right?"

I need to get a grip. I'm talking to a wolf.

This time he remains silent, eyes riveted on the rabbit instead of me.

The flesh cools enough to pull off a piece, and I stuff it in my mouth without overanalyzing. Tastes like chicken, but plain and a little dry. No doubt due to my less than awesome cooking skills.

I pick around the outside, still unwilling to encounter any organs, and my stomach is full to protesting before the meat disappears. I lick my fingers clean, feeling sated for the first time in days. The wolf's gaze remains fixed on what's left of my dinner. His silent begging makes me smile. No threatening posture, sound, or move has emanated from him in two weeks. The rabbit is technically his. I suppose sharing the rest is just good manners.

To be honest, if I'm going to die, I'd rather my furry friend kill me instead of the Others. The image of

Ko, bound and tortured, flits through my mind, bringing with it a shudder of revulsion.

Definitely better to be eaten by a wolf.

Caution painting my moves, I cross the room to the wolf. I stop a foot away and gently lay the stripped carcass on the floor of the cabin. His hopeful eyes flit between the meat and me, and his long, pink tongue snakes around his mouth. I watch as he lifts his black nose, sniffing the air.

"It's okay. Come get it."

He checks for permission one more time, and for some reason I nod as though he knows what that means. My breath catches in my throat as he stands and creeps toward me. His head is low and he swishes his tail back and forth, looking for all the world as though he expects me to hit him.

The wolf lays in front of the rabbit, sniffs it from head to toe, and then picks it up in strong jaws. From inches away—the closest we've ever been—the movement provides a terrifying glimpse of his teeth and it backs me up a little. Without so much as a thank-you, he turns and trots back outside. The sound of crunching bones jerks me into a wince. At least he went outside first.

Fed and sleepy, I settle by the fire and warm my fingers and toes. The wolf returns within minutes, having made a neat meal of his prey. I don't see a speck on him, at least not from here. He doesn't sit, as has become his custom, but stands and stares. "What do you want? I don't have any more food."

He makes that playful, responsive noise again, regarding me with expectant eyes. The words slip out before I know they're going to. "What, you think you deserve a spot by the fire now?"

I hold my breath, wondering if he really can understand and whether or not I want him at my fire. I'm too tired, too full, and too pleased with myself to take back the question. He puts one huge white paw inside the door, nails clicking on the wood floor. Summoning bravado, remembering Lucas and his pet fish and the envy I felt over his love for the animal, I nod encouragingly and pat the ground. "Come on. It's okay."

He pads to the opposite side of the fire, stopping a couple feet back, and drops to the floor. His huge head rests on his paws and his eyes slip closed with a contented sigh. His relaxed posture makes me smile. It looks as though he's made himself at home.

4.

It stops snowing over the next week, and pale sunshine melts much of the accumulation on the ground. Patches of brown grass emerge in the clearing. The wolf, who I've taken to just calling Wolf, is my daily companion. He brings fresh meals, which we share, every couple of days. So far I've skinned a couple of squirrels and another rabbit. He brought me a raccoon last night but it's still lying just outside the door, intact. It's big. It probably has fleas. I'm not sure I want to skin it, even though it's fat enough to feed us both for several days. Every couple of hours Wolf wanders over to the carcass, whines at me, and gives me a look that says, *I went and got this; aren't you going to cook it?*

I shrug at him and he gives up. I'll probably do it. Maybe.

The Clarks' water bottles have proven useful. I fill them up with snow or water from the creek and keep them in the house. I taught Wolf to drink out of one yesterday. He seems delighted with his new trick of lapping the flowing stream as I pour it in front of his nose.

A frown pulls at my cheeks when Lucas's face flashes through my mind as it does multiple times a day. I can't sit here on my hands. I've got to find him, and the other two. Cadi said there are four of us, four half-Other and half-human kids. Four of us with the power to control the elements. Four Dissidents, as Ko called us. Still, the little cabin, and Wolf, are safe havens I'm reluctant to leave. Especially since I don't know where to go or what to do.

It's winter, and since we never travel to our home seasons, Lucas won't be easy to locate. To find him, I'll have to travel to a different season, and to do that, I'm going to need help. Easier said than done. With Cadi captured by Chief last autumn, I don't know where she stands. She might not even be alive, and since the Others know she and Ko were helping to hide us all these years, I'd say there's a good chance I'm on my own.

Lucas and I traveled without their help once though. If I could find another kid like me—the one who belongs in Autumn or Spring—then maybe I could get back to Lucas. I don't know how to go about finding them, but the first step is probably to leave the loneliness of the Wilds.

Late in the afternoon I scrounge up the nerve to skin the raccoon. The fleas have abandoned its dead skin, but other infestations may have set in, especially since the weather has improved a bit. Although it's not warm, the wind no longer bites my skin. I wash the silver-and-black striped fur in the creek before hauling the rigid body inside, every moment recalling the baby raccoon Lucas tried to help in the woods before it attacked him when we escaped Danbury. It feels so long ago now, though it's only been a few weeks.

Its body is heavy. Wolf prances around, apparently excited that I'm accepting his latest gift after all. Once inside my little hideaway, I drop it in my bloody corner and strip off my clothes. It's a strangely freeing feeling, being naked.

I wonder if I'm becoming some sort of wild woman.

Probably.

I started skinning Wolf's gifts naked to avoid ruining any more clothes, and the wracking shivers encourage me to do it quickly. This raccoon will be messier than the squirrels, no doubt about that. I get halfway through, stopping every couple of minutes to gag and cart pieces outside, before a low growl rumbles from Wolf's throat. I've never heard the sound before, not from him, and fear shoots through me.

But Wolf isn't staring at me, ready to rip out my throat. He's concentrating on the opening to the outside. The fur along his back stands up in spiky tufts as he repositions himself between the world and me. He growls again, and then a face appears in the doorway.

My heart stops, then drops like a rock into my belly. My legs freeze, unresponsive.

An easy grin lights the stranger's face, wiped away immediately at the sight of Wolf. His sky blue eyes, replicas of Lucas's and mine, register at the same moment I remember I'm naked. Perhaps I should be more frightened of the stranger, but the power of my embarrassment overshadows everything else. In fact, I kind of want to die.

I snatch up my clothes and shriek at the intruder, "Turn around, for Pete's sake!"

"I would, honest, but I'm afraid your dog will take a bite out of my backside."

His fear may not be unfounded. Wolf stands rigid, unwilling to take his eyes off the boy, who returns the animal's gaze. I take advantage of his distraction and toss my jeans and sweater on as fast as possible. Dressed, I make my way to Wolf's side and twist my fingers in the fur at the back of his neck. My face flames. In fact, all of me is red-hot, and I let go of Wolf after the scent of burnt hair lifts to my nose. Out of the corner of my eye, the flames reach higher in the fire pit.

They lower a moment later as I blow out a breath and regain control.

Once calmed, or at least calm*er,* I peruse the stranger. Aside from his eyes, nothing about him reminds me of Lucas. His skin is a tanned brown and his hair is a messy, deep-chestnut mop atop his head. He grins at me in a lazy way, as though the smile has all the time in the world. My heart pounds hard, making breathing a chore, and even though I want it to be the result of the startle, it's something more.

The fact irritates me. "He's not a dog; he's a wolf," I snap.

Until a few days ago I'd never seen either, but that's not the point.

"Can I come in?"

"No."

We square off in silence for a minute while options flutter near and then away. It's obvious he's not going to leave, and I have no desire to sit out in the cold. Wolf is inside, and even though there's no guarantee he'll defend me if the boy attacks, the stranger doesn't know that. If I'm being completely honest, I don't want him to go. I've been alone too long, and the fact that he's out here in the Wilds by himself prickles curiosity along my skin.

I'm sure he can't be an Other until the memory of how the Prime's son wore Barbarus skin, disguising his alien self with somewhat more familiar yellowed skin and bright tilted eyes. We ate together, chatted, walked through the park, and neither Lucas nor I suspected what he was underneath until it was too late.

With Wolf between the boy and me, I sidle to the window and peek out, scanning the trees. Nothing moves in the white and brown landscape. Wolf's gaze pins the boy in place inside the doorway; he seems unconcerned that more intruders might lurk in the Wilds.

I sigh. "Okay, fine. Come in."

I motion him over to the fire and plop down with a clear path to the door. He follows, easing onto the floor and propping his back against the flimsy wall. A strong breeze blows in his wake and nearly extinguishes the flickering flames. He smells spicy and sweet, a heady combination that soaks my blood with a dizzying syrup, but the wind gusts the scents away before I can define them.

The utter quiet in the cabin grates on my nerves as we fake smile at each other across the fire. I have no idea why either of us is pretending this is normal, since we're both in forbidden territory. People don't walk in the Wilds. Before last autumn, I would have figured the fact that he's alone proves he's not human, but I'm no longer sure what's true. I've been through too much in the past few weeks to beat around the bush.

"So what are you doing out here?"

One corner of his mouth twitches. "Let's say I got lost."

I snort. "What's your name?"

His eyes meet mine and the smile takes its time reappearing. He's handsome, in a rugged way, with a sharp jawline and broad shoulders. The confident, assured quality surrounding him sucks at me, pulling me toward him like a magnet. The memory of Cadi telling Lucas and I that there are more half-Other beings like us skips through my mind. The idea that he could be exactly who I've been wondering how I would find skips ripples of excitement through my mind, like a rock skimmed across water.

"Pax."

"Althea."

A couple of beats go by before I realize we're staring at each other. An odd shyness comes over me, like I'm worried about embarrassing myself. Well, embarrassing myself *further*, given that he's gotten an eyeful of me in all my naked glory already. Electricity zips over my arms and races down my spine at the memory.

Pax tears his gaze from my face, nodding toward Wolf. "You know that's not a wolf, right?"

"How do you know?"

He shrugs, his eyes still grinning as though he's making fun of me. "I pay attention at Cell. It's a dog, though there are similarities, I'll give you that."

"Wolves are dogs," I mutter under my breath.

He barks a laugh. "Got me on that one, Allie. So what are you doing out here?"

"Don't call me Allie. I hate nicknames."

He returns my earlier snort, not seeming to notice that I didn't answer his question. "What were you skinning over there? Care to share?"

"You can have whatever's left after Wolf eats."

Pax stands and bends over, reaching beneath his pant leg. I think he's scratching his ankle, but when he straightens up again steel glints in his palm. I scramble backward and press against Wolf, my panic ripping another menacing snarl from his throat.

"Shit, you're jumpy. I'm just gonna take that carcass outside and finish dressing it for you. Earn my chunk."

He drags the raccoon's body outside while I calm down, wondering how he knows about fixing dead animals into food. Wolf leaves my side and pads to the doorway, watching Pax with suspicion in his posture. I build the fire up a bit while Pax isn't inside to watch, then clean up my pile of cans. It's not that I care if he thinks my housekeeping skills are lagging, it's more that sitting around with nothing to do makes me anxious. And this boy does make me nervous.

Because as always, even though I hate it, being alone is safer.

It's not long before Pax hollers from outside. "Call off your dog, Allie. I mean, providing you actually want to cook this raccoon."

For the life of me I can't figure out why my blood sizzles at the sound of his voice instead of cooling in irritation. I must be lonelier than I thought. "Only if you promise not to call me Allie again."

"Uh-huh."

It sounds like a lie, but since my other option is letting him make off with my dinner, I ignore it. "Wolf, come here."

He turns his head and searches my face. I pat my leg and he comes, but only after glowering at Pax for another several seconds. Our guest strides through the door, raccoon parts neatly chopped up and cradled in his jacket. He also gathered several strong sticks and whittled off the ends, making far stronger and more effective roasting instruments than mine. With his sleeves pushed up, the muscles in his arms ripple as he

47

carries the load, and Pax tosses a playful wink my direction when he catches me staring again, flushing my cheeks with heat. I glare back in an attempt to cover up my stupid body's reaction to his presence.

Pax stops beside the fire and sets the raw meat on the ground. Without a word he plants his feet, catches my gaze, and raises his arms to shoulder level, palms facing the walls.

In the next instant a gale blows through the cabin.

Wolf flattens himself against my side, whipping his head around in agitation. My spare clothes and the discarded cans whirl in a mad circle as I hit the ground in order to avoid a knock on the head. Wind howls, sending my ponytail and loose strands of hair whipping into my face and mouth. I notice, in an odd moment of clarity, that the wind beating against me isn't cold like the air outside. It's cool and bright, with a hint of sunshine.

Just as abruptly as it began, the dizzying storm ends. Cans clatter back to the floor and an extra T-shirt falls onto Wolf's back. He turns in frantic circles in an attempt to catch it in his teeth. The fire is gone, extinguished. Sticks and embers scatter among my meager possessions, clothes dotting the cabin floor like haphazard rugs.

The room no longer smells crisp and cold, with a hint of pine needles and snow. It's doused in the scents of apples and cinnamon, with the slightest hint of burning leaves. It's the same spicy, sweet smell that wafted off of Pax earlier when he walked past me.

Pax is the picture of composure, never moving from the spot where he stood before the incident. He gives me a small smile. "Now, why don't you show me what you can do?"

5.

It seems impossible that the two of us would find each other without even trying.

Then again, Lucas and I fell together in a similar manner. Before last autumn, I had never met anyone else like me, and even though my original note from Ko promised there were more, most days I had trouble believing it. Then all of a sudden, Lucas was there.

Now he's gone, and Pax is here instead.

We haven't said a whole lot since his little demonstration, but I did tease the fire back to life so our dinner could cook, proving I am who he thinks I am—another Dissident.

Juices slip off the fatty meat like tears, splattering on the rocks ringing the fire pit with tantalizing sizzles. Wolf's tongue works without ceasing, wetting his lips in anticipation of the meal to come.

As promised, I give my wolf his portion before letting Pax tug some meat free. It doesn't seem to bother him, being made to eat after an animal, and his calm demeanor and lazy smile get under my skin. He tears chunks of meat way from bone with his teeth, chewing and staring into my fire with a distant look in his eyes.

"So, how did you get here?" I venture.

Pax slides his gaze from the flames to me. "I walked."

"Walked?"

"Yeah, you know, like with my feet."

I roll my eyes, perfectly aware that the reaction is what he wants. Pax can't fool me with his smart-aleck comments and cheerful banter. As an expert in building walls to keep people at arm's length, I recognize the work he's putting in to do the same. "But where have you been until now?"

"I landed in winter about, I don't know, three weeks ago? I've been wanting to escape Des Moines the whole time, but the storm . . ." He shrugs. "I finally got away a day ago and walked west. This little place looked pretty good until I stuck my head in the door and realized it was occupied." A different grin, a wicked one, spreads his lips this time. "Then it looked even better."

My head swims at the reference to my earlier display of nudity. Despite my understanding of the wall Pax is keeping between us, my anger boils because he's using my embarrassment to do it. I bite back a retort, unwilling to play into his hands. "How did you know who I was?"

"Well, you're out here all alone, in the Wilds. You have a dog for a pet. What about that seems human to you?"

Tears fill my eyes for no discernible reason. The not being totally human, the being part Other . . . it still sneaks up on me.

Even though I look away, he sees, and for the first time, chagrin pinches his handsome face. "Plus the way you smell. Also your eyes. Our eyes."

The Elements' eyes. They're the only Others with blue pinpoints, with eyes that are not all-engulfing black holes.

Getting upset wastes energy. It's time to start accepting the way things are, starting with the fact that Pax is here with me and not Lucas. It's better than nothing. Perhaps together we can formulate some sort of workable plan. If I can get him on my side, we could find Lucas. "Where were you before this?"

"Summer. Portland. It was my first one there. Then Atlanta for a few days."

The tidbit sparks recognition. It had been Lucas's first autumn in Connecticut, too, and it had happened because we were supposed to meet; Ko and Cadi orchestrated it that way. Maybe Pax and the elusive fourth were together, too.

Without making it seem intentional or awkward, he finishes eating and shifts closer to me. We can see each other better without the flames flickering between us, but his advance makes Wolf's muscles tighten against my back. I pat his head and he goes back to eating, albeit with one eye on our guest.

Pax and I are the same. Dissidents. There's no reason to keep anything from him, yet it feels a little like a betrayal to share the experiences Lucas and I had while he's not here. When he might be alone and scared.

I bury the sentiment. It's not the time. Maybe it never will be. It was never meant to be only Lucas and me; Cadi and Ko have rested the fate of Earth on the *four* of us, not two.

Pax clears his throat, breaking the silence. "Why are you out here alone?"

"They found us last autumn—the Wardens. We escaped, but they know who we are now. My note said to run." I don't bother explaining about the note.

He most likely has one, too, and his nod confirms it. "Who's 'us'?"

"Winter—" His name gets caught in my throat for a few seconds. "His name is Lucas."

Pax doesn't answer, just cleans the grease from his hands using his pants and reaches for his pack. Wolf watches every movement but isn't coiled tight anymore. When the boy—Autumn, I'm pretty sure—straightens up, he's clutching a book in his hands. Unlike the hardback volumes the Others give us at school, this one is covered with paper. The picture on the front is of a boy with bare feet sitting in a giant tree overlooking a green lawn. The sky is blue, so clear it looks like it goes on forever. Pax turns it toward me, showing off the title. *A Separate Peace*, by a man named John Knowles.

He offers it up and I run my fingertips over the rough, wrinkled cover. The lower right-hand corner is ripped and the spine is so worn that the book falls open to the center when I set it in my lap. Operating on instinct, I flip to the front and find Pax's note. It is identical to my and Lucas's original notes, save his name.

> *Pax,*
>
> *You feel different because you are Something Else, a Dissident. But you are not alone. There are more, and you will find each other when it is necessary. In the meantime, trust no one.*

I close it and give Pax a wry smile. "That's familiar."

As a return gesture, I unhook my necklace and hand it over. He inspects it for a minute, and then gives it back. For the first time, I notice a bracelet tied around his wrist, made from a pretty braid of colored threads. They're vibrant shades of blue, red, orange, and green woven together in a flowing pattern that looks like it formed spontaneously. It must be homemade, even though I've never seen anything like it—ever.

He catches me staring and pulls his sleeves down over his wrists. I'm not sure what we're supposed to do now, but sitting here staring at the floor isn't going to accomplish anything. "What happened to you last season?" I ask, on the off chance he'll tell me.

"Well, let's see. I learned that my real mother fell in love with a stinking Element—Air. I found out the Others use mind control to keep the rest of the humans from questioning their power. And I found out what they can—and will—do." He doesn't elaborate. A strange tightness squeezes his words, the opposite of the loose grace he's exhibited up until now.

There's no need to push it. Thinking back over my autumn, there are certainly events I'd rather not think about, or talk about, or remember at all. The memory of what the Others are capable of—the pain, the violence, the relentless pursuit—pops electric shocks of fear through me. If Pax knows enough to fear the Others, he's experienced at least some of those same things. We don't need to relive it.

"So, where were you headed when you stumbled in here this evening?"

"Nowhere special. Hiding. Staying away from the Wardens. I'm not surprised to see you, actually. After last season, the way Deshi and I were thrown together and Ko saying things had changed, I figured Summer might be around."

The name Deshi rings in my ears, vibrates all the way into my toes. A cold fear swishes in its wake. "How do you know Deshi?"

The Prime's son had pretended to be human, to be our classmate. Watched Lucas and I, then reported back to the Prime Other that we were the ones they wanted. He'd been in Danbury with us all autumn; he couldn't have been in Portland with Pax.

Emotion twists Pax's red, chapped lips into a grimace. "He was with me in Portland until the Others took us. They . . . I don't know what they did to him."

The implications of his words roll around my head like marbles, but eventually I gather a few into my palms. "You're saying Deshi is one of us?"

He nods. "Spring."

The information sounds wrong until I remember how the Chief had told Cadi she couldn't protect us . . . or protect Deshi. I couldn't figure out what he had meant then, but it's starting to make sense.

Pax stares at me, his eyebrows knitted together. "You're really pale, Summer. What's wrong?"

"What does Deshi look like?" The fact that he broke his promise to not use a nickname barely registers as an annoyance. The need to confirm my suspicions hums like the generator in the Cell basement.

"He's a Barbarus. Slanted eyes, really shiny black hair. I mean, not dark brown like mine—really *black*. He's got our eyes, but they look wrong in his face. Short." He jaw clenches when he pauses. "Nice guy."

It makes sense after a few silent rounds of question and answer with myself, and confirms what Lucas and I suspected last fall—that the Others had somehow discovered that we smell different than regular people. It had just never occurred to me that they uncovered that fact by kidnapping another Dissident and then replicating his appearance.

57

Never once had I guessed that the yellowish skin, the glossy black hair, the short stature of the Other Deshi were simply a replica of a boy named Deshi. Our fourth. Spring.

I take a deep breath. "I think the Others copied him to try to find the rest of us. A boy who looked just like that came to Upper Cell in Connecticut, and he smelled like spring. We found out he was an Other in disguise, but not until he figured out who we were." The story tumbles out, and I'm unsure whether it will make Pax feel better or worse.

He doesn't respond at all, or volunteer any more information. Not how he feels about what happened, or that the Others can copy people, slide inside their skin. I wonder how much he and Deshi managed to figure out before they took him. Probably not much. Other Deshi showed up in Connecticut a few weeks into the Cell year, right at the beginning of autumn. The real Deshi and Pax must have met in summer or winter, where they could be together.

There's a lot Pax needs to know. About Cadi and Ko, how they're captured and maybe dead. How they might be telling the Others everything they know about us and our "talents." He might even be blessedly in the dark about how our human parents are dead. He knows his dad is Air—Vant—and I'm curious to find out how that piece of information found its way into his clutches.

Lucas and I only found out about our parents because Cadi schemed her way to Danbury. I bite my lip to keep it from quivering as I think about that last night, about Lucas. Then I realize Pax's arrival could mean there's a chance to find him, and soon.

Before I figure out the best way to broach the subject of travel, though, Pax sets his leftovers in front of Wolf and stands. When he stretches his arms over his head, a glimpse of the tanned, hard muscles of his stomach makes my heart leap into my throat. I divert my eyes before he can catch me, but my face feels like it's going to melt off. When his gaze does land on mine, it darkens with an indefinable emotion.

"Are you going to invite me to stay or send me packing? Because even though we have a lot to talk about, I'm beat."

I haven't been "beat" for weeks, but that's because I haven't done much of anything except keep warm and feed myself. If there's one thing that's struck me most about Pax in the last hour, it's that he won't be rushed into anything. His entire attitude mimics his smile, and every last inch of me knows that trying to coax information out of him will result in the opposite. That character trait is going to drive me to Breaking, to falling completely apart in a way the Others don't bother to fix—it's the exact opposite of Lucas's willingness to brainstorm, to share.

The barrier between Pax and I brews apprehension, but the idea of turning him out doesn't even cross my mind. "Of course you can stay. But first thing in the morning, we're going to figure out what to do next."

"Thanks." He tugs one of my blankets to the opposite side of the fire, not asking permission first. After a moment he gets comfortable, his pack propping up his head, and closes his eyes.

It doesn't take long to clean up the leftover pieces of raccoon. Wolf drags the last of his portion outside and crunches away, as well-mannered as ever. When I lie down across from Pax—who isn't fooling anyone with his fake sleeping—I wonder what will happen now. The immediate relief that came with finding Lucas isn't attached to Pax, and whether it's because I already knew of his existence or because it means something different now, it's hard to say.

He frowns, not opening his eyes. "Stop staring at me."

"I'm not. I was thinking." Flustered heat floods my blood. I'm not going to need a coat if he sticks around.

"Were you thinking about why you built a fire in the floor instead of using that stove over there? It would heat the whole room." Even though his eyes stay shut, that infuriating smile returns.

I glance at the metal box under the window. There isn't anything else in this place that could be a stove. It certainly doesn't look like the ones people cook with inside the boundaries.

Wolf pads back inside, his big pink tongue cleaning grease off of his generous lips. Usually he stays a safe distance away, probably more for my comfort than his, but with Pax invading our space, he drops onto the floor at my back.

Instead of giving Pax any sort of satisfaction, I roll over and pretend his attitude doesn't bother me in the slightest.

6.

Pax wakes before I do, and his banging around the metal box—the stove, I guess—shoves my eyes open a few hours earlier than normal. The Others in my dream try to follow me into wakefulness, but disappear like wisps of night banished by sunlight. They were talking about the blizzard, about how they told Apa to make it stop so they could find me. When I tried to wake up, they chased me through the tunnels that connect their minds, the ones that I accidentally invaded when my skin touched a Warden's.

They're gone now, but I lie still for a few moments and catch my breath. It's still dark outside, and moonlight tries to wriggle through the dirt smudged on the windows. The fire has died to embers, allowing the chilly winter into the room. Wolf presses harder against me now, and his thick fur keeps me warm. His pale eyes follow Pax as he shoves wood through a little door on the side of what he claims is a stove.

"Why on earth are you making that racket before the sun even comes up?" In spite of everything, the taste in my mouth makes me hope he doesn't come too close.

"I wanted to show you how to use the woodstove before I leave."

That sits me straight up in my blankets, morning breath forgotten. "Before you leave? Where are you going?"

"Back to Portland."

"But . . . we haven't figured out what to do about the Others yet!"

"Come here and light this thing."

Distracted by his declaration, I get up and cross the room without protest. Cold wind immediately cuts through my clothes, eliciting shivers, speeding my steps. He points inside the stove, where there are some bigger branches and a pile of smaller sticks. Pax has also torn up some of my bloodied, discarded clothing from my first attempts at skinning animals.

The strips of cloth catch quickly under my palms, and after the sticks glow red, Pax closes the door, turning a knob on the door until it won't go any farther.

"It lets oxygen into the stove. The more air, the hotter it gets. If you get too warm, close it a bit—at night, too."

"I don't care how the stupid thing works. It's not like I plan on staying here for the rest of my life either—no matter how short that might be. What's in

Portland that's worth us splitting up? Ko and Cadi said—"

"What's anywhere?" he interrupts. The stubborn set to his jaw returns as his eyes flit everywhere but to mine.

"Okay, fine. What about the Others? They know about us, and they obviously think we're a threat. Lucas and I want to figure out how to save us. All four of us."

"First of all, there's a good chance there's only three of us now. They've had Deshi for months. Second, you and Winter can do what you want. Leave me out of it."

"But I need your help to find him; I can't travel alone! And if we're going to die because of what we can do, don't you at least want to know why?"

"No. I want to hide long enough for the Others to forget I exist. That's all."

Without a backward glance, Pax shrugs into his coat, jams a gray stocking cap over his mussed hair, and stalks out of the cabin. I watch him through the open doorway until he disappears into the trees. After a few seconds, Wolf leaves to take care of business. The solitude pricks my eyes with tears. I've tried traveling on my own; nothing happened except my skin producing buckets of sweat, followed by an emotional breakdown.

I need Pax. I have to convince him to help me find Lucas. If he doesn't want to stick around after that, he can go his own way. The realization pushes me to my feet, despite the fact that the stove spews enveloping heat into the cabin.

The warmth abandons me as I step outside and tug my hood up over my hair. Pax turns at the sound of my running footsteps, expression determined. I stop at the sight of the first serious emotion he's shown me since seeing me naked yesterday evening.

Pax moves closer, until the smell of apples and cinnamon lodges in my nose, until the heat from him and I winds together. Too close, really. His lips are full and red, chapped from the wind. Our eyes meet and he holds mine with an intensity that traps breath in my lungs.

The moment freezes in time, so still and quiet that his deep voice sounds like a dream when he finally speaks. "I'm sorry if it's not what you want to hear, that I don't want to fight. I tried, last season. When they took Desh, I . . . tried. It's hopeless."

A million questions burst in my head, but the pain in his apology twists my throat closed. It stops me from worrying about me, about Lucas, about all of our problems for a second. Instead of getting angry I reach out to touch him, but he jerks his hands away. It feels a little like a slap in the face, and icy fingers slide around my heart. *He's not Lucas,* I remind myself. *You've only just met him.*

I drop my hands to my sides. It's not only that I need him. We need each other. That means building trust, and the fact that he's trying hard to hide his hurt tugs on my heart. "I'll go with you. To Portland."

Surprise lights his blue eyes. "Why?"

"Because I'm sorry that something bad happened to you last season. Bad things happened to me, too. I respect your opinion about the Others, but I'm going to change it. We're going to find Lucas, and the three of us are going to fight. So the bad things stop happening to all of us."

A slow sigh of surrender whispers from deep in his chest. A flock of birds take flight a little way off, their red wings flashing against the graying morning sky.

He scrunches up his face, resigned. "I'm not sure you understand the meaning of respect."

"Well, you're stuck with me. At least for now."

That mysterious emotion skitters through his gaze again, the one that looks as if he's pushing aside what he wants to say or do. It tugs at my center as though it wants to yank us together. Flustered, I step backward and offer a small smile. Avoiding his gaze calms my breathing. "I'm going to pack up. We can leave soon."

"Okay, sure. I'll just scout around a bit then."

Wolf joins me inside after a little while, watching with curious eyes as I stuff my belongings back into one of my duffel bags. The second one is extra now, since there's no food left. The trash needs to be hidden, maybe buried, in case the Others happen past. The less they know about where I've been, the safer I'll be. Pax, too.

Wolf hears Pax before I do. When the sounds grow loud enough to catch my hearing, though, panic isn't far behind. I run to the doorway in time to see him crash out of the underbrush, eyes wild, hair snagged with pine needles and snow.

He doesn't speak until he's closer, and the forced whisper swells my fear. "Wardens. In the woods. They're not far; we have to go."

"But how did they find us?"

"Summer, we can chat it up later. Right now, we gotta move."

Pax snatches the duffel bag and grabs me by the hand, propelling us both into the woods at the rear of the cabin. Wolf keeps pace at our side, and gratitude at his loyalty chokes my throat with tears. At the edge of the clearing, the scent of apples and cinnamon swells as leaves and debris lift off the forest floor. Pax whirls and stares back the way we came, hair whipping into his eyes, but I tug hard on his arm.

"No. If you start a windstorm they'll know you're here. Right now they think it's just me."

"How do you know?"

I *don't* know what made me say that, but then the memory of my dream assaults my senses. That's why I think that. Because the Others in my dream said Apa should stop the storm so they could find *her*. That means me. I'm the only her, the only female Dissident. There's no time to explain that to Pax.

Besides, I'm still convincing myself it was just a dream, despite the clarity of their empty black eyes and the grim disgust in the Prime Other's voice when he ordered his Wardens to hunt me down. "I don't, but why confirm anything for them?"

He grunts, lowering his free hand and setting down the pieces of forest prepared to do his bidding.

"Fine," he says. "Let's go."

***

We don't stop for hours, not until the sun's started to dip toward the horizon. The ground is frozen and cold, the landscape flat once we emerge from the forest. It's not smart to be out in the open like this, but we're surrounded by miles and miles of nothing but empty fields. The sky is gray, the ground is white, and it feels as though there is no color left in the world. Even Wolf's black-and-white coat blends in to the countryside we're traipsing across.

My feet and legs are completely numb by the time Pax stops at the edge of a park. Weeds crawl over the space like a tangle of snakes; it's nothing like the manicured parks inside our boundaries. He hasn't asked if I need a break, and I'm determined not to be the first to suggest one. We've passed a crumbled structure here and there the last couple of miles, as though this was once a town where humans lived. Before the Others.

A thin yellow-striped cat with violet eyes studies us from a low tree branch, bushy tail twitching back and forth and knocking snow onto the ground. I expect Wolf to give chase after spotting the thing, but he doesn't. In fact, if anything, he acts wary of the emaciated creature, even though it's smaller than the raccoon he caught for dinner. Its grape-colored eyes follow our every move, disturbingly human in the way they don't look away.

Pax's hoarse voice distracts me from watching the creature. "We need to find shelter. Once the sun's gone we won't be able to navigate so easily."

All day, I waited for the Others to come up behind us, to take us away. Pax must have given us a decent head start. "We could travel. I could show you how Lucas and I did it. We could make sure they can't follow."

Pax's teeth clamp together. "No. We lost them. They were about half a mile away when I spotted them, and your dog doesn't hear anything. We're good."

"But they're going to know we were there. We didn't have a chance to get rid of any of the cans or the fire—"

The determined flash in his eyes silences me.

"Look, Summer, I told you I have no interest in searching for Winter Boy Wonder, so don't think you're going to trick me into traveling to find him. I'm going back to Portland because there's something I need to do. You can come or not, but it's going to be a long trip with you being disappointed every time we have this conversation."

He's right. Not to mention I'm too tired to fight right now. "Fine. So, where are we going to stay tonight?"

"Just keep those pretty blue eyes peeled."

I've started to think we're never going to find a place to sit down when we finally run across potential shelter. There are two wooden doors, slightly slanted up, built right into yet another wide expanse of barren land. Several paces away are piles of exploded timber,

70

perhaps once a house or outbuilding, but now reduced to firewood.

The doors into the earth stop us both in our tracks and we stare for several moments. The baffled look on Pax's face makes me smile. No one's going to explain it to us, so I stride up and grab one of the metal handles on top. The right door, then the left, pulls upward easily, belching a cloud of wet-smelling dust into my face. It forces a series of sneezes, and when they finally dissipate and I blink away the tears, Pax is grinning at me.

"You sound like a squirrel when you sneeze."

"Um, thanks?"

He strides to my side and peers into the hole in the ground. There's a wooden ladder leading into the dark interior that looks too fragile to hold our weight. Wolf whines, and to me it sounds like he's not keen on the idea of being underground. I turn my back to the doors and reach out a leg, feeling for the first rung.

"Wait, what are you doing?"

"Going to check it out. What, you think you should go first because you're a guy?"

"No, by all means, go right ahead." He runs a hand through his brown hair, but it's too fine to tousle. The wind rearranges it in the next second anyway, and makes me shiver.

My bones suddenly ache all the way through, and nothing is scarier than having to stay on my shaking feet while we continue to search for a place to crash for the night. Without waiting for him to stop me, I keep backing down the makeshift stairs. They creak under my weight but don't snap, and after only twelve steps I feel solid earth under my feet. It doesn't take long for my eyes to adjust from the gray day to this dark space, and when the image of a bed melts out of the darkness, happiness makes me want to cry.

"It's like a little bedroom! Come on down!"

Pax grunts in response, which I assume means he's going to acquiesce.

Shelves line the walls, stacked with cans of what appear to be food, although the labels are faded and dirty. There are bottles of water stacked in a corner. Those are labeled as well, and it's not the water the Others deliver. The bed is covered in a patchwork quilt made of browns, reds, and oranges—it reminds me a bit of something Mrs. Morgan would buy—and little tassels pop up in the center of each square. The errant thought of the mother I Broke in Danbury last autumn punches the air out through my stomach, dampening my elation. Lucas's earnest face, urging me to believe that it wasn't my fault, hovers in my mind, bringing the smallest bit of comfort along with it.

I sit on the edge of the bed and run my fingers over the colored pattern. The repetitive motion slows my heartbeat and shoves tears back into my head where they belong before Pax sees them and I have to explain.

He's not ready to talk about what happened last season and neither am I.

A loud crack interrupts my sorrow, jerking my head the direction of the stairs. Pax flails the last couple of feet to the ground, landing on his rear in a cloud of dust with a loud groan.

"Are you—" Giggles overtake me, refusing to be swallowed. Eventually I manage to gasp out the rest of my question. "—hurt?"

Pax is already on his feet, glaring at me while he brushes debris off his backside. My giggles continue, and after a moment Pax's mouth twitches into a smile. He laughs, too, and the tension from the day melts off of us. Every muscle in my body throbs with fatigue, aching as I thaw from the cold hours and hours of traipsing across the hard earth.

"What is this place, do you think?" Pax studies the shelves, squinting through the darkness at the provisions lining the walls.

"Good luck, if you ask me. We'll have some food tonight, even if Wolf doesn't catch anything."

"True. I wonder why it's underground like this, though."

I push my legs out, pointing my toes and stretching out the stiffness. Wolf whines from the top of the hideout, but there's no way to get him down here. He'll have to fend for himself, at least for tonight.

"So, how do you know we're going the right direction? Can we really walk to Portland from Iowa? Is it close?"

The thought of walking more makes me want to shut my eyes and sleep for a week.

"We have to walk the direction the sun goes over the sky. East to west. Portland is all the way on the west side."

"How do you know that?"

In Cell, we're taught about the universe, about planets and stars, but never about the specific makeup of our planet. I have no idea where Connecticut is in relation to Iowa, or Portland.

Pax slides a suspicious glance my direction. "Everyone knows where the Sanctioned Cities are, and where the Other Core is—otherwise how would we all get to the Summer Celebration?" He seems to realize the answer to his own question. "Oh."

I've never known the layout of Earth because I've never traveled—not in the human sense. Unless they're relocating for their Careers, humans only travel in the summer. And I don't have any summers. It's stupid to feel sad about it. I know now the Summer Celebration is nothing more than an excuse for the Others to gather people together, to reinforce the veils keeping them content, keeping their emotions in check like well-behaved children, but there's still a longing to truly be connected to these people who raised me. Lucas, Pax, Deshi, and I—we don't belong anywhere.

"I'm sorry, Summer." The words are gruff, like he resents having to spit them out, yet they're also sincere. Somewhere, wrapped inside layers of deflection and lazy smiles and charm, lurks a nice boy.

"You know, you promised no nicknames."

"Not true. I promised I wouldn't call you Allie."

Then again, maybe there's nothing inside Pax's charm except an obstinate boy who lives to irritate me to death. "I hate nicknames."

"Why do you think it's so much fun to use them?"

He winks, and my infuriating body can't decide whether to stop breathing or kick him in the face. Instead of doing either, I ignore him. Maybe if I act like it doesn't bother me he'll give up the game. I'm suddenly sure it's a game to him, charming people into liking him, and wonder if he's had success connecting with humans over the years. His personality is much more conducive to making friends than mine, or even Lucas's. Lucas and I played it safe, and that meant being alone.

"I'm going to go out for a while, maybe scout around. I'll take the dog with me, if he'll come, okay?"

The idea of being down here alone swings a pendulum of conflicted emotions inside me. On one hand, separating is probably the worst thing we can do. Lucas and I learned last autumn that we're more powerful together, and if the Wardens show up again, we'll have a better chance if we're both in the same place. But being around Pax isn't as easy as being around Lucas. I could use the time alone to sort out my feelings and figure out how to convince Pax to help me find a way out of this mess.

Pax doesn't wait for me to approve. He simply hauls himself up, past the broken ladder rungs, and disappears from sight.

7.

The sound of Pax grunting as he lands at the bottom of the broken ladder jars me out of a disturbing, looped dream. It takes a little longer than usual for the present to solidify, for me to recall exactly where and when I am. I must have fallen asleep after Pax went out.

In my dream, my mother came to find me. She wanted to talk, maybe even to tell me her secrets, but when she opened her mouth, no words came out. Frustration wrinkled her pretty forehead, but no matter how many times she started that sentence, I couldn't hear her.

Pax's indolent smile helps anchor me, flooding me with such gratitude it catches me off guard. It's not that I don't like him—I think I do, actually. He's different from Lucas, more willing to just tell it like it is, less inclined to protect me. But that's an okay thing to be, really, especially in our situation, and I don't need to be protected. It's not knowing his plan, his intention and agenda, that sends nerves hopping like a circus of fleas in my belly. Part of me wondered if he would come back at all, but now that he has, I realize that I wanted him to. Badly.

"Your dog wouldn't go with me. I found a pile of bricks around the back of what used to be the house and built him a little wall to keep out the wind. He seems to like it. He'll be okay up there tonight."

"Wolf."

"Look, he's not a wolf. He has a blue eye, and—"

"No. His *name* is Wolf." Lucas named his fish; I can name the dog. If it is a dog.

My smile catches him by surprise, and he blinks a couple of times before returning it. "Oh. Sure, whatever."

"Did you find anything?"

"Yes, actually. There's a road—a big one—less than a mile away. The asphalt is cracked with vegetation and big holes sink in lots of places, but it heads the direction we need to go. With any luck, we'll be able to follow it a long way."

"Do you think it's safe, walking out in the open like that?" Iowa is the worst place to be right now. There's no place to hide in the endless flat landscape.

He plops down on a collapsible cloth chair that sits near the packages of bottled water and unlaces his tennis shoes. The sight of his bare feet, chewed up and red from our hike, catch my breath.

"You don't have any socks?"

"Nope. It was summer, remember? I'm lucky I had shoes on when I traveled."

"But your blisters—"

Pax waves a hand, cutting me off. "Don't worry about it. Anyway, we can probably find at least a little cover and just keep the road in sight. That should be good enough. There's a few destroyed buildings closer to the road, but nothing better than here. We should spend the night and then get moving again in the morning."

"Okay." The mention of the destruction brings the Others instantly to mind. Not only have they left parts of this planet to fend for themselves, but they've destroyed the lives of every inhabitant in those areas. Even in the Sanctioned Cities they've stolen the humans' lives. People live with veils in their brains, separating them from strong emotions. They take humans who Break—whether they are injured or their minds can no longer handle the invasion—and no one ever hears from them again.

The Others tortured Ko until blood poured from his face, and a single look from the Prime's son seized Lucas with horrible pain. I want to forget those things happened, imagine we're not up against a force greater than we can hope to defeat. It might not even be possible, but for the moment we have to focus on something semi achievable. "Let's see about dinner, then, shall we?"

Our shelter gets darker by the minute as night falls. We're not going to be able to see our faces in about half an hour, so getting settled for the night is a priority. Pax and I peruse the containers on the shelves, each pulling a few down, then comparing. I grab familiar items that would be safe if they came from a kitchen inside a Sanctioned City but are more risky out here in the Wilds.

Pax holds out his hands, showing me cans of tuna and something called Spam, which I've never seen before and have zero intention of putting in my mouth. He grins as though he knows exactly what I'm thinking.

Some of the cans don't have a pull tab on top, so in the end we're relegated to the food inside the containers we can open. Some corn, two cans of a soup called Mexican tortilla, whatever that is, and the Spam.

"You're really not even going to try it?" Pax holds out the dented blue can full of some kind of pink mush.

"There is nothing you could do to make me eat that."

He hasn't tried it either, I notice, but a thoughtful look ghosts over his features at my emphatic statement. It turns mischievous in an instant. "Really?

Nothing?"

Something inside me snaps at his attitude. It's exhausting babying his feelings, not addressing my wants, and never really talking about anything important. So I refuse. "You could say you'll help me find Lucas."

A thick, writhing silence invades the distance between us, a corporeal entity that displaces the once empty space. Pax doesn't answer, digging into the Spam with a plastic fork. His immediate grimace says my decision to stay away is the right one, but he eats the entire can anyway. If he gets sick later, I'm making him sleep outside with Wolf.

It would be nice to bail him out, to take it back, to change the subject, but now isn't the time to be nice. All four of our fates are on the line—not to mention that of the entire *planet,* according to Cadi—and Pax wants to ignore that fact, as though it will go away if we pretend we're not who—no, *what*—we are. The Others aren't going to forget about us. Chief's face looms in my mind: leering, bent on killing Lucas or me before we could escape Connecticut last autumn. The way he called us *abominations,* the hatred dripping from his voice when he said we should all die . . . I know they'll never stop looking.

Pax needs to understand that, too. Because with Lucas away and the real Deshi captured, Pax is my only ally in this fight.

Tears fill my eyes at the hopelessness of it all. Who's to say Pax's way won't let us live longer than mine? Whether we run or fight, the outcome is likely the same, at least the way the odds are stacked at the moment.

To hide my emotions, I pick up my empty soup and vegetable cans, stacking them in a corner. The toe of my shoe clinks against glass, and when I bend down to explore, the fragile object snags my interest. I hold it under the last streams of late evening light where the ladder comes down, puzzling over what it could be. It has a brass handle and bottom, but the middle is a globe of glass. There's a piece of cloth standing up from the base, and the sound of sloshing liquid is loud in the uncomfortable silence.

It looks like the porch lights on our houses inside the boundary, only instead of a twisty bulb, it has the cloth.

Light the cloth.

"Stay away from me," I growl at my mother's voice. Even to my own ears, the command is weaker than it should be, making it clear I no longer know if her going away is what I want. During my nap, I would have given anything to hear the words Fire wanted so desperately to communicate.

"You're stuck with me tonight, but if you want me to stay away, tomorrow morning we'll go our separate ways." Pax's voice makes me realize I spoke aloud, nearly causing me to drop the brass and glass contraption to the ground.

The piece of cloth lights behind the glass, heated easily by my embarrassment and confusion. It burns steadily, casting flickering shadows on the dirt-packed walls of our little hideaway. After I settle it in a safe place, on the trunk at the foot of the bed, I give Pax an answer. "I don't want you to stay away. I was talking to . . . I don't know. Myself, I guess. I just want to understand why you're so sure figuring out more about ourselves and our abilities won't do any good."

The word *talents* sticks in the back of my throat. Lucas called our abilities talents, but it's hard for me to see them that way. They destroyed Mrs. Morgan and almost Leah, too, not to mention Emmy and Reese and who knows how many more. Even though they helped us escape the Wardens, our powers can hurt people.

I push those memories away and sink down onto the bed, slipping off my shoes and tucking my cold toes under my knees. Pax clings to his silence like a shield, grabbing a bottle of water and unscrewing the cap. The instinct to tell him not to trust water that didn't come from the Others leaps to the tip of my tongue, but there's no point in giving it voice. We're no longer part of the world where the Others make things safe. If they ever did.

From across the room, even in the dim light, Pax's violent shivers are easy to see. His whole body trembles, and it shakes pity loose from my frustration.

I sigh and pat the bed. "Come on, Pax. You're going to freeze to death down there."

Gratitude and something brighter shines in his blue eyes while he studies me from the floor. It takes him about a split second and another wracking shudder to realize my offer is a good one, and he lands on the bed at my side. His skin is chilled and the tiny, flimsy mattress vibrates until worry skitters around me like raindrops. Either of us getting ill could be the end of any plan at all. Without Healers or remedy tablets, we'll die out here in the cold.

"Lie down," I command.

Pax starts, as though my voice attacked him, but quickly recovers and shakes his head. "No, there's only room for one of us. You should keep the bed."

The sleeping space is small, that's true, but I'm willing to share. Just because we don't agree doesn't mean I want him to get sick. Our body heat will accomplish warmth faster than the blankets alone, so I ignore the weird sensation tickling my chest, the one that feels like betrayal as my heart conjures memories of snuggling with Lucas, and roll my eyes. "Pax, we've got to stay warm. We can't afford to get sick. Lie down; there's room."

The fact that he obeys without further protest gives me more reason for concern. He's hardly done anything I've asked since interrupting my raccoon-skinning adventure yesterday evening in the cabin. The casual thought of the heat propelled by that stove brings about an unexpected longing for the place I called home for a short time.

Pax pushes against the wall, leaving me as much space as possible. As a nod to my conflicted feelings, I settle in the opposite direction, my body tight and rigid, my head by Pax's bare feet. With four blankets piled atop our bodies it only takes a few minutes before he stops quaking.

When my leg bumps his, Pax flinches away. The bed is too narrow for us to relax and stay separated, but apparently he's going to try. I probably should have been the one to put space between us, given my autumn with Lucas, but my body continues to betray my heart. A few weeks ago, Lucas and I were courting, and the way he smiled and kissed me took my breath away. But Lucas isn't here, and even though Pax and I are a long way from even being friends, we are alike, connected. We are Dissidents, and the heat of him next to me, the sound of his breathing, spreads a comfort so complete I want to cry from the sense of belonging.

"Did you meet Cadi?" His voice drags over the question, soft and unwilling.

It's Pax's peace offering, this conversation. It gives me hope that he does believe some good could come from our existence.

"Yes. She came to collect my Connecticut mother's belongings after she . . . Broke."

After the Others *disposed* of her.

"Your mother Broke? What happened?"

The answer is too much all at once. *I* Broke her. With my mind. It's better to avoid stories that could make Pax run away just as he's taking steps my direction.

"I'm not sure, really. It all happened really fast." Not a lie. Technically. "How did *you* meet Cadi?"

The pause is so long and complete I worry it might be forever.

"I didn't. Ko told us about her. He was there when . . . when the Wardens captured us."

"Us? I thought they only took Deshi?"

Pax blows out a breath, as though it can expel the horrible truth from his body. "They took us both. It was the first week of Cell and I'd noticed Desh, but hadn't decided if I was really seeing what I was seeing, you know?"

I nod. He can't see me since we're both staring at the roof, but he continues anyway.

"The Wardens appeared out of nowhere. There were ten of them, led by one they called Chief. He nabbed us outside Cell one day, told us to come along for questioning. I mean, I wanted to run, but where would I go? And for all I knew, they were questioning all of the students, and I had no idea about anything. I mean, I had the note and knew I was different, but not that I wasn't human or that the Others would do something worse than Break me if they found out."

I struggle to keep my attention on the ceiling and my voice calm as he finally lets me in a little. "So then what?"

"They drove me past the Portland boundary to this crazy tall black glass building. Deshi was there, and they left us locked up together for days and days. There were cameras and they kept coming in and out, taking blood, hooking us up to machines; they studied us the whole time. Anyway, Ko was there, too. He was different than the rest. Nice." The next pause lasts longer than the previous, and when Pax does finish the thought, the words drip with regret. "He filled in a lot of gaps. When he could talk."

When he stops this time, it feels as though the story is over, at least for tonight. I wait, wondering if he'll pick it up again if I stay silent. My patience is not rewarded.

"I can't tell you the rest right now. I will, though. Promise."

It's enough for tonight. Instead of making him feel worse, I tell him what Cadi taught Lucas and me. About our parents, Other and human. About how she and Ko came from a planet called Sprita but are like us, half-breeds who want to help us try to save this planet. That they can make the world change with a snap of their fingers, create something out of nothing and make you believe it.

I'm not sure how much of the information is new to Pax. He doesn't interrupt but occasionally makes responsive noises. As my tale winds down, his leg rests against mine and the space under the blanket heats up even more.

When our bodies touch he sucks in a sharp breath, then talks again as though he wants to cover it up. "Ko told us that, too, about how he wants us to save Earth from Sprita's fate." He pauses, his tangled thoughts almost tangible in the deepening dark. "It's too big to make sense, though. Does that sound stupid?"

"It doesn't sound stupid at all." It sounds exactly like what my own brain has been trying to articulate since Cadi told us about what happens to the Others' host planets after they leave. That no one and nothing survives. But how can Pax and Lucas and I save an entire planet?

"I don't see how we can beat them, is all. When we try, people get hurt."

No matter how long I wait, he won't elaborate. There's no way he can know I hurt Mrs. Morgan, that Lucas screwed up Leah when he damaged the Others' veil in her mind. About how our fooling around in chemistry resulted in Emmy's and Reese's disappearances.

It sounds like he knows, though. If not about those things specifically, then about something else, something similar.

Something bad.

8.

The next morning comes early. The little lamp with the oily cloth sputtered out in the middle of the night, leaving us once more in the pitch dark of our underground hole. The last thing I want to do is get out from underneath the blankets, made warm by our shared heat. We made progress last night, I think, as far as building some kind of friendship. Instinct says trust rests outside our grasp, at least for now. Pax harbors secrets, as do I, and our paths seem determined to diverge. Mine heads toward Lucas, and hopefully a solution to the situation on Earth. Pax's feet follow a road to Portland and an unknown task.

Surprise wakes me all the way up as I realize how badly I want to be able to call Pax a friend. It's not enough to be kindred.

He sits up before I do, propping his back against the dirt wall and giving me a sleepy smile. The sight of it, along with his disheveled hair and rumpled shirt, drops my stomach into my toes. The physical intimacy of this moment, waking up together, outstrips anything I experienced with Lucas and pushes Pax and I into territory too familiar for a day-old friendship.

Yet something about the magnetism between our bodies feels older than a day. Older than a lifetime, as though it existed even before we were here to experience it.

Pax pulls his gaze from mine with what looks like effort, then crawls over my legs and off the bed. "Thanks for keeping me warm, you little furnace."

For some reason the statement heats my face to an unbearable temperature, even though being compared to a furnace isn't exactly sweet. "No problem."

I run my fingers through my tangled hair, then jam it back into a ponytail, trying not to notice that Pax watches the whole process with an indefinable expression. When I've finished, nothing sounds better than finding my toothbrush. The Wardens pre-empted my daily hygiene when they showed up yesterday. Which wasn't great, in the middle of nowhere, but I did bring toothpaste and a brush. "I think we should take some things when we go. I have another bag; it will hold some of the food and maybe another blanket."

"Yep, good idea. I'm going to use the wasteroom." He pauses on the ladder, turning back with a serious expression. "Don't pack the Spam. It's not worth it."

Pax laughs from his belly at his own pride from the night before, infecting me with his ability to be amused by his own faults. I smile, too, our laughter tumbling together and making the dank hole briefly cheerful.

While Pax hauls himself aboveground, I climb out from under the covers. A chill immediately infects my bones. Socks help, and a fresh sweatshirt and my coat almost thwart a new round of shivers. My cold toothbrush makes my teeth ache as I brush with some of the suspect bottled water in the corner, spitting into the empty soup can from last night. Since I'm as ready as I'll ever be and Pax is taking his time outside, I open the extra bag and scour the shelves. The Spam can stay, but that soup was pretty tasty. I add the remaining cans, along with the vegetables and a couple containers of tuna. We need food other than vegetables until Wolf can catch us more animals.

Pax clatters back down as I test the bag's weight, trying to make sure we keep it as light as possible. He tosses his pack on top of the mussed covers, then strips off his hooded sweatshirt and the plain white T-shirt underneath. The sight of his skin, with its warm, olive tone and the way it stretches perfectly across his chest and shoulders, steals my breath. Muscles are stacked like blocks down his stomach and as he turns to grab a fresh shirt, more ripple across his back. My body feels like it's melting as I watch, and heat spills downward, trickling into my knees and making them weak. It

92

doesn't seem to faze Pax, but I have trouble averting my eyes from the first naked skin I've ever seen. Besides my own, of course.

I manage to look away before he catches me practically drooling, and dig through the wooden box at the foot of the bed where Pax found the extra blankets instead. There are a few sweaters that reek of dust and mildew, but underneath those are books. The covers are paper, like the book holding Pax's note, and look as though they were designed for children. Three of them huddle inside the trunk, intact but musty. I set them down beside me and return to my search. It's a good thing, too, because at the very bottom are four plastic containers holding a liquid that, when I lean in close, smells like the lamp. I've decided that's what makes the cloth catch fire and keep burning. Now we can have light to carry with us without having to make a fire.

Pax peers over my shoulder, the nearness of his body bringing back the mental image of his bare chest. I try to scoot forward, but there's nowhere to go.

"What'd you find?"

I clear my throat and twist to the side so that we're face-to-face and a few feet separate us. "Books and the fluid that makes the light work. So that's good."

He crouches in front of me, still barefoot, and while he peruses the books, I scoot away and rummage through my bag. I find what I'm looking for and crawl back to Pax's side, my feelings of embarrassment under control, at least for the moment.

"Here. I have an extra couple of pairs." I hold out my hand, and Pax looks as though I'm giving him the ability to take out the Others with a single blow instead of a pair of gray socks. A grin lights his face from the inside, eyes shining, as he dumps the books on the dirt floor, grabs the socks, and pulls me into a hug.

"Gosh, they're just socks," I murmur into his shoulder, but I'm smiling, too.

He pulls away, tugging my socks over his tanned, blistered toes. I rescue the books from where he dropped them, reading the titles before stowing them in my duffel: *A Wrinkle in Time. Anne of Green Gables. Harry Potter and the Sorcerer's Stone.*

It will be nice to have something to help pass the time if we're going to traipse over this entire planet to get to Portland, where apparently Pax has something quite important to take care of. At least I can read. On the second page of *Anne of Green Gables,* by a woman named Lucy Maud Montgomery, there's a series of paragraphs basically saying that the pages are full of not-true things, and that they were written in 1908.

That seems like too long ago to have existed at all. A lady filled these pages over one hundred and twenty-five years ago. The Others have been on Earth a bit less than twenty years now.

The books reach out to me with promises of not only stories, but also a glimpse into the place Earth was before the Others invaded, before they reached into our minds and stole our autonomy, our feelings, our ability to fight.

I keep thinking *our,* but that needs to stop. I'm not one of them. The Others stole those things from *them*—the humans. I wouldn't even exist had the Others not committed those unthinkable acts. Plus, unlike the humans, I can overcome the Others' mind control. My mind has always been my own.

Pax boosts me up the ladder, and the sight of Wolf's animal grin when he sees me pours what must be love straight into my heart. It feels like it will burst open, and even though it comes as a surprise to both me and my dog, I drop to my knees and hug him. He licks my face—not as though he's trying to get a pre breakfast snack, but as though he's happy to see me. Pax stares, shaking his head while I pour water out of a bottle and Wolf laps it up.

"Oh, no. He's certainly not *your* dog."

I shrug in response to his teasing tone and re-cap the bottle, stowing it in my bag. It pleases me that Wolf sticks close to my side as we head toward the road Pax found, though, and having him here does more than make me feel safer. It makes me feel wanted.

Pax didn't lie about the size of the street he found; it's six lanes across and a mess, as though chunks flew apart in a million different directions. We stay several feet away, walking in ditches or among trees when they're there. The road heads west and we follow it until the sun begins to disappear under the horizon.

The night is horrible—freezing cold and windy. There's nowhere to shelter, so Pax, Wolf, and I huddle together under four blankets, and I stay awake most of the night so I can keep us warm enough.

It gives me the time to read the first of the books, *Anne of Green Gables*. I've never read a story before, not one with made-up characters with their own problems and friends. I suppose the book isn't meant to instruct, not in the way our Other textbooks are, but Anne and her adventures teach me about the life that must have existed on this planet before the Others redesigned it to fit their needs.

Anne, with her red hair and her tendency to say the wrong thing, wriggles her way into my insides and I doubt she'll ever leave. It's easy to see myself in her struggles, and she's so real it's almost like having a friend. The concept of adoption, that human beings before the Others would take in children that didn't belong to them and love them like their own, comforts me. Perhaps all of my parents really did care about me deep inside, behind the Others' control. Maybe in another world, they would have truly loved me.

So many of the ideas in the story are foreign. I figure out that Cells used to be called schools, and that kids went away to learn even more after they completed Upper Cell. They got to choose what they wanted to do, and who they loved, or even if they wanted to Partner at all. Anne's adoptive parents were a brother and sister that lived together.

I must've dozed off, but when Pax shakes me awake it feels as though I haven't gotten any sleep at all. No dreams invaded the night, which is a relief. It's hard to get good rest while my mother, who might get me killed with her intrusions, pesters me with fruitless conversation.

By the time the sun begins to set once again, Pax must wish he had left me behind no matter how warm I can keep us. In spite of how many times I tell myself to, I can't stop blathering about Anne's life in Green Gables, about how it's so different from the humans' lives now, but somehow more like ours. He listens with a polite smile, and some of the details raise his eyebrows in interest, but it's been hours since I started talking.

In the end, it's not my good sense that shuts me up, but the sight of a city. It's not like a Sanctioned City—there's no boundary and there aren't even houses. Buildings stretch toward the sky like silent sentinels, reminding me of the night Mrs. Morgan Broke and they took us to an Other facility, even though these structures are neither black nor intact. The whole place is deserted, a fact I sense not because of any physical indicators, but more due to the air of complete abandonment.

All of the glass has been blown out of the windows, and it litters the street like crunchy carpet. The majority of the buildings are at least half toppled, but there are a few that appear to remain at their full height. Businesses that sat closer to the street have been completely decimated, reduced to rubble like the house we stayed beside two nights ago. Empty windows make me feel watched, as though anything or anyone could be hiding within the darkness. The whole place makes me want to whisper, but it also inspires awe as I try to take it all in.

A few miles later, the city disappears and we're back in what was probably a residential area before the invasion. Structures that are recognizable as houses droop in various stages of collapse, but even so it's clear they didn't all look the same, and they weren't made of brick, either. Unlike our neighborhoods, each house displays character; I wonder whether their exteriors might have reflected the personalities of the families who chose to live within their walls.

It's hard to study them as much as I'd like because not tripping over the rubble takes a significant amount of concentration, but my favorite house so far is a pretty yellow color, with a painted white porch and a matching swing that remains intact. It's like a dream, and when I close my eyes for a brief moment, Lucas and I sit under a dusky, star-brushed sky as we swing back and forth on a summer night, the sound of those singing bugs—cicadas—filling my ears.

When I open my eyes to reality, shadows encroach on the stretches of concrete sidewalk and the pretty yellow house is missing half its roof. This city is so unlike the pristine environments maintained by the Others.

Pax walks ahead as we struggle over and around chunks of debris, trees sprouting from the middle of what used to be sidewalks, and I try to stick close as the sounds of the night press nearer with each passing moment. I trip on the corner of an object that escaped my notice, falling to my knees and scraping the heels of my hands. Sitting back on my butt, I give Wolf's neck a squeeze when he pushes his cold nose against me like he's worried, then give the offending corner a kick. The whole obstruction comes loose under the force of my shoe, the painted words on broken wooden planks sizzling excited discovery through my mind as I crawl to my feet:

Walt Disney Elementary School.

"An old Cell," I whisper.

The building is mostly gone, but the piles of bricks are a tan color, most of them smudged at the edges with evidence of fire. What used to be a Cell—a school—is reduced to several heaps of wreckage. All the way off to the right side, three walls and part of the ceiling are still standing and have protected at least some of the contents from the weather.

Pax follows as I start toward the intact part of the building, curious about what's still inside, what else I could learn. It's as though reading *Anne of Green Gables* opened a hole in me and made me aware of how empty my life has been, and it seems nothing but more knowledge can fill it. Wolf comes, too, unwilling to go far from my side even though he must be hungry. My stomach cramps as well, but this could be as good a place as any to settle in for the night.

The interior of the room disappoints me. Burned remnants clutter the floor, and the scorched walls smell like wet firewood. In the farthest corner, two shelving units sit upright and unharmed, a picture hanging between them. More books like Pax's, like the ones we found two nights ago, rest on the shelves. Another unit is toppled on its front, and as I look around, it dawns on me that the entire room was full of shelves full of books. As far as I can tell, only a few remain.

All of those stories lost forever.

For some reason, my most recent classmates' faces scroll through my mind, kids who will never know what it's like to read a book that makes them feel as though they've found a friend, or causes them to finally realize that their struggles aren't unique. Right now, it feels like the most depressing aspect of this entire life under the Others, the loneliness, but that's not true. Even though it's never happened to me, I think not being able to feel must be the worst part for the humans. They don't feel the bad things like fear or sadness or anger, but they also never experience elation or love.

I comb through the remaining shelves. The volumes still stacked on them are tattered and torn, missing pages and chunks from their spines. I doubt they'll be readable. I'm digging through the books on the floor under the tipped unit when Pax calls my name. He's standing at the picture hanging at a crooked angle on the cracked wall, which at closer inspection isn't a picture at all.

Blue, black, and green lines squiggle across the white background. In the center is a red pushpin trapping a square piece of paper that reads YOU ARE HERE. We both reach for the bright pin, our hands brushing. It feels as though an electrical charge bites into my skin, and we both yank away. My stomach tightens and all of the words in my head flee like startled birds from a tree.

Pax sucks in a ragged breath, stepping away from me and nodding toward the wall. "It's a map. Like the ones of the universe."

As soon as he says it, I know he's right. During our two hours of astronomy every day for the past twelve years, we studied maps of the stars and planets. I can look at the night sky and name most of them, but we also learn about galaxies we can't see from ours, such as where Deaspura used to be, before war destroyed it and forced the Others to leave. This is a map, and if the pushpin says we are here, then it's a map of Earth.

After a minute, I see the name Iowa to the right, and make out the area that seems to belong to the word. I'm shocked to see that Des Moines, the

Sanctioned City, is a tiny speck in the center. Pax and I are in a city called Omaha, in a bigger place called Nebraska, which I've never heard before in my life. In fact, the majority of Earth that's drawn on this map is made up of places I've never heard of. Connecticut is far away from where we are, all the way to the east. The sight of Portland, as far west as it could be, deadens my limbs. We can't possibly walk that far.

Pax's finger trails along a wide line. "This is the road we've been following. Look—we can take it all the way to here before we'll have to go north."

He points at a place called Salt Lake City, in a humongous area labeled Utah, but it's still far from Portland. Looking at it makes me want to lie down and sleep. The idea of trying to travel there using our powers burbles up toward the surface again, and we're going to have to discuss it at some point. The only thing is, I have no idea if we can control where or when we go, and Pax seems intent on not only getting back to Portland, but getting back there this winter. Then again, what's to stop Cadi from yanking us around, assuming she's alive and capable?

I think of her eyes going dark, of the Wardens and the Prime's son telling her they know she's a traitor. Cadi might have been able to change my note, but it doesn't seem like they'll leave her unattended for long enough for her to orchestrate anything larger. Pax and I are on our own, but traveling is something we could maybe use to our advantage. If I can get him to try.

"So, we keep following it." I notice several larger names set in the big road's path. The road called I-80. "These bigger cities should give us places to stay, at least. And maybe we'll find more clues about how Earth used to be."

Pax gives me a look that's a funny mixture of longing and disdain. "Why does that matter? I mean, what good does it do to make yourself sad about how things used to be? It's better to accept the way things are now."

Irritation at his attitude finally breaks the surface, and I don't shove it back. "Because, Pax, you heard what Cadi and Ko said, and all you have to do is look up all the Others' previous host planets to figure out that their occupation *destroys*. When they decide they're done with Earth and move on, everyone will die. All of your parents, the kids at school. Me, Lucas, Deshi. Isn't there anyone you care about enough to try to stop that from happening?"

"I thought you agreed—"

"I *do* agree that it sounds crazy and impossible! But we don't even have a chance if we don't try, and to do that we have to find out why the Others want us so badly. Doesn't their pursuit make you hopeful at all?"

"Hopeful? No, I can't say that idea ever entered my mind." Bitterness freezes the words to his lips until they shatter away, scattering pain like snowflakes in the winter breeze. Pax's anger shows up in the unnatural wind tossing his hair even though we're protected, swishing the scent of apples and cinnamon and burning leaves into my nostrils until a sneeze threatens.

My own impatience lifts my body temperature, spreads the sweet scent of jasmine until it collides with Pax's spicier flavor. "I'm asking you to consider it, Pax. Consider that they might be scared. Of *us*."

It never occurred to me that they might be until the words slide from my lips. Pax's wide eyes meet mine, and we stare at each other for a moment while the suggestion solidifies into what sounds like the truth. Cadi said the Others want to know what abilities we inherited, to study us or punish our parents with our deaths. But what if it's more than that? What if they're afraid that we could really undo their hold over humanity and lead an uprising against their occupation?

Lucas and I both proved last autumn that our thoughts can somehow take down veils inside human minds. We did it on accident, and then on purpose, with varying results. We spent days wondering what we might be able to accomplish if we could find a way to wake up everyone at once, if we could ready more than four of us to fight the Others for this planet. We could never figure out how to resolve the tiny issue that people go completely insane without the veil, at least at first.

But Cadi pretty much said we can never reach our full potential unless we're all together. I don't know if Pax knows about taking down the veils, but for now, it looks as though I've at least convinced him to think about the potential in our lives instead of focusing on the desolation.

"I don't . . . I never thought of it like that." Pax takes a few steps toward me, stopping a foot or so away with his hands clenched into fists at his side. He leans into my space as though he's being pulled against his will, as though it's almost impossible not to take that extra step and slide his skin against mine. "I'll read your book, okay? I'll try to see why this place might be worth saving. If we could."

9.

In the end, we decide it's not safe to stay in the crumbled Cell. It's my thought first, but it doesn't take long for Pax to agree that if the Others are searching—and they are—that they'll expect us to seek comfort and shelter from familiar things. Houses and Cells top that list, since they've stolen pretty much everything else from our world.

Night falls as we find a place to stop and then worry over shelter. Wind that's so strong it makes me stumble, so cold that every inch of exposed skin chaps and numbs, whistles through the fields along I-80. I'm starting to think staying at the Cell would have been worth the risk when Pax turns to me, shouting over the gale.

"These grasses are tall enough to hide us. We could just stay along the road tonight!" His teeth clatter together, cheeks red like apples.

I shake my head and crane my neck, preferring another option even if searching for it means staying out here longer. We need a fire, and with the wind the open fields will turn to flames in an instant if we both fall asleep. A large outcropping of rocks rises in the distance, blacker than the night. "Look! Those rocks are big; they'll block the wind. We can maybe even find an overhang and use the blankets to close us in!"

My throat goes raw from shouting; Pax follows my pointed finger and hears enough of my suggestion to nod and lead the way. He never looks back, even though his steps are longer than mine and I lag several paces behind, struggling against the headwind. Wolf stays at my side, appearing at home in the freezing weather. His fur sure comes in handy.

For a while, I think my mind imagined the rocks because it takes us more than an hour to reach them. Once we do, though, we have our choice of little nooks out of the wind. The largest overhang we can locate is only about four feet deep, not offering much space, but after Pax crawls up and secures three blankets under some heavy rocks, and I do the same to anchor them to the dirt, the space at least keeps out the wind.

While Wolf wanders away, hopefully to find dinner, Pax and I gather sticks and I start a small fire. The nice thing about our nook being so tiny is that the smoke and flames heat it up within minutes, and the lazy crackle loosens my frozen, aching muscles.

Wolf returns with mournful eyes and empty jaws a half hour later, but Pax and I already shared cans of tuna and corn, anyway. My eyelids droop; hiking the last couple of days has been relentless, and Pax hasn't slowed his pace for my benefit one single bit.

Pax's eyes rake my face as he opens a can of tuna for Wolf. "I'm going to read for a while, but you should go to sleep. You look dead on your feet, Summer."

He doesn't have to tell me twice. Even though the icy wind finds its way into our makeshift shelter, I take care to nestle against Wolf and not Pax. The weird sensation that draws my body toward him disturbs me as much as it entices me, and I fear touching him once would make it impossible to stop.

Pax seems to feel the same, always keeping an intentional distance between us. He's clearly focused on getting to Portland, though he still hasn't confided in me the reason why, and doesn't seem to be distracted by the energy that flies between us without permission. Or by anything else for that matter.

Sleep finally steals the chilly discomfort. Pax and Wolf fade away as I drift.

Then dirt-packed walls surround me on three sides, and the world outside the open fourth wall is dark. I crawl over and look right, then left as my eyes adjust to the dimness. Tunnels reach in every direction, even up above my head and angling down in an abyss. No other alcoves like mine are in my line of sight, but I sense that I'm not alone. If I went searching down the endless hallways, I would find others.

The thought stops me. I wouldn't just find others. I would find *Others*. This is their hive, their connected mind. I know this without being told, as though the knowledge resides deep inside my blood and pumps through me with every heartbeat. I'm not really here, though; this place exists inside my head, but that doesn't make it any less real.

The night I realized that Lucas and I had access to their connected minds comes rushing back. When I touched one of the Wardens intent on bringing us in to the Prime, my mind connected with his and I could hear what he heard, see what he saw. They meet in here, in these tunnels, so they can communicate without being physically together. And since I am part Other, they can't keep me out. Likewise, I suspect Fire uses the tunnels to talk to me when I'm upset or stressed.

The alcove I find myself in must be in a corner of my mind, a place she can get to, but this is different. I'm here, and they're here, and if they see me . . . I don't know what will happen.

All I know is that I don't want to find out.

Before I can figure out how to disconnect from the hive and wake up, Fire appears a step outside my alcove. A brief smile turns up her lips, revealing a beauty so stunning and intense it fills me with awe and pride. I've never seen her smile. She's my mother, and even if she's an Element and helps the Others destroy planets, part of me wants to know her. So I smile back, even though the twist in my gut says it's dangerous. *She's* dangerous.

Fire comes into my alcove and sits beside me, putting a hand on top of mine. Our pale skin is the same warm temperature. She opens her mouth and speaks, but again, no sound accompanies her words. Frustration wrinkles her nose and she taps a finger against her lips, like she's trying to figure out why we can't hear each other.

For the first time, I try my own voice, but keep it to a whisper. "Hi."

Tears fill her eyes at the word, which met my ears as well. I feel a strange brush of sound in my mind, akin to the soft noise a shirt makes when I whisk it over my head, and I can hear her.

"Althea, baby." She puts out her arms as though she wants to hug me but then drops them, unsure.

I'm not sorry. I want to know more about her but jumping into a mother-daughter relationship like the one Anne formed with Marilla Cuthbert will take time. It might not even be possible, given what she is, but a piece of me deep inside threatens to shatter with the wanting of it. "Why am I here?"

"You're not. You're asleep. We're simply communicating through a specific part of your mind. You are a part of this hive, which is dangerous, my daughter. I love that we're able to converse in this manner, but you should avoid this place. Let me find you from now on. The more time you spend willingly in your sinum—" She pauses, seeming to realize the word doesn't mean anything to me, and struggles for a moment to translate. "Your bay. Pocket. At any rate, the more you are here, the bigger trace you'll leave. It took me over four years to find you, and I'm your mother. They've been searching, too; they'll find your sinum, your alcove, eventually, and then you'll never be safe. Whenever you sleep, whenever you are not in control of your consciousness, you'll be vulnerable."

"How do I know you're not trying to trick me?"

She tries to mask the pain that darkens her expression before answering. "It's a fair question. I've . . . we've all changed. Someday I hope to tell you about Ben, your father, and how he altered me to my core, but now is not the time. Don't come back, Althea. I'll find you. I promise."

As though she summoned them, the sound of pounding footsteps thuds in the tunnel outside my

112

nook. She places two fingers inside my palm, heating them until the burn rips a scream from my throat. The sound is loud, and for a moment I'm sure she did it so they could find me, but my eyes open to a panicked Pax shaking me awake.

"Summer, what's wrong? Why'd you scream like that?"

Sweat soaks the hair on my forehead and the back of my neck. Wolf moves away from me and watches from several feet away, head cocked to one side as he reconsiders befriending a girl who screeches in her sleep. I suck in a few deep, calming breaths as I tell myself it was just a dream, another dream about my mother, about the Others.

Only what if it isn't? What if they can use the hive to find me, just as Fire suggested? To find us both? The desire to tell Pax everything lights inside me, but one look at him talks me out of it. His handsome face, those blue eyes that remain so guarded, so unsure of how to react around me. The way he promised, just tonight, to rethink his convictions because of the things I said. If I tell him about my dreams, how my mother told me the Others can use them to find me, he could decide he's better off alone. He might think my presence will betray him.

"Althea, please tell me what's wrong." His voice drags over my real name, as though having to use it, to face me and what's happening, hurts him somehow.

It almost changes my mind. Except the idea of being alone in the middle of this big, wintery planet is the scariest thing I can imagine, infinitely more frightening than even the idea of facing the Prime's son again, so I push a wobbly smile onto my lips. "It's fine. A bad dream, that's all."

Skepticism is at home on Pax's face; in fact it's the expression he chooses most often, so it's not a surprise right now. Especially since it's warranted. To distract him, I ask about the book, which lies on the ground at his side.

In spite of the way we seem to know each other on a deep level, the reality is that we don't, so Pax drops the inquisition. Instead, he tells me what he likes about Anne and what he doesn't, how he hopes the other stories we brought along have more boys in them. While he talks, I curl my fingers around the two round, red burn marks in the center of my palm.

***

Over the next ten days, sleep becomes a luxury I can't afford. The thought of my mind accidentally going back into that hive, giving the Others permission to enter my brain, keeps me awake more often than not. I catch a few hours here and there, but by the time my eyes fall closed I'm too exhausted to dream at all. I can only hope that means my mind stays in the blessed emptiness along with me.

It's funny that the pressing nothingness of traveling used to be the worst thing imaginable. The memory of that feeling, that I don't exist in this world, fills me with familiar dread, but if I *could* go to the nothing place, maybe I could get some rest.

The nice thing about all the extra time is the reading. I've read *Anne* twice more, and *Harry Potter* and *A Wrinkle in Time* two times each. I love them all, for different reasons, but I've been harping on Pax for the last two days to read *Wrinkle,* which was written by a lady named Madeleine L'Engle. There's a scene toward the end that reminds me of the humans on Earth, and I love that it acknowledges the existence of species besides humans but doesn't assume they're all bad.

Pax likes *Harry Potter* so much that he keeps re-reading it. My favorite thing about that one is how the kids end up saving the day, and that's the bit I'm hoping Pax likes the best, too. All of the magic opens my mind to so many ideas, even though I'm pretty sure the Others don't have access to that kind of power. That's why they needed the Spritans and went out of their way to create beings such as Cadi and Ko. So they could do those spells and things. It's interesting that the humans who wrote the stories imagined the possibility before the Others came, though.

Pax said he finished *Wrinkle* when we woke up this morning. According to the map we took from the Cell in Omaha we're somewhere north and a little west of a place called Denver. We're getting closer to Salt Lake City, where we'll go north while I-80 continues its relentless journey west, but it'll still take us at least another two weeks to get to Portland, we've guessed. It's been snowing like crazy, making the miles we cover slower and harder than they were in the plains. Mountains rise up out of the ground to the north and south of us, their beauty alone enough to make me want to fight for this planet.

"The part you were telling me about was the one on Camazotz, right?"

It takes me a moment to realize he's talking about *A Wrinkle in Time,* about the scene at the end where Meg has to go alone to a weird, terrifying planet to save her father. "Yes. I mean, obviously the Others aren't giant brains pulsing and controlling everything, but . . ."

A shudder rolls through Pax, strong enough to see. "The kids bouncing the balls in time with one another?

It freaked me out. Like the way we all watch the same movies at the same time every Saturday in our identical houses in our matching towns."

I've thought the same thing a million and one times. Even though humans aren't doing every single thing in unison, it's creepy that people aren't in control of their lives. I wonder again why the Others need to keep them alive, what resource Earth has that they need. Why they don't simply kill everyone and use the conquered planet for themselves.

"And the one kid on Camazotz who didn't bounce his ball the same as the rest of them, who got taken away for not falling in line—" I pause. "—do you think he's us?"

"Yes. The pain they inflict to force him into submission, the Others can do that, too."

It's a statement, not a guess.

I suspect Pax knows about the agony the Others can cause without lifting a finger. They infiltrated Cadi and Ko's minds in front of me, then the Prime's son tried to Break Lucas the night before we escaped. They haven't done it to me, and I hope they never do. But they captured Pax. There's a good chance he has firsthand experience.

The conversation about the book takes us until lunch, which turns into more of a stop than usual when

117

Wolf appears with a fat rabbit clutched between his strong jaws. Pax takes it from him, and it strikes me how Wolf has become kind of his, too, these past several days. The dog no longer trusts only me, and will sit next to Pax when he stays up late reading by the fire. It's hard to believe, sometimes, that the Others could find us out here. The land is completely deserted, and we haven't seen any large cities since leaving Nebraska behind.

It's been snowing all morning, and for the past half hour the winds have started to really blow. It could be Air and Water working together, trying to strand us or kill us or make us surrender before the latter happens. Or it could be that it's a normal winter in a place that seems pretty harsh as it is. From the places we've walked, treading west, it's easy to see why the Others didn't choose to place a Sanctioned City out here.

The wind and snow nip at my face until it feels tight and dry. My feet and hands tingle, then go numb, even inside socks and gloves and my coat pocket. Visibility drops, and when Pax turns, he shouts to be heard over the howling.

"We need to stop! I think we're going off course; we can't see well enough to keep straight! Look for a place to get out of the snow!" His face betrays nothing, but panic trips under his words.

118

Even though I tell myself he's not scared, my stomach ties itself into knots, pulling tighter and tighter as the world goes white and the drifts stack up past my calves. Pax and I have to hold hands to stay on course, and I snag the stiff fingers of my opposite hand into the fur at Wolf's neck, not wanting to lose him, either. We haven't seen anything for miles—days maybe—but before that we would occasionally stumble upon half-standing buildings. Most nights we've built our own shelter either out of the growing number of hills and mountains or out of blankets and sticks. Together we've gotten pretty good at fashioning ways to keep the wind and snow at bay, if nothing else, and the fact that I can prevent frostbite comes in handy.

When a sign made out of thick stone, still standing in the deep drifts, appears in front of us, it looks as unbelievable as Cadi's magic.

Fort Laramie National Historical Site.

I have no idea what a fort is, but we have to get out of the snow, now. The sight of a pretty solid-looking building standing several yards behind the sign loosens the fear threatening to tear me apart. With the howling wind pushing us backward, it takes Pax and me another fifteen miserable minutes to shove our way to the one-story, white building. When we push inside, out of the cold, it feels like we've discovered the best place on this

119

entire planet. Wolf shakes from head to toe, dismissing snowflakes and water in every direction until Pax and I are soaking wet and shrieking with relieved laughter.

We settle down and explore our temporary home. My stomach grumbles at the thought of Wolf's lunch offering, but there's nowhere to make a fire, at least not at the moment. The building's walls are lined with glass display cases. Some hold weapons, others strange-looking leather clothes with turquoise and fringe, and another has some sort of ancient uniform inside. There are framed maps and quotes from people I've never heard of about what I assume is a race called Native Americans. Apparently they had some kind of quarrel with the people who lived in this place before, when it was called Fort Laramie.

At one end of the creepy ode to the past is an expanse of soft leather wrapped around three upright sticks. It's roped off, as if it's some kind of display, and the floors inside are covered in animal fur. In the center is a fake fire pit, and I wish more than anything I could start a real fire there. The opening in the top of the structure, which the sign calls a tepee, looks like it's meant to vent smoke, except we're not outside.

Instead, Pax volunteers to go outside to clear a spot for a fire after we find a broom in a storage closet. The south side of the building is semiprotected from the huge drifts piling up against the north wall, and I get a pretty good fire going after a few tries. Between the three of us, the rabbit is gone within ten minutes of being cooked, and then we stretch out on the furs inside the tepee for a nap. It's cold inside the building, but not terribly so once Pax, Wolf, and I are under a couple of blankets.

Pax's breathing evens out, then Wolf starts to snore. My eyes grow heavy, even though I'm trying not to sleep, so I pick up one of the books touting the past of Fort Laramie that we found in a little store at the front. It doesn't take long before the words begin to blur and I can't remember why fighting the heaviness is so important.

10.

Thankfully, this afternoon's slip into the unconscious doesn't result in any forays into the Other hive. That I can remember. Pax's snores make me smile as I lay in the darkness, then I roll over and press my nose against Wolf's. He pants, which makes him look as though he's smiling, and pleasure crawls under my skin.

"Hey, bud. Think it's stopped snowing? Maybe you can go out and catch some dinner."

He and I extricate ourselves from the tepee without waking Pax, but the windows reveal the opposite of no more snow. We can't have slumbered that long, but a white blanket smothers the world as far as the eye can see. Branches of the huge pine trees hang heavy with mounds of fluff, the ground is covered, and it's still coming down hard. There's no way we're going anywhere tonight. Probably not tomorrow, either. This fort is a lifesaver, plus it has more books than I know what to do with. Although if they're all going to put me to sleep, I'll stick with the made-up stories.

Outdoors is silent under its frozen cover. The lack of noise is strangely comforting, as though the storm insulates us from the rest of existence, wraps us in a cocoon that can hide us away. I know that's not true— the Others are part of me, and they're part of Pax. It's not fair to him to keep the secret of the hive mind from him, to hide that they're looking for us inside our subconscious, too. I'm being selfish, afraid he'll leave when he finds out.

But he's keeping things from me, too, and we're never going to be able to move forward together, or apart, if we don't find a way to face each other without secrets. Even though we've been thrown into each other's company, there's no implicit alliance the way there was with Lucas. I knew instinctively he'd always be on my side, that we'd find a way to align our visions for the future. But it's different with Pax. In some ways, more exciting. And more infuriating.

Pax appears at my side as though my musing called out to him, jarring me out of the warring thoughts in my head and heart. For a long time we stare outside at the weather that's going to trap us for days. Our breath fogs circles on the glass. A sideways glance at his strong profile, the determined set of his jaw, and his dark hair tightens my chest, and I have to resist the urge to reach out and touch him. When he meets my eyes I see the same smothered desire trickling through his carefully constructed façade and a deliciously warm pleasure fills me. My mind slogs through what it wants, groping for a safe topic.

"Seems like we're not leaving this fort anytime soon," I remark. Boring, but safe.

"Looks that way. Come see what I found in the shop."

We'd found the store during our initial sweep of the building, but what Pax shows me now is a game, played with small rectangular pieces of laminated paper—cards. While we read the instructions, Wolf goes out into the storm. Whether he's looking for food, making waste, or simply stir-crazy remains a mystery, even though we've traveled together for weeks now. I think animals aren't meant to be cooped up, is all. He gets restless.

Pax and I play a silly game called Go Fish, then another called Old Maid until we get bored. Wolf returns again with sad eyes and no food, so we eat some green beans and split another two cans of tuna between the three of us. We're almost out of the provisions we took from the underground room in Iowa. "We're going to need food soon."

Pax spreads the map out on the floor, walking his fingers between Laramie, Wyoming, and Salt Lake City. It's at least as far there as we've come from Omaha, which means another ten to fourteen days, depending on the weather. But another rummage through our supplies reveals perhaps only another four or five days of food. If we stretch.

More than we have been already.

With the winter weather, Wolf's had a harder time finding animals to kill. I've lost so much weight my filthy, permanently wet jeans slide down my hips all day long. The shop where we found the books and cards also has clean clothes, so I change out of my stiff jeans and into a pair of soft pink sweatpants and a matching hooded sweatshirt with FORT LARAMIE written on the front. All of the clothing smells musty, but at least it's dry.

I don't like this place, or what it seems to represent—a fight between different kinds of people who all wanted the same land. It reinforces the questions Lucas and I kicked around after seeing a news report about a couple in Portland. The man had Broken and killed his Partner, then himself, leaving their young son alone and probably half Broken, too, after witnessing all of that. I wondered whether humans weren't better off the way the Others kept them. Sure, they're cut off from the good emotions—the ones that flood me in the presence of Lucas and Pax come to mind—but humans are also incapable of the violence that I'm beginning to fear once ruled them as a species.

I wonder if Pax knew that family, since he was in Portland last season. Probably not, though. There must be hundreds of families in Portland. I never knew them when I spent seasons there.

Back in the tepee in our warm, clean clothes, Pax surprises me when he puts down the thick tome about Fort Laramie he's been reading and voices my train of thought. "This place kind of makes me feel like humans aren't any better than the Others. I mean, according to the plaques on the walls and this book, the guys in the fancy uniforms tried to take the land from the American Indians, but who knows who *they* took it from before that. Were humans always fighting wars?"

The word *war* rings a bell, and after a moment I remember I saw it in Lucas's note holder; it was part of the words I liked:

A time for war, a time for peace. To everything, there is a season.

I recite as much as I can remember for Pax, and although he gets the gist of what they mean, his lips pull down into a distasteful frown.

I redouble my efforts to show him an opposite opinion. "Look, I'm not saying that I *want* to fight the Others, but Ko said the time has come. And the words, they say there's a time for everything, even to fight." The sentiment tastes sour on my tongue. Last autumn, I was the one telling Lucas we needed to tread carefully so the humans wouldn't suffer because of our actions. "We could keep the humans safe, maybe, if we understood our abilities better."

Pax studies me for a minute, then digs *A Separate Peace* from his pack. He keeps it close to him, so it's the one book among our things that I haven't read. He hands it to me, letting go a little bit reluctantly when I tug it into my lap. I feel the same way about my locket. It's never away from its place around my neck.

"You should read it. It might change your mind, about people. About war."

"It's about war?" Curiosity needles, urging me to open and start reading right away.

"It's about a lot of things, and most of them aren't very nice. I've spent years figuring Ko picked it for a reason, that there's something about the story or the people in it that are supposed to teach me something particular."

"And have you figured out what it is?"

His voice hardens around the edges. "Maybe. It doesn't mean I agree."

Pax gives me a tight smile before getting up and going outside to take care of personal business. When he comes back, I'm sitting in the glow of the lantern we brought from Iowa, already on chapter two of his book.

"'Night." Pax lies close enough to keep warm but far enough to avoid touching me. The scent of minty toothpaste, the fresh outdoors, and his particular mixture of spicy sweet smoke makes me dizzy.

I hold my breath, withstanding the war between the fading memory of Lucas's affections and the nearly frantic desire to feel what it's like in Pax's arms. Not that he would invite me in; Pax seems as intent as I on not crossing any kind of line past traveling companions or casual friendship.

Wolf pads in between us, flopping down with a great sigh and closing his keen eyes. Left alone in the silence and flickering light, I return to the story of Finny and Gene, which has already captured my attention with the wavering trepidation spread through its pages.

***

The Prime's son finds me in my alcove. He doesn't look like the Deshi we knew last autumn; he looks like the Other who grabbed Lucas and would have killed us both when he shed his disguise. I don't remember getting to the hive tonight, or whether or not I saw my mother. When Chief's painfully cruel face pops into my space, it's as surprised as I feel. He doesn't expect to see me here.

The ensuing panic startles me into motion in the same second he reaches out to grab me. His long fingers slide through loose strands of my hair, grasping enough to rip at my scalp. I scream because of the scorching pain, because of the fear, and my brain struggles to extricate us from this place where we aren't present, not physically. He can't follow me into consciousness, but if he gets enough control to keep me asleep, they'll find a way to make me tell them everything. Where I am. Who I'm with.

Pax. I can't betray him. I struggle harder, until hair rips free from my scalp and my attacker is left standing with nothing but a fistful of red strands.

Right before I wake up screaming, I see Flacara— my mother—standing behind him, as calm as can be. Maybe I don't try hard enough to block her from my mind. In spite of everything, Fire is still my mother— which in no way means she won't get me killed.

"Summer! Althea, wake up!" Weariness and concern, a strange combination, infuse Pax's urgent request.

It's no wonder, given that he's woken me like this at least three times in the past couple of weeks, and I always say it's nothing but a bad dream. This time, terror throws my soaking wet body into his arms. My scalp burns where Chief ripped out my hair, but it must not be missing in reality because Pax doesn't exclaim that I'm suddenly half bald.

After a moment, his arms lift and wrap tentatively around me.

The heat between us catches me off guard; it's stronger than even I suspected. Like we're melded together, tied to each other deep inside, and before I know what's happened, our mouths press roughly together.

The sweet taste of apples tickles my tongue as his lips part, mingling with the swell of jasmine and cinnamon tangling in the air. My recent fright melts away, replaced by the intense desire yanking my heart into stutters and turning every slide of his hands, every slip of his tongue against mine into bursts of pleasure.

It feels so good to let him hold me, for us to finally connect, but at the same time it's frightening—the desire to be even closer, that there's still too much between us even though I'm sitting in his lap—so strong it makes me want to rip at his clothes. I lose myself further in the smell and taste of him, and Pax groans into my lips as his hands tangle in my hair. My hands roam under the hem of his thin shirt, and I gasp against his mouth at the feel of his taut skin against my hot palm.

When I do think about something besides touching every square, hard inch of this intoxicating boy, Lucas's face pops into my mind. His sweet dimpled smile, the way the wind tosses his blond curls, how he wants so badly to figure out how we can help the humans find a way to survive.

We break apart at the same time, not gently but as though someone turned the magnet between us around, repelling our bodies back with a shove. Pax's face twists, a mask of horror and something else I can't quite read. My heart pounds and tears fill my eyes at what I've done, what I've allowed to happen here with Pax while Lucas waits somewhere else, probably scared and alone. The hem of Pax's shirt smolders where I had hold of it; he notices and dampens the smoking fabric before it burns him.

Confusion sweeps through me in a mad swirl, caused by the frantic kiss and my lack of immediate regret. Guilt, yes. Regret, no. I'd been sure I was falling for Lucas last autumn—only a short number of weeks ago—and together we had a plan, we supported each other. Now Pax is here, and despite the fact that he doesn't seem interested in a future and hasn't even told me what we're on this quest to find, a piece deep inside of me wants him, without question.

It's more than the insane, instant attraction, though. Pax doesn't baby me. He pushes me, questions me, and forces me to figure out why I believe the things I do. These past weeks I've felt stronger than ever; even if he does decide to go away and leave me alone, I'll be able to survive.

"That can't happen again." Pax's words cut the silence and pummel my pride, even though I'd been thinking the exact same thing. He grimaces at my expression. "I have a plan, Summer. You have a different one, and yours obviously includes Winter. Nothing is more important to me than getting to Portland and finishing my business there. So, you and I? We're both Dissidents. We can help each other, but nothing more. I need you to tell me right now what you're hiding. Your dreams scare me—you never sleep, you look like hell. We have a long way to go, and as strong as you are, you'll never get there like this."

"Leave me behind, then." I bite off the words, heat pooling in my palms as I try to control the burning humiliation. "You've just made it quite obvious you're not interested in being my friend or in what happens to me. Go to Portland and let me to deal with my own problems."

A sigh winds out of him and into the space between us, now a widening gulf. "Of course I care about what happens to you. We've been kicking against the current dragging us together since the first moment we met, and just because I'm not going to drown in it doesn't mean I don't *feel* it. I promised I'd think more about you and Winter's idea about saving Earth, and I am. But you and I . . . I'm not sure just friendship is an option. I'm not leaving you, though. We're in this together, as long as you're still coming to Portland, so please let me help you."

The words press a cooling salve into my assumption that I just threw myself at an unwilling body, even though the heat of the moment proved otherwise. A few deep breaths calm my pounding heart as Pax waits, maybe for me to realize I can trust him to stay beside me even after he knows everything.

In some ways, the breaking of the tension between us makes things easier. He's said he's not leaving. So it's time to tell him everything and let him make an informed decision about whether to hide his head in the sand or to help Lucas and me come up with a plan.

Wolf whines, agitated by the emotions flying around the room like a storm of birds. Pax and I take turns patting him until he settles between us. I relight the lantern, taking the time to organize my thoughts and figure out the best way to explain the hive mind, if he doesn't know about it already.

Pax takes a deep breath, blows it out, and then surprises the snot out of me.

"I have to go back to Portland because the last thing I did when I was there was get my summer parents killed."

11.

The confession makes the world go black for the briefest of moments, but not for the reason he might assume. The memory of Mrs. Morgan, of her easy smile and graying hair, assaults my battered heart. I don't say anything because nothing can make it better, but don't drop his gaze so he knows I'm not scared to hear what's coming next.

"It all happened like I told you before—the capture, the torture, Ko. He showed up late one night, after they'd gone after Deshi's mind so hard I thought he'd turn into a puddle of himself before morning. He hadn't moved since they brought him back, just stared at the walls and leaked water. I had the chance to escape, but Deshi wouldn't move so I left without him."

Pain squeezes his eyes closed and he pinches the bridge of his nose as though he can push himself back together. "I just left without him," Pax mutters again, almost to himself. "By the time I got back to the Sullivans', I was out of control. All I could think about was telling them—and then everyone—what the Others were doing to our minds. Mr. Sullivan saw me, I mean, really *saw* me, as though he heard the frantic thoughts racing through my mind. He went insane, his eyes rolling around in a panic, and nothing I said after that even registered. He tried getting his Partner to shed her veil, and finally I tried just thinking at him. That's weird, right? But I thought that he should calm down, and that it was me who was wrong, not him. Not the Others. He stopped screaming nonsense, but he wasn't . . . he wasn't right. I traveled that night to winter in Georgia, but right after I got there we saw a report on the news. It was the Sullivans' house, and he'd murdered his Partner." Pax's eyes flutter to mine, despondent and wrecked. "It's because of what I did to him. His mind couldn't make sense of it, and he Broke."

The bloodstained sheets covering the dead bodies on the news, the Warden's baffled face, the human journalist's cheerful reporting of the incident had chilled Lucas's and my blood and led to our questioning the goodness of humanity. And Pax had made it happen.

"I'm so sorry, Pax." There is one thing I can say. I can tell him I understand, because I do. But this is Pax's moment, and the fact that he's finally sharing it with me proves that he meant what he said about the two of us sticking together. Maybe it even means he's

136

reconsidering his position on our purpose here on Earth.

"Me, too. Their deaths are horrible, but nothing is worse than the fact that I left Tommy, their son, alone. Without parents. They were all he had, and the news report didn't say what happened to him. I shouldn't have left him, and I shouldn't have left Deshi, but I did . . . I left them both."

The guilt soaking his confession hurts my chest. I want to plug my ears so I don't have to hear it. Pain vibrates through the inside of the tepee, pouring from Pax and swirling toward me until we share it, although I know the brunt of the agony isn't something I can take away from him. Instead, I get to my knees and inch toward him, careful to leave distance. "That's why you want to go back to Portland?"

He nods, wiping at cheeks stained pink with embarrassment. "I want to make sure Tommy is okay. He's not my real brother or anything, I know, but he doesn't have anyone now because of me. And I don't know, I thought maybe together you and I would be strong enough to help Desh."

"We *are* stronger together. It's how Lucas and I traveled." I try to distract him. Tommy is probably Broken, maybe disposed of, but that's not a truth Pax needs to hear right now. And maybe he isn't. There

137

could be a nice, childless couple in Portland who took him in. The situation falls too far outside the norm to guess how the Others would handle it, but with his parents Breaking under such suspicious circumstances, it's hard to believe they simply let the boy be. Even on the news report, he hadn't seemed okay.

"How?"

"Remember how I told you about my Connecticut mother Breaking? That was my fault, too . . . I didn't know about the veils at the time, and we had only guessed about the mind control. No idea we could undo it, or even mess with it. I snapped and accidentally decimated her veil. . . . The Others came and they took us all to a facility—it looked like the one you described, where they held you and Deshi—and they refreshed my dad and the Healer who attended. Just gave them new memories, like the whole night never happened. They tried to do it to me, too, but it didn't work. I've never been so scared in my life." I squeeze my eyes shut for a second and then continue. "The Others disposed of Mrs. Morgan. *Disposed*, that's how they put it. She never came back. The kids at school had all heard that she Broke."

"That's terrible." Shared regret shines in Pax's eyes.

"It is. It is terrible, Pax, and the Others are going to keep doing it unless someone stops them. You know

138

about the veils, you know that we can undo it. But you also know human brains can't cope with the loss of the Others' control, at least not immediately." Understanding dawns, and I hold his gaze. "That's why you don't want to fight. You're worried we'll be the cause of everyone's death, instead of giving them back their lives."

His eyes glint with hard determination. "Why are you so sure I'm wrong?"

Leah's black curls and pleading eyes spring to the forefront of my mind. The fact that she survived after the Others had her, after Lucas poked holes in her veil, after I took it all the way down and left her in Danbury. "Maybe I've seen enough to believe it's worth trying."

A sigh so deep and thick it sounds like the entire world settling on Pax's shoulders envelops the tepee. Maybe it is, but if the world rests on him, it rests on all the Dissidents. A fourth of it is mine to bear.

"You don't have to do this alone. There are four of us, and Lucas and I doubled our power by pooling it. Cadi said our—the Elements together are stronger than all the rest of the Others."

He doesn't respond, but interest lights his face and a little bit of hope springs up, like the first plants to push through spring soil. Traveling to find Lucas will have to wait, even though I'd feel better about our chances with three instead of two, because I see now why Pax wants to get back to Portland. The longer we wait to return, or if we travel and end up skipping another season or two, it will be harder to learn what might have happened to Tommy, or to stop what might still be happening to Deshi. Every hour we leave them in the hands of the Others means a smaller chance they'll be okay when—if—we manage to free them.

I'll have to trust Lucas to be the smart, self-reliant boy I knew, and to take care of himself for a little bit longer. A throbbing piece of me misses him so much in this moment, forlorn over not knowing where he is, if he's safe. If he's sweating to death in summer or hiding in a spring Wilds full of flowers. Or if he's been caught and is rotting in a prison alongside Deshi.

Lucas would know what to say, how to convince Pax that we should have hope, beyond a shadow of a doubt. Or maybe he would talk Pax out of the crazy idea of going anywhere near the Others until we have a solid plan of action. Lucas would know, and I don't, so all I can do is follow my gut.

"I said I'd go with you to Portland, Pax, and I will. Please promise me we'll be quiet about it, though, and not make any hasty moves. If we find Deshi or Tommy, and the Others have them, we'll need a plan. I know you think I only want to find Lucas because of our . . . friendship, but he could help us get them back."

"It's not that I'm against finding Winter. If he can help, then that's what we'll do. But I need to see for myself what's happened to them first. Before the Others find us."

Those last five words bring the whole reason for this conversation crashing back down around me, and it steals the hope that's sprouted between us in this place full of pain. Pax confessed his secret, that he's responsible for two human deaths, that he knows our ability to unveil the humans leads to little more than their quick disposal by the Others. It's time to tell him about my dreams, about my mother's voice, and what Cadi said about our private niches inside the Other hive. Our sinum.

About how earlier tonight, Chief was waiting for me when I closed my eyes.

In the silence, I find some scraps of courage still inside me and wish for them to tide me through the coming confession.

It scares me that Pax might see the same thing I do—that the Others can find us wherever we go. That sooner or later, there won't be anywhere we can hide.

12.

"Have you ever touched an Other?" The question emerges as a whisper, even though I meant it to have more confidence.

"No. Even when they locked us up and tortured us, they never touched us. Why?"

"Cadi explained something to us about the Others, about how they communicate. They don't have to talk; all of their minds are connected like tunnels in a sort of hive, they call it, and every Other has their own alcove or cave thing in their mind called a sinum that lets them in and out." I take a deep breath, then lock my eyes with Pax's to make sure he's keeping up. A nod encourages me to continue, even though I'd rather not. "We each have a sinum, too."

"I don't understand. We have what? A place in their tunnels? What does that even mean?" He doesn't sound as upset as he does confused.

Then again, he hasn't heard the worst part. "It means our minds are connected to theirs, but since they weren't aware of us until last season, they never thought to look for us within the hive. Except Fire found my alcove years ago . . . she's been talking in my

142

mind, only I didn't realize it was her until Cadi showed a memory of the Elements to us and I heard her speak."

"Your mother talks to you in your mind." The repeated fact stumbles from Pax's lips, as though he's waiting to believe it before he finishes talking.

"Yes. Usually only when my guard is down, like when I'm losing control or I'm sad. The last couple of weeks, though, she's been visiting while I sleep."

"That's why you stopped sleeping? Because you don't want to talk to your mom?" Pax's trademark skepticism is back, knitting his dark eyebrows together.

"It's not only my feelings about Fire. It's that Cadi thought if the Others suspected they could find us this way, they would look. Fire's knowing where to find me scared me, and the last time I went there, she told me to stay away. That they were looking for me, for us." It takes a minute to find the bravery to continue, but the encouraging expression on Pax's face helps. "And tonight, he found me. The one who looked like Deshi. The one they call Chief. He knows he can get into our heads."

"You saw him? He saw you?" Pax pauses for a moment, opening and closing his mouth like he can't figure out which question to ask first. "If he knows where to find you, why can't he talk in your head all the time like Fire can, then?"

"Maybe we have some kind of built-in defense when we're awake and in control that blocks them? I don't know. All I know is that I'm terrified that the next time I fall asleep and the part of me that's connected to them goes to the alcove, that horrible Other is going to be waiting. And he's going to make me tell him where we are. How can we hide if they can simply read our minds?" My voice rises, panic and desperation fighting for dominance.

"Maybe they can read our minds, Althea. But they can't *control* our minds. We know that. It's the most important thing that makes us different. Which means we can find a way to stop this."

Confidence snags thin fingers in my desolation over betraying us to the creatures we're trying to defeat. Maybe Pax can help me sever the connection. The thing he said about them not being able to control us, about it making us different, lights a flame of relief in my exhausted mind.

"That's true. Cadi said the Others even control their own race. That the part of their minds that knows what they need to survive is cut off from their ability to communicate, so they can't give away the secret. So, we're not just different from the humans; we're different from the Others, too."

"Summer, please tell me you already knew that in your big, stubborn heart. We are different from *everyone*. We are Dissident. Something Else. Being half Other doesn't make us like them . . . not unless we want to be." Pax's eyes have never been less conflicted, and his words might be the most beautiful I've ever heard.

"We're not like them."

"No, we're not. Now, why do you think you dream yourself into the lion's den but I don't? Did Winter?"

"No. I think it's because she found me. Since Fire communicates with me, and I've spent time there, I leave some kind of trace behind or something." The last bit is the hardest to say. "I'm not sure if she betrayed us, or if they followed her, but she was there, too, tonight. With *him*."

Pax's face softens, and he pulls me tight to his side with one arm. The smell of spicy cinnamon and sweet apples kneads my bunched muscles in the brief moments before he releases me.

"We're going to figure something out. If you can keep her out when you're focused, there must be a way to do it all the time. Close off your sinum, somehow." He lies down and holds the blanket up beside him in invitation.

The comfort of being next to Pax isn't something I'm going to turn down tonight, conflicted feelings about Lucas and our relationship or not. Thankfulness for Pax's presence starts in my head and trickles down to my toes. He knows about Fire, and that maybe I'm going to lead the Others right to us, but he's still here. In the dark, with Pax on one side and Wolf at my back, I feel safe. I feel cared about. And even though we're in an abandoned, ancient fort in the middle of nowhere, it's nice. Maybe it will never be with Pax the way it is with Lucas. Every last piece of me accepts the knowledge that it will never be easy to be with him, whether we're companions, friends, or something more. But we've had a breakthrough tonight. Kissing him eased the tension between us, if only a little, and I'm more comfortable now that we've acknowledged the spark we've been ignoring for weeks.

"It's not your fault, what happened to the Sullivans," I whisper. "I feel that way, too, about Mrs. Morgan, but we have to put the blame where it belongs. Because the Others did this. Without the veils, there wouldn't have been anything for us to accidentally take down."

He regards me in silence for several seconds, before a smile drains the uncertainty in his eyes. Then Pax sits up and reaches for his bag, rummaging for a minute before coming up with a pretty rainbow bracelet like the one he hasn't taken off since the day I met him.

"Hold out your wrist."

I do as he asks, curiosity thumping through me. It's too much to bite back. "It's just like yours. Where'd you get them?"

"Deshi has one, too. We . . . we found them." He finishes tying the bracelet around my wrist, the waterfall of woven colors beautiful against my pale skin.

I think again how it looks as if someone rolled the earth and the sky into perfectly balanced threads. That they don't look possible, somehow. "Thank you."

"If I have to be in this with someone, I'm glad it's you."

***

Three days drag past before the weather allows us to leave Fort Laramie and head west. Mountains begin as rocky brown foothills but climb higher as the days pass, snow turning their crests white. It's cold; I've never felt anything as bitter as the winds that numb me within a minute of stepping into them, and we haven't found shelter in a building since leaving the historic site. It's safer—and more miserable—but the insane chill helps me stay awake.

Our next major stop is Salt Lake City, and if everything goes well, we're less than three weeks from Portland. Even though we've been walking though barren countryside and abandoned cities for what feels like forever, the remaining time suddenly doesn't seem like enough to figure out how to find out what happened to Tommy or where the Others are keeping Deshi. And rescuing Deshi might be as important as finding Lucas, feelings aside, if we're like our Element parents and gain power when all four of us work together.

Since I confided in Pax, the dreams have stayed away, but I've only slept a total of nine hours in three days. If I wait until the exhaustion is so complete there's no way to fight it, I don't dream at all. Pax stays awake and watches me in case he can see some kind of clue that I'm sinking into the hive mind so he can wake me up. It's weird, knowing that he watches me while I'm asleep. The discomfort makes it even harder to close my eyes, which is fine except for the fact that I look terrible. The fort had an old wasteroom, and even though it wasn't functional, the mirror reflected my haggard appearance. I'm starting to resemble the little raccoon that attacked Lucas at the end of the autumn, black rings around my scared eyes.

The snow has stopped, but the two-foot-deep drifts still slow our progress. We have fresh clothes thanks to the shop full of items, and in the maintenance closet we even found three pairs of snow boots. Pax's fit pretty well, but mine are huge. Still, they save me the discomfort of traipsing across half the planet in wet shoes.

On the fifth day since we left Fort Laramie, when I think we must be getting closer to Salt Lake City, the woods next to the highway grow dense. It's lovely in the uncomfortable, quiet way winter can be beautiful, and I'm staring up at the snow-covered treetops when Wolf growls. Not a warning like he issued Pax that first day, but more menacing. Pax digs in his heels at my side, yanking me to a stop and behind a big tree.

A hulking catlike animal waits ahead, maybe twenty feet from where Wolf stands. My dog's entire body tenses, tail and head lowered toward the ground and the fur between his shoulder blades thick and spiked. He growls again as the tan cat, at least twice his size, takes a bold step forward, then another. It slinks toward where Pax and I are hiding, black eyes flashing, like it plans to avoid Wolf and go right after us.

Wolf clearly isn't going to let that happen, which should make me feel better, since the cat's long, sharp front teeth are visible from here, but all I can feel is ice-cold dread running through my veins. Powerful muscles ripple under the animal's thin fur as it sinks into a crouch.

"Pax, we have to do something. If they fight, Wolf will get hurt." My whispers draw more attention from the predator, his gaze latching on to our hiding spot as he slides another few steps our direction.

Then the big cat leaps at us.

Wolf reacts, launching into its side and knocking it into the underbrush. I hear a scream, realize it's mine, and sprint toward the ruckus before Pax can stop me. There's nothing we can do. The animals are locked together, all snarling teeth and flashes of brown, black, brown, black as they tumble and snap, swipe and bite.

Wolf yelps, a pain-laced sound that reverberates straight through to my heart. The giant cat disengages and limps off into the trees. The whole fight lasted less than fifteen seconds, but Wolf saved our lives.

And now he's not getting up.

13.

I fall to my knees in the snow at Wolf's side, relieved to see his eyes open and watching me. The red spots dotting the ground catch my breath in my throat, and the gash across the right side of Wolf's chest and down his leg leak more blood onto the snow underneath him.

Pax crouches down beside us, assessing the situation with an enviable calm. My breath pants out in frantic white clouds. Helplessness tightens my chest as I watch my best friend bleed, and a quiet whine full of discomfort wheezes from between his jaws.

"We have to help him."

"Okay. First, we have to stop the bleeding." Pax sounds a little as though he's reciting from a textbook, although not one we read in Cell. He offers a tight smile in response to my curious glance. "My Atlanta father is a Healer."

He grabs a blanket out of my bag, quickly tearing three thin strips from one edge. "Wash off the blood, if you can. Use the snow."

A couple of weeks ago fear would have stayed my hands, worry over the unpredictable nature of a wounded animal, but Wolf isn't any animal now. He's mine, and he needs me. Our eyes meet, his filled with trust and pain, mine surely reflecting horror. He doesn't move as I grab a handful of snow and rub it across the deep gash. The cold clump in my hand turns watery and pink as blood continues to pump from the wound. "It's not stopping."

"Pack some in there."

I do as I'm told, then move to the side as Pax ties two strips around Wolf's chest and winds another down his leg. Thankfully, blood doesn't soak through the material, at least not right away, but the fact that Wolf hasn't tried to stand up snags worry deeper.

"What do we do now? He can't walk."

"Stay here with him. I'll scout around for somewhere close we can shelter."

"Wait. What if you get lost? What if that *thing* comes back?"

He winks, but his heart isn't in it. "The answer's the same: Use your fire hands."

Guilt digs under my skin when I realize Wolf's lying here injured and I could have prevented the whole thing. Why didn't I think to burn the attacker? Everything happened so fast and the huge predator was scary, but I need to be better about thinking on my feet. If I can't even protect my dog from an aggressive animal in the woods, how am I going to shield an entire race of people from the Others?

Instead of sitting here fretting about my many shortcomings when it comes to protecting anyone, I get up and gather some sticks and logs, then build a fire beside Wolf. Ice crusts up around his nose and eyes, a strange sight because usually his face stays dry even when the snow blows from every direction.

The fire seems to help, to calm him, and he even moves a little so he can press closer to me. I get out the thick tarp we took from the fort and spread it on the ground, then tug him onto it and stretch my legs out in the snow. I pull his head into my lap and scratch behind his ears the way he likes. His breathing sounds ragged, and I wish there was something more we could do to take the pain away.

Wolf closes his eyes, denying me the ability to verify that life continues to stir inside them, so I've been staring at his rib cage, making sure it rises up and down, for at least an hour. Even though there's nothing I can do if it stops. I'm beginning to understand how Lucas felt the day we found Fils dead on the radiator—helpless and angry. And he had that fish for years; Wolf's only been with me around a month.

It's a strange thing, loving an animal. I remember wanting to know that love so badly when watching

Lucas, but now that I have it, it's terrifying. Wonderful, true. But the idea of having it ripped away is accompanied by so much pain it's hard to fathom surviving it. The strength of my emotions surprises me. In some ways it's even stronger than what I feel for Pax, or even Lucas. Because Wolf doesn't want anything in return for caring about me. He almost died for us today. And he would have, had it come to that.

In this moment, it's brilliantly clear to me why the Others chose to keep the animals separate. It's not because of fear, or danger. It's because of love. The emotions their unconditional devotion can inspire are too much to purge or to block, I bet.

Footsteps crunch through the snow and push me into a defensive position on my knees, but it's only Pax. He shakes his head, warming his blue hands at the fire.

"Can't find anything nearby, and the sun's going down. We'll have to make do here." His worried gaze slides to Wolf. "How is he?"

I shrug. "Sleeping."

"We should change the bandages again." Pax kneels and rips apart more of the blanket, talking softly to Wolf as he unwinds the soaked crimson strips, cleans the wound, then rebinds it.

The trees offer some shelter, blocking the worst of the wind and creating a dark canopy above our heads.

It's still freezing, but that's become a bit of a relative term these past weeks. Instead of complaining, Pax and I simply gather more wood. We drag the tarp bearing Wolf's weight to the largest fir tree we can find, then settle on either side of the injured dog. A new fire springs to life under my trembling hands, and my jumpy emotions make it a little too big at first. It's been a while since controlling the heat has been an issue, the mistake reminding me how much we still have to learn.

Pax falls asleep, but I can't. Watching Wolf breathe does nothing but grind concern deeper into my patience. He'll never be able to get better without resting, and every sound that emanates from the forest shakes him awake with a start, eliciting a whine of pain at the sudden movement. The fire stays strong, so at least he's warm enough, but we need shelter.

When the night sky fades from black to blue to gray I ease to my feet, shaking the kinks out of my back from sitting against a tree trunk all night. Pax is slumped sideways, his right hand tangled in the thick fur across Wolf's shoulders, and he frowns in his sleep. The expression shoots a new feeling into my heart, at least where Pax is concerned—tenderness. Since we met, so many of our interactions have popped and sizzled with attraction or conflict, but ever since that night at Fort Laramie, my emotions have managed to slip toward affection. We still keep our distance, physically, but it would rip me in half if something happened to him. As much as if Lucas were hurt or Broken.

A smooth piece of hair falls over Pax's eye. I turn away, fighting the urge to brush it back, and start scouting the area for a usable sanctuary.

It's amazing what trekking halfway across the planet on foot will do for a girl's ability to navigate on her own. While Lucas and I couldn't go in one direction without the aid of the stars, my brain now catalogues landmarks and senses when we've moved off course without me asking. This morning I take note of the rising sun's position, then start looping in a circle around where we settled last night. Pax was gone about two hours searching yesterday, so I go farther. Four hours later, I find what I'm looking for and then make my way back to my friends.

Pax is awake, and the relief that washes out of his golden tan at my appearance warms me from the center. "Where have you been?"

"Looking for somewhere we can stay while Wolf heals. There's something called a ranger station about an hour north of here. The windows are all busted out but the walls are standing." I kneel next to Wolf, who gives my hand a halfhearted lick. "Do you think he'll walk?"

"I don't know. It doesn't seem like it."

"Well, we can pull him on the tarp, then."

"That dog's got to weigh seventy pounds, Summer."

"I don't care. We're not leaving him. I don't care if it takes all day." My voice rises with irritation.

He frowns at the determined set of my jaw. "I was only making an observation. I wouldn't leave him out here either. He saved our lives."

Decided, we prepare to leave. Getting him to the station doesn't take all day because Wolf reacts to our movement and struggles to his feet. His long white legs are a little wobbly, and we do set a slower pace than the one we've fallen into these past weeks, but it takes us less than three hours to reach the ranger's station.

The interior of the building is cold because of the missing windows, but rugs cover the floor and there are bedrooms with actual beds. Furniture adorns the living room, arranged around a cutout in the wall that makes me squeal.

Wolf's ears prick and Pax shoots me an irritated look. "What are you so excited about?"

"I know what this does." I stride over to the cutout, crouching down to peer inside. The bottom is covered with piles of gray ashes, reminding me of the magicked room where I met the Elements for the first time.

Well, not technically *met,* since they didn't know I was there, but still. They had one of these, and my mother controlled the fire they built inside it. I peer up, finding a wrought-iron handle that's chilly under my palm. The sound of grinding cement meets my ears when I give it a push, and winter air flushes toward me from above.

It's the same as the stove in the cabin, the way it piped the smoke outside, or how the window drew it away from my floor fire. These things are neat. "You put wood inside, then light it, and the smoke goes up there."

Pax leans his hands on his knees, peering up into the darkness. He grunts. "Like the stove. I'll go get some wood."

Wolf looks as though he's ready to collapse again, so I make him a bed of dry blankets in front of the fire holder. He lies down and I scratch his ears. A small, flat creature, an amphibian or reptile of some sort with bright yellow scales and purple spots, peers at me from the arm of the couch. Pax comes running in response to my shriek, shaking snow out of his hair, but the thing scrabbles down to the floor and disappears. I describe it to him, and we hunt it for five or ten minutes but find no trace. Exhaustion takes hold, even with knowing a scaly little creepy-crawly is lurking about, and we give up.

While I take care of the fire, which is crackling happily within minutes, Pax rips more strips from the blanket and changes Wolf's bandages again. A closer inspection reveals the wound still weeps blood, but it has slowed considerably.

"Do you think he's going to be okay?" I ask, not sure I want to know the answer.

"I think so. It's a deep cut, but if we keep him still and clean it, it should heal."

My heart swells at Pax's willingness to care for Wolf, and the fact that his injury is going to keep us here at least a few days doesn't seem to irritate Pax at all, even though we both know he's in a hurry to get back to Portland. I lean over and press a kiss to his cold cheek, pulling away before it can turn into something more.

"Take your shoes off," I say. "You're getting puddles everywhere."

Bright emotion shines in his eyes as he gets up and puts his boots by the door. "I'm going to take a look around."

As reluctant as I am to leave the fire, it could be interesting to see what a ranger's station entails. I don't

159

know what a ranger is, or why he lived out in the middle of nowhere, and it's frustrating that I might never find out. Snooping around could offer a few answers, though.

It's the first intact building we've run across in a long time, but every time we encounter signs of a previous life in the Wilds it reminds me that the perception the Others give off, that there's nothing outside the Sanctioned Cities, isn't true. They destroyed a lot, especially the interiors of the large cities they didn't keep, but humans inhabited every corner of this planet. There have been more cabins alone in the woods and more tiny little towns along the big road than I ever would have believed. The Others stole more than the humans' mental freedom; they took their space, too, and the ability to fill it how they chose.

I can't help but wonder how many people must have died when the Others first came here. Cadi said they'd never encountered a species with as many emotions as humanity and that they Broke many before figuring out how to keep them both controlled and alive. Now that I've seen the size of Earth, I know a good portion of them must have been killed off at the beginning. The land we've traipsed through, the number of ruined homes we've passed . . . there is room for more people to survive than the number that live in the four Sanctioned Cities. Many, many more.

The ranger's station has a bedroom with a regular-sized bed covered with a black comforter. Clothes hang in the closet, mostly uniforms for a man named Ranger Wearn. Clean socks and underpants and T-shirts for a man stuff the drawers, and there are more boots in the closet that will probably fit Pax. They'd fit Lucas, too. I sigh as the ache for him opens up and tries to swallow me. I push it away and grab a pair of socks, stuffing them in my pocket.

Pax is back in the living room, enjoying the fire. His feet are propped on the table in front of the couch and his eyes are closed. He's covered the two windows in the room with blankets I've never seen, and they're secured with some shiny silver tape. The room is warmer already, and as much as I want to crawl up next to Pax, I sit on the floor by Wolf. Memories of Lucas spin through my blood and empty my insides until nothing sounds better than being in his arms. Pax's would be a replacement right now, and that wouldn't be fair. The more my feelings change toward Pax and become grounded in experience and respect instead of wild, almost unwilling desire, the more I wish Lucas were here.

"Hey, Wolf." I snuggle up next to him, letting the heat from his body and the fire comfort me as much as they can. He rolls his head my direction and licks my cheek, buoying my faith that he'll be all right in a few days.

A pile of bottles and packages next to Pax's feet catch my eye. "What's that stuff?"

Pax opens one eye and smiles at me, the sparkle in his gaze making everything better for about ten seconds. "Medicine to clean Wolf's wound the next time I change his bandage. It's old, and probably not as good as what the Others supply the Healers, but it's better than nothing."

"Oh."

Pax stares at me for several minutes, heating my cheeks with his bare perusal. A wrinkle appears in between his eyebrows, signaling an unspoken turmoil that I'm not ready to inquire about or even wonder over in silence.

Finally he closes his eyes again, shoulders relaxing into the sofa. "I'm glad your dog is going to be okay, Summer."

"Me, too. Honestly, he's probably as much your dog as he is mine now."

Wolf doesn't lift his head but his eyes flick between Pax and I, following our discussion as though he knows it's about him.

"No way. I mean, if I attacked you he'd eat my face off. And if it came down to you or me against that giant lion cat thing today, he would have chosen you."

His sentiment stretches a smile across my lips. I really do love that dog. "He's a good dog."

"Yeah, he is."

The warm room makes my eyelids heavy, and when I startle awake a few seconds later, Pax's steady gaze lands on me again.

He picks up *Harry Potter*, opening it to a folded page. "You can go ahead and sleep, Summer. I'll keep watch."

14.

When I open my eyes, the sight of the packed dirt walls of the hive curl dread into my abdomen. The scent of moldy earth fills my head, and the sight of Chief's face explodes flashes of pain in my head. It's like nothing I've ever felt before in my life, as if he takes a knife in each hand and shoves it into my brain through my ears.

But he doesn't hold them still. It's as though those knives are twisting, tearing tissue and ripping into the backs of my eyes. *It doesn't stop, it won't stop, what if it never stops,* repeats in my head until finally, it does. And everything goes black.

The next time I open my eyes, it's like déjà vu. I'm in the room Cadi showed Lucas and me, the one where they had Ko tied to a chair while the Prime Other tortured him for information about our whereabouts. Except this time, I'm the one bound to the chair.

The same Others sit on the raised bench in front of me, the one they call the Prime in the center. The one I knew as Deshi—Chief—sits on the Prime's left, and a girl with shining blond waist-length hair and a manic, gleeful expression stands on his right. Their distinguishing marks—three thick black bands looping the Prime's neck, single bands marking the boy and girl flanking him—set them apart from the rest. I've never seen the girl before. She looks like she might be my age, and her obvious agitation as she prances behind the Prime's chair pummels me with unexpected fear.

Others fill the rest of the room, some dressed in the tan and black uniforms of the Wardens, others in the all-white outfits of the men who refreshed Mr. Morgan, but all of them are staring. At me.

Like they're waiting for the show to begin.

Their nearly identical faces, hair, eyes, and expressions swamp me with dizziness, and the room swims. It doesn't make sense; I'm not really here. I'm curled up in a warm room in the middle of nowhere, with Wolf asleep at my side and Pax keeping watch. He hasn't noticed anything's wrong or he would wake me. Unless he fell asleep, too. Or if the Others found him and are holding him captive somewhere in his own mind.

I shouldn't be forced to stay here, and it's strange feeling as though my mind won't do what I tell it to. I want to wake up but no matter how hard I wish for that to happen, it doesn't.

"Don't bother. Those threads binding your wrists were made by the Spritans and are powerful magic.

They'll hold your mind in this place for as long as they're touching you," the Prime's silky voice explains.

They just read my mind. Knew I wanted to wake up.

Shudders crawl upward from my toes and won't stop. Panic quickens my breath until I can't breathe, and my mother's voice isn't there to tell me to calm down. She could be working with these Others, could've betrayed the location of my alcove.

Or maybe she really is nothing more than a prisoner, too.

"Where are you?" The Prime's voice is smooth and sweet.

It's easy to see he's taller than the rest, even seated, and a muscle in the back of his jaw clenches as he clasps his hands in front of him. His posture conveys impatience, but not anger. His eyes glitter like black jewels, which should be pretty but instead make him appear entertained by the entire situation. In spite of my desire to stay strong, a tear slips down my cheek.

A firm jab into my brain tissue snatches a gasp from my chest. Instead of encouraging more tears, the Prime's eagerness makes me angry. When I raise my head to glare, Chief's sick smile tells me he dealt the pain, not his father.

"I'm in your hive." Being smart probably isn't the best plan right now, but it just pops out.

Chief leans forward, annoyance twisting his handsome features into a horrid mask, and takes up his father's line of questioning. "No. Out there. Where are you *out there*?"

"I don't know." It's the truth, actually. I know where we've been and where we're headed, but we got off track today because of Wolf. The fact that I can't reveal what I don't know brings a smile to my face, which is rewarded with a series of three knives to the brain.

Someone screams as the last one twists as though it's going to pop out my eyeball. A few seconds after the pain recedes, I realize the audible evidence of agony came from me.

"I want you to understand, daughter of Fire, that what you're feeling right now is a small fraction of what my son is capable of inflicting." The Prime waits until I raise my gaze to his. "And I promise you don't want to find out what my daughter enjoys."

The breathtaking girl at his right grins, then her tongue lolls out and she pants at me, tiptoeing forward. When her father snaps his fingers she stops in her tracks, shoulders drooping, and shuffles back beside his chair. She emits an irritating clicking sound, like the movement of her tongue against the roof of her mouth.

The Others don't allow any sort of mental deviation among humans; they cart anyone who shows signs of being incapable away, labeled as Broken. Until now, I assumed that the intolerance applied to their own race, as well, but this girl—the Prime's beautiful daughter—is definitely not right in the head. It takes a moment to tear my eyes away from the disturbed girl.

"I can't tell you what I don't know," I say.

"Son, the council and I have some business to attend to. We'll be back in an hour, and if she hasn't told you anything, we'll try alternative means of convincing her to share." The Prime rises, the rest of the Others following suit.

The room empties, leaving Chief and me alone.

My fear ramps up, dampening my body with sweat, but no good can possibly come from losing my cool here. I've got to focus on keeping my mind blank, the way I did that night during the refreshing. It worked to imagine a white board, to use a mental eraser to swipe it clean, a technique I employ again now. Pax's and Lucas's secrets are mine, too, and the thought of betraying them is worse than any pain the

Others can inflict. I hope. Because it looks as though we're about to test that theory.

Wake up, Althea. Wake up!

I try pushing thoughts at myself the way I did when I Broke Mrs. Morgan, but Chief's gorgeous, cruel face stretches into a wider smile, his black eyes endless black pools. Pain that feels like nothing more than a pinch now stabs my eyes when I look right at him, and the star-shaped scar below his ear—the one that looks like the locket Ko left me as a child—seems to writhe and pulse with the radiating waves.

"It won't work. Talking to yourself like you're a moron human. Last autumn I thought perhaps you would be a worthy adversary, but you are not. No more than Ko turned out to be."

The agony begins anew, and it's fire instead of knives this time. Licking the inside of my skull, burning my flesh to ashes. When Chief lets up, I taste blood. It's trickling from my nose into the corner of my lips like snot. The back of my head aches from my neck up, and the memory of Ko, Cadi, and Lucas banging their heads in keening misery slams into my mind.

I can't think about that; I have to get back to Pax.

"Pax? Oh, you've found him, then? That's convenient."

Tears mingle with my blood as they run down my face. More hot liquid drips down the back of my shirt; the banging must have ripped open my scalp. It's hard to think between the throbbing headache, the fear of the next bout of Other mind torture, and the ravaging guilt over giving Pax up to these monsters.

"You care about him. What would your Lucas think of that, hmm? You're nothing but a little tease. Like your mother. Do you know she and I were to mate, before she met your disgusting, unworthy, human father? I took great pleasure in killing him. Slowly." He watches me as he speaks, that languid, malicious smile eating away at everything good in this world, as though his existence is so terrible it can consume all of the light and kindness.

"I care about them both. Because they're my friends," I gasp out. "We're not like you. And I didn't know my father but I am sure he was worth about a hundred of—"

I break off with a shriek as Chief comes at me with more this time, the blades joined by pliers twisting and ripping off chunks of my mind a piece at a time. He waits for perfect intervals, until the pain from the first begins to ebb before he tears off another. What feels like freezing liquid comes next, and it burns holes in my brain tissue.

Somewhere inside me, in a place that still fights, I know he's not really damaging me. He can get to a place in my brain that issues pain signals but still leave my mind untouched. I know this because he tortured Lucas in the woods, too, but as soon as I lit Chief on fire, Lucas came back exactly the same. At least physically.

The knowledge gives me strength for a minute, but the next dousing of acid rolls opaque black clouds through my field of vision. A sharp slap across my cheek brings tears to my eyes and the world back into focus, although the room still wobbles a little around the edges.

"What's your name?" My voice is raspy, as though he took my throat and ran a cheese grater over it. My whole body feels a little bit like a block of cheese that's been shredded, now that I think about it. The image won't go away, and the confused look on Chief's face is almost enough to amuse me. It hurts to be amused. It hurts to be.

"Chief."

"No. Your real name. Hobej? Boboj? Jerkfacej?" All of the Others' names end with the letter *j*, but I've only known him as Deshi or Chief. The idea of calling him either doesn't sit right with me, though. "What's the matter, ashamed of the name your daddy gave you?

Maybe he likes your sister better and she got the good name." He still doesn't answer, which is interesting, but I shrug. "Jerkfacej it is, then."

I don't know how many more times he pushes the pounding, gnawing wretchedness inside my head. I think about trying to summon enough heat to perhaps melt my bonds, but it takes all of my energy to keep hold of a blank picture, and even so, the effort fails a couple more times. When the Prime returns with the rest of the council, my vision is thin. Too bright in the center, too dark around the outside. The throbbing never leaves, even when his son stays out of my head, and even though I swear I'm concentrating on sitting up straight, my cheek keeps banging into my shoulder.

"What have you learned?" The Prime seems more annoyed than ever, and my torturer sulks at his father's expectant tone.

"She and Vant's bastard, Pax, are together. She hasn't told me where they are right now, but he's taking her back to Portland."

"To Portland, the rain the rain, I can make pain rain, pain in the rain." The Prime's daughter intones nonsense interrupted by fits of giggles, twirling in circles around her brother. The sweet notes of her voice belie the sickening words.

When did they all return?

"Why?" The Prime ignores her, as though she's said nothing at all.

"I don't know."

"What has she told you about their plans? About their abilities other than the element control?" A deep and fluid anger infuses his melodious tone, snapping me to attention.

"Nothing."

The fact that those two pieces of information, so precious and indispensable to Pax and me, remain secret causes a mixture of pride and determination to flow through my screaming body. I've done something well, even if they know we're going to show up in Portland sooner or later. We can fix that. If I can just get out of here.

"Very well. If you're not persuasive enough, we'll move on to something else." The Prime raises his voice to a commanding pitch, catching the attention of the two Wardens stationed inside the door. "Fetch Ko."

15.

D read, new and fresh and strong enough to wake me from my half-passed-out stupor, arrives with the sound of that one name. Ko is still alive. I feared the worst, and Cadi did, too, after he was tortured so much that he gave up at least some of our secrets last season. They're going to use my soft spot for him to try to make me tell them the rest. I don't know if I'm strong enough to sit here and watch Ko, the being who gave up everything to get me this far, suffer the kind of distress I've survived the past hour. Hours. Especially since I know for a fact he's already been through so much.

When they bring in Ko, two Wardens have to drag him between them. His feet try to keep up but stumble continuously, and he appears half dead already. The yellowed bruises beneath his eyes have deepened, as though his lifeblood is draining, puddling above his cheekbones. The midnight blue of his eyes is dim; the light behind them flickers dangerously close to going out. Tears and undiluted love fill those eyes at the sight of me, followed closely by a sorrow so deep it aches in my chest, too.

"My life means nothing compared to yours, Althea. Remember this."

Ko pays for his selfless statement with a crack to the jaw, delivered by one of the Wardens holding him upright. To my horror, the Prime's daughter spins toward him after a flick of her father's finger. Her feet seem to barely touch the ground, as though she's floating across the glossy floor. One finger rests in her mouth, ruby lips pursed tight around her skin, and her black as night eyes shine animalistic hunger and expectation.

She bends at the waist until she's eye level with Ko, but if she's looking for his fear, she's disappointed. Instead his gaze hardens, as though it can prepare him for what's coming. "Kendaja, dear girl." Her name sounds lovely even on his exhausted tongue, making me wonder for a moment if Chief really did get the raw end of that deal. Ko holds her gaze, an expression like sorrow infusing his features. "It doesn't have to be this way. You don't have to be what they expect."

Apparently unmoved by his heartfelt sentiment, Kendaja pulls her finger out of her mouth with a slight pop. It glistens with saliva as she reaches it toward Ko slowly, licking her lips and panting hard.

A hairbreadth from his forehead, she pauses. Her voice, dainty and as sweet as sugar, hums through the cavern. "Give it to me, little magic man. A small touch, He says, but worth it. Oh ,worth it, for you, too. Feel me, magic man, feel my magic."

Her wet finger brushes Ko's skin by his right eyebrow, then traces a line down the side of his face. He screams, tears gushing from his eyes, body twitching and jerking so hard the two Wardens have to plant their feet and hold on with both hands to keep him from wrenching free. It goes on for minutes, until her nail slides off the end of his chin and he slumps forward. Skin gapes open on either side of the gash, golden blood bathing his neck like a scarf. He might be dead.

Honestly, for the sake of his relief, I almost hope he is.

Sitting here, clamping my teeth shut to avoid crying out and telling them everything they want to know, is the hardest thing I've ever done. Harder than watching Chief torture Cadi last autumn, or even the night he forced me to defend Lucas by hurting Others.

Because they're destroying Ko over and over again because of me.

When Kendaja turns to face me, her smooth alabaster face betraying nothing but ecstasy, a new kind of fear slices me open. This is a creature with no anchor to reason. She hurts because somewhere deep inside, she needs to. She craves the pain, although it's hard to believe she understands or cares why. As I watch her tilt her head back, eyes rolling up in her head while she licks her lips until drool runs down her chin, terror like I've never known threatens to tear me apart. Unlike her volatile brother, there's no way around what she is, no hope of distracting her with anger or irritation.

No hope of wriggling out from under her insane grasp, once she's got me in her sights.

It crosses my mind for a brief moment that perhaps I could turn the mind-invasion trick on the Others, overrun their thoughts to gather information or cause pain. If my situation spirals into something more dire, or we're confronted in reality, that might be my final card. I don't want to play it right now, not when they still think our only advantage is our control of fire and wind and water.

The frightening girl steps closer, making the hairs on my arms stand on end as though she's surrounded by an electrical charge. Then a strange event occurs. The smell of apples and cinnamon dances on a slight breeze that shouldn't be in this room that's not really here. A moment later, the burning scent of leaves singes the inside of my nose when I suck in a deep breath, and a pair of invisible lips press hard against mine.

It's Pax. The unmistakable smell of him, the overwhelming reaction of my body to his, lights my frayed nerve endings on fire. The desperation he must be feeling at not being able to wake me up pours through my veins like a windstorm. Increasing breezes whip my hair around my face as the Others yell and shout, but it's far away. Kendaja puts a wet finger on my face but nothing happens, causing surprised rage to flicker in her manic gaze.

The invisible kiss deepens, drowning out this room and my team of torturers. His hands trail down my arms, around my waist, up my neck, caressing me the way I longed for the first time we touched. The pull toward him heightens further than I expect, is more than I can stand, and with my last bit of clarity, I know what he's doing—or what he's helping me figure out. He's aware of the chemistry between us, too, and his relentless attention heats my blood to a degree that doesn't seem safe.

It loans me the extra boost of power I need to melt the bonds at my wrists and ankles. I barely have to try to let the mixture of need, desperation, and horror come to the surface before the magic ropes drip from my wrists.

And I'm gone.

***

I open my eyes to find Pax's lips pressed against mine, his tanned face pale and frantic. When he opens his eyes and finds me awake, he stops kissing me and crushes my body to his in a bone-breaking hug. Wolf limps to us, licking my face and Pax's.

"I'm sorry. I'm sorry, Althea. You wouldn't wake up, and you were jerking and screaming but you . . . you wouldn't wake up."

For the first time, I notice that I'm sprawled in a snowdrift. The exposed skin on my hands is blue, and all of my muscles are spasming. From the cold. From the pain. There's an ache in my head that throbs with every beat of my heart. When I struggle into a sitting position and Pax backs off a little, the reddened snow where my head rested stirs nausea in my gut.

"How long—" My voice is a croaky whisper, so I clear my throat and try again. Talking makes my head pound harder, until my teeth ache. "How long was I gone?"

"A day."

It doesn't make sense that I could have been out for a day. "I want to go inside."

"Here." Pax helps me stand up, then loops a strong arm behind my knees and one underneath my back, cradling me to his chest like a baby.

I try to protest, indignant at being carried, but nothing comes out of my mouth. I have nothing left, and if he hadn't picked me up, I'd have had to ask him to. My limbs are limp noodles, floppy and outside my control, so instead of worrying that Pax will think me weak, I press against him and draw on his strength and warmth.

He places me gently on the couch in front of the fire, then piles every blanket on top of me. Wolf pushes into my side, leaning over to lick me every couple of seconds.

Pax falls to his knees beside the sofa, his face a heartbreaking mixture of fear and guilt. "I'm so sorry. I'm sorry. It's my fault, I fell asleep just for a minute and when I woke up you were screaming. I tried everything to wake you. There were times you were still, so I left you alone in case you were resting, but . . . I'm sorry."

His horrified, despairing expression splits me in two. Pax looks as though he can't bear to know what his transgression has cost me. Cost us. It pushes tears down my face as I unearth my hands and tangle them roughly in his hair, forcing his eyes to mine.

"Pax, stop. You fell asleep. It's not your fault. Please. It's not your responsibility. I can handle it."

He takes a deep breath, expression calming into a more familiar mask of confidence. "You can handle anything, I know that, but watching scared the life out of me, Summer. I don't know what I would have done if you never came back."

"I did. You got me back, it was all you. I didn't have enough strength left to melt my bonds until you, um, heated me up."

Pax tucks my hands back under the blanket, then runs shaking fingers through his hair. "I'm sorry I had to kiss you again. It was the only thing I could think of that could make you hot enough to save yourself."

That smile, the slow, sneaky one, steals onto his lips and crushes the breath from my chest. We're going to be okay, the smile says. Together. If that's what I want.

I'm too out of sorts to think about what I want from Pax. The way he's looking at me heats my face again, and I lie back against the couch with a teasing sigh. "Well, since it probably saved my life, I'll forgive you. This time."

16.

I debrief Pax on the happenings in the hive, softening the torture experience as much as possible. He doesn't need to feel worse than he already does, for one, and for another I'd rather not remember it too clearly, either. We're going to have to face the Others again at some point, and the kind of fear I felt with Kendaja bearing down on me isn't going to be helpful when I need to call on courage.

His eyes cloud over at the news of Ko. The disgust swirling in my stomach turns into a furious storm when I think of the months he's been used as their leverage.

"So, they know where we are?"

"No, I don't think so. But they know we're together. And that we're headed for Portland."

"We'll stay here like we planned, then, for a couple of days while you and Wolf finish healing. And we'll figure out what to do next." Pax runs his hands through his dirty hair, pinching the ends in frustration.

Disappointment that I couldn't have held out longer breeds a growing anger inside me. We have to find a way to protect our thoughts all the time, even while asleep. But if Ko and Cadi can't withstand the Others' mind torture, maybe that's shooting a little bit high. An idea flashes like a bulb in my brain and I chew my lip for several minutes, making sure it's sound before blurting it out and getting our hopes up for nothing.

"If they get us in the tunnels again, or if they find a way to restrain us in the real world, we can't fight the torture. The pain is . . ." His eyes cloud over and I finish quickly. "It's too much to think about blocking them at the same time."

"Okay, so, we have no chance of hiding."

"Well, we know Cadi said the Others can wall off certain things from their ability to communicate. What if we, I don't know, walled off our sinum so they're disconnected from their tunnels?"

It sounds naive now that it has voice, but Pax doesn't laugh. "That way even if you went there when you fell asleep, they couldn't get in?"

"That's the idea. But I haven't the slightest idea how to accomplish such a thing."

The silence claiming the room tells me he doesn't either, but we can't figure it all out at once. Sometimes, when I was younger and the homework for Cell was new, it would take time for the lessons to make sense. It would worry me when I couldn't figure it out right away, but then I'd be taking a walk or staring at the ceiling before bed and it would all just click, like my mind worked out the problem without my knowledge.

Maybe the answer lurks in there somewhere now, waiting for me to relax. "I'm going to take a soak, if you'll help with the snow."

The best thing about the ranger's station is the cleansing room. Instead of a shower, which graces every cleansing room in the Sanctioned Cities, it boasts a long basin with clawed feet, similar to the one Cadi had in the building outside the Danbury boundary. She let me soak in the hot water while she scrubbed the skunk smell from my skin, and the experience of being submerged in warm, fragrant water ranks among the most pleasant of my life.

Pleasant is something I can use right now, and thinking hurts.

We can't magic water into the basin like Cadi can, but if we haul in the snow I can heat it up, no problem. It works as well as I expected, although my muscles are too weak to give Pax much help with the carrying part. Twenty-five full buckets later, I've got a steaming basin of water to climb into.

"Need help?" The mischievous twinkle returns to Pax's blue eyes.

Its appearance fills me with relief even as the suggestion twinges something strange inside my abdomen, but I don't let him see either reaction. Now isn't the time to worry about boys or my romantic future. If we manage to live another ten years, or figure out how to find a way to return the Earth to the humans and they let us live among them, I'll figure out how I feel about Partnering then.

I roll my eyes and push Pax toward the cleansing room door. "Nice try."

"What? You're the Meg to my Calvin, what can I say?"

Pax is nothing like Calvin from *A Wrinkle in Time.* Calvin's limbs are too long, his hair too orange . . . although, now that I think about it, they do share an easy confidence.

I shake my head, smiling. "I prefer Gilbert from Green Gables."

"You *are* more of an Anne than a Meg. Although you're not as awkward as either of them."

Pax turns just outside the threshold, grinning while I shut the door in his face. Honestly, if he were a girl, the offer of help would have been accepted. I bite my lip to keep from whimpering as I shrug off my layers of clothing and ease into the steaming water. Silence slides over me, offering comfort with its simplicity. I let my mind shut down, thoughts drifting away like the tiny ripples in the dark water. My hands reheat the basin twice before I finally get out, toweling off with the bath sheets tucked under the sink.

The ranger, or whoever lived here before, must've left in a hurry—everything is still in place. It's not the first time I wonder what happened to him, and to be honest, it's a little creepy staying somewhere that looks as though the occupant could come waltzing back in at any moment. As comfortable as this place is, I'll feel better when we can move on.

Except we have no idea where to move on to now that the Others know where we are headed, and gnawing worry encroaches on the pristine separateness in the tub until there's no point in staying submerged.

After I dry, I watch as Pax reclines on the floor in the living area, his back propped against the couch as he pours some medicine on Wolf's cut, still open but no longer bleeding. Wolf watches Pax with reproachful eyes as the liquid runs across his exposed blood vessels. Once it's re-bound with fresh strips of blanket, we heat up some dinner of canned vegetables and the last of the tuna.

"I'm starting to think we should have brought the Spam," I joke. It would be funnier if we weren't running out of food again.

There are provisions stocked in the ranger's station but the supply of edible bits is low. We found some bags of flour, pasta, and sugar, some spices, and a few cans of fruits and vegetables, but nothing more substantial. Wolf better get well enough to hunt soon, or we'll be in trouble.

Remembering all I didn't do for him in the woods, I decide it's time to step into the role of protector. Wolf has been there for me, so why shouldn't I return the favor? Between our two abilities, Pax and I should be able to corner some game in the woods. Maybe we'll go out tomorrow and give it a try.

Or tonight. I won't be sleeping any time soon.

Not wanting to lose the feeling of warmth from my soak, I curl under the blankets on the couch. Pax leans back against my legs, and the weight of him anchors me here in this place. It's still not easy, like it was with Lucas, but being together gets more familiar with each passing day. My heart only pounds for a few beats now when we touch, instead of minutes on end.

It might not be a good thing, the intimacy. If Pax and I are going our separate ways eventually, if he won't be convinced that fighting—that *war*—is necessary, then being happy with him will make things harder. Trust has never come easily to me because I've always been alone and Ko had instructed me not to trust anyone in the first note enclosed in my locket. But now I *do* trust Pax not to leave me, to do his best to keep me safe and get us to Portland. It's the part that comes after that worries me, and it keeps me determined to leave as much distance between us as possible. It's going to hurt to lose him, to leave him behind if he won't come with me to find Lucas.

Pax interrupts my spiraling train of thought. "I was thinking about what you said earlier. What if creating a physical barrier is easier than we're making it? You said that once you're in their hive, it's like everything is actually happening. Not like a dream, right?"

"Yeah . . ."

"So, what if you literally build a wall?" Pax sounds a little like I felt earlier, as though his thought might be the silliest idea ever uttered aloud.

It does sound too simple, but maybe it's not. "Where would I get materials?"

"You're in your mind. Won't they just be there if you imagine them?"

We sit in the quiet for a long time, hearing nothing save Wolf's breathing and the crackle of the logs burning in the wall. It's not uncomfortable, though, as if we should fill it up with more ideas or blather. More like this is exactly the right thing to be doing in this moment.

My whole body still aches from the catastrophe in the Others' hive. The residual pain and stress make me long to close my eyes and rest, to build my strength back up, but I just can't imagine being able to sleep anytime soon.

"Hey, Pax. Do you want to read *A Separate Peace*?"

He twists a little so one sparkling eye is visible. "I've read it. About three thousand times."

"No, I mean together. And we can talk about it."

I've been meaning to bring it up for a few days, since I read it for the third time, but to be honest it's a lot harder than the rest of the books to understand. Not that I don't get the words or the story, but it's that they go deeper and mean more than they seem to on the surface. To be fair, there are a lot of foreign concepts involved, too, chiefly the distant but looming war.

It turns out war means a giant fight between countries—I'm not entirely clear on what those are still—with weapons and huge armies of men killing one another. The whole business sounds terrible when described that way, boiled down to its essence, but in the story the idea is abstract and far away. A little easier to swallow.

We read the book through the night, and in the morning, our eyes bloodshot and weary, we watch the sun spill rays of winter light around our blanketed windowpanes.

"Who do you like more, Gene or Finny?" My voice sounds rough to my ears, tired. I don't even want to think about what I look like.

"I don't think I like either of them."

The pause is full of unspoken clarifications, ones he's maybe trying to figure out, so I wait in silence. Pax has read this book so many times; he probably knows Gene and Finny so well they feel like friends maybe he'd rather get rid of, if he had a choice. Still, envy tickles me at his having friends of any kind his whole life. Characters in a book are better than nothing. In my limited experience, they're better than some people, too.

"Gene, he's a liar, I think. Like a lot of the story is all skewed because he's telling it the way he sees the world, as a place where everyone is out to get you. But Finny, he's in denial. Gene thinks Finny has it right, the way he never sees anyone as an enemy, but that's obviously not the answer. Some people *are* enemies." Pax shrugs. "If they were one person, they'd be pretty solid."

He's right about both characters, although I had more of an affinity for Finny than Pax seems to, but maybe that's because, like the carefree character, I want to believe beings are essentially good. That the Others might have that capacity, even. The idea that we're headed for a battle—the three, maybe four of us against them—seems like an impossibly tall mountain to climb. I want to bury my head in the sand like Finn, like if I say the war doesn't exist, that it's made up, then maybe we can find Lucas and rescue Deshi and the four of us can live happily ever after in the woods for all of our lives.

Pax looks at me, sadness weighing down his gaze as though he can read my mind. "We can't ignore the fact that the Others are stronger than the humans. They're in control of this planet now, and you know as well as anyone what happens when we get in their way."

"But how does that make you better than Finny? Not fighting what you know is wrong is the same as pretending the fight doesn't exist, isn't it?"

"Not if it wouldn't make a difference if you fight or not."

"How do you know unless you try?"

Silence returns, this time thick with disagreement. *A Separate Peace* gets under my skin and festers. The more we talk about it, the more I think I agree with Pax about not really liking the story—it's sad, and no one is right, and the entire situation is rife with grief and the loss of innocence. Yet their tale will never be far from my heart, which makes it a worthwhile thing, even if it's hard to read about.

Pax interrupts my thoughts again, and his words are strangely along the same lines. "Maybe the humans are better off. They're innocent, like the boys were before the war. Happy. Who are we to take that away from them?"

"They didn't choose it, that's why. And because we know something they don't. That the Others have no intention of leaving this planet inhabitable when they leave." I wait for him to give some sign of agreement, but he doesn't. I remind myself of what he's been through, that he's sure that trying to tell the truth cost little Tommy a family. I understand his hesitance, but it's not going to change my mind. "They'll never give up, Pax. They won't leave us alone, not even if we stay out of sight for the rest of our lives."

"I just don't know what's right anymore. Let's keep taking this one day at a time, okay? Right now, what I know is that you can't stop sleeping. It's impossible. So for you, Althea, and for today, I'll face them. We'll figure out how to keep them out of your head—or keep you out of theirs—and we'll at least discuss our options as far as waking up the humans. After we find out what happened to Tommy."

Gratitude floods me from head to toe until I want to collapse into a puddle of relief. Pax presses his shoulders back into my knees, his version of a handshake, I suppose. I'm relieved he doesn't turn to face me, because I doubt I'd have the willpower to keep my hands to myself and then who knows where we'd end up. The whole building could go up in a storm of fire and wind.

A noisy yawn, attended by an exhausted gurgle, escapes his hold and makes me giggle. I get up. "Here. Get some rest."

"Are you sure you're going to be okay?"

Pax would stay awake if I asked him to, but he's already climbing onto the couch hoping I won't. It gives me a little bit of happiness, to be able to do something for him. "Yes. I'm not ready to sleep yet, anyway. I'm going to read, or sit outside for a while. Or just be thankful I'm alive."

"I really am sorry, Summer. About letting you down."

"You didn't let me down, Pax. You saved me."

17.

When Pax wakes up later, we take a walk into the woods to find something for dinner that doesn't currently reside in a can or jar. I would do terrible things for a slice of bread, so killing a squirrel or rabbit doesn't seem like such an abhorrent prospect. Until now, Wolf has done the dirty work, but that's really not fair.

We stumble across three deer grazing near an almost frozen stream. Two have antlers and one doesn't, and the memory of the deer Lucas and I met in Connecticut lifts wistfulness through me like a breeze. She was the first animal we met, the one that proved the Others had lied, and the gentleness in her eyes stilled my heart.

Pax quirks an eyebrow in a silent question. My stomach and heart and brain wage a silent battle: one begging for food, the next arguing for mercy for an animal who would never hurt me, and the last lecturing that people eat meat. A rabbit or squirrel wouldn't hurt me, either, but I've eaten plenty of those. What stops me is the fact that we're planning on leaving this place, maybe tomorrow if Wolf can travel, and we can't carry meat with us. I'm not going to take a life and then waste it, leave it behind to rot in an abandoned ranger's station.

I shake my head, putting a finger to my lips so we can watch them for another couple of seconds. The deer sense our presence before long, evidenced by their twitching tails and pricked ears. A few minutes after the last one disappears into the trees, we spot two gray squirrels—much more reasonable—on the lowest branch of a tree. This time I nod in response to Pax's silent question, and he begins like we discussed before leaving on this mission today.

He raises his palms upward, and within seconds the squirrels' perch whips violently, creaking in the unnatural wind. Nothing is burning, but Pax's scent of smoky leaves threads through my hair and I know it's going to smell like that until I wash it again. The small animals freeze, uncertain and fearful, and drop toward the ground with the branch when it snaps free from the trunk. Pax lowers his hand and I run toward the falling animals. Before the squirrels can smash into the ground and feel pain, I shoot what I hope is the right amount of heat at them.

I get one right, but the second is a blackened husk. The good one's fur smokes a little bit, but otherwise it looks simply dead. Pax comes over and grabs them both by the tail, which is also part of our agreement, and we trek back to the cabin.

Wolf is in a tizzy about being left behind, and licks our hands, sniffing the already-cooked animals curiously. He's moving better, though he still limps on his bad leg. It worries me, when he forgets he's hurt, that he's going to rip open the closing wound if he gets too excited.

Pax and I share the meat of the nonblackened rodent, pairing it with our last can of corn. Wolf seems perfectly happy with the crispy one. Even though the sound of his chomping makes me a little sick to my stomach, it pleases me to have been able to catch him dinner for once.

After we eat, my eyes feel heavy but my heart can't settle down long enough to fall asleep. Pax tries to talk me into it for a while, promising a million different ways to stay right by my side and wake me up every hour, but when I don't take him up on the offer, he changes tact.

"Let's try the wall thing, then."

"No, I told you. It's too soon. I'm not ready to go back there." I don't even know if I *can* go back there, but my mouth feels like someone stuffed cotton into it at the thought of trying.

"We can do this."

"What do you mean *we,* Pax? It's me that has to go, and I can't. Not yet."

"Summer, you can't keep this up. You want me to say I'll fight? Well, we can't fight anything if you're not at full strength, and you haven't slept a whole night in weeks. How are you going to hike anywhere tomorrow or the next day?" He takes a deep breath, his mouth set in a determined line. "And I meant *we.* I'll go with you. Or I plan to try."

"How?"

"The same way you and Winter traveled. We share our power, and let it take us away."

All of the moisture goes out of my mouth, making it hard to swallow. After a moment, I force myself to nod, fighting with the strange mixture of thankfulness and terror closing up my throat.

We arrange ourselves on the floor in front of the fire, facing each other with our crossed legs barely touching at the knees so we can't get lost. My hands hold tight to his. Our eyes meet for a minute, then we close them. On the count of three, we push a little bit of our power through our hands, until mine are hot but not scorching and a sweet, burnt-smelling breeze sweeps ashes out of the fireplace.

I turn my mind inward, searching for the area where Fire talks to me. I don't feel alone, but once I let go of reality, there's no way to tell whether or not it's Pax with me in the ranger's station or Chief and his creepy sister waiting for me on the far side of this experiment. There's nothing concrete in this place— this hollow, black cavern of my mind. In a moment of sudden, terrifying clarity, the crushing emptiness of my travels slams into my chest and I know this is how Ko and Cadi move us around—through the tunnels. I don't know how it works, but this solid belief that I don't really exist has never taken hold of me anywhere else.

My stomach clenches and fear spins alarm down my legs. What if I get stuck in the blackness? We're not supposed to be in here on our own, I'm guessing, and the anxiety over being trapped here forever makes me want to turn around and fumble my way back to the station in the woods. It might be my imagination but support blows against my back, smelling briefly of cinnamon, and I stop fighting. Pax is here. I have to sleep. There must be a way to keep the Others out while I'm not protecting my consciousness.

It dawns on me again that if we can get into human heads, and if I can enter the hive, then we might be able to invade the Others' minds, too. It's already been established that we're linked, but what if we could hear their plans or know if they're close to discovering us?

What if we could cause *them* pain instead of the other way around?

I'm not sure what good this would do, because Cadi said no one had figured out how to defeat them, and she and Ko have had years of practice. As far as torture, I doubt I have the stomach for it. But right now, with my lack of sleep, I think maybe I could do anything.

I'm literally stumbling around in here like a person with no eyes. Instead of trying to move my feet, which isn't doing any discernible good, I concentrate on my sinum, what it looks like, the way the tunnels stretch outside the opening. How the packed dirt smells faintly loamy, and what my mother's face looks like when she smiles at me.

It works. Not only that, but when shapes melt from the pressing blackness, I can feel Pax's hands still clutched around mine. And to my utter astonishment, a pile of red bricks, like the ones that build our Cells, fill up a corner of my alcove. Next to the stack is a bucket of some gray goop and a tool, probably to stick them together.

That my mind can build a wall with my hands is too much to comprehend. In fact, a year ago I would not have believed a tenth of what my brain is apparently capable of. Pax doesn't speak, just catches my gaze and then points down the tunnels, then to his eyes.

He goes to the opening, putting his back to me. He's keeping watch, I guess. We need to work on our nonverbal communication. Only not the kissing kind.

I get to work on the wall, stacking layers of bricks and smearing gray, sticky stuff in between them. No noises beside the occasional scrape of a brick filter down the tunnels, which should calm me down, but it shakes my nerves instead. It's not that I want the Others paying attention to what's going on in this corner of the hive, but where they all might be instead concerns me. They could be out looking for me and Pax, or hunting down Lucas. Getting rid of Ko or Deshi. Anything. Anywhere.

As the wall grows, a feeling that this will work fills my fingertips, and strength flows into my hands. I'm not constructing it with bricks, but out of fierce determination.

When only a couple of columns remain, Pax backs inside and helps me finish. We're trapped inside my little alcove, and a strange claustrophobia like I haven't felt since the night I took my first trip in a hot, stuffy rider claws at my lungs. My breath chokes out in gasps and the tiny space heats to an uncomfortable degree.

Althea, honey. Calm down. All you have to do is imagine where you want to be instead. No one is keeping you here against your will.

My mother's image shimmers in the wall, then disappears. It's working. She can't get in, even though she knows I'm here.

Flacara. You betrayed me. If you had never found my alcove, none of this would be happening. I hope she can hear me.

I'm sorry. I'm not as strong as I should be, and what happened to you is my fault. But you must know I didn't do it so I could lead the Prime and his children to your mind. I only wanted to know you. To help you if I could. I thought I could be careful.

I grind my teeth together. *Well, you were wrong.*

I hear her sigh. *I know. I won't come to you again. The wall won't hold forever. Your strength of will keeps it intact, but they are strong willed, too. Especially Kendaja. They'll get through, eventually.*

What's wrong with her? I ask.

She's been Broken since birth. Were she not the Prime Other's offspring, she would have been disposed of as an infant. Kendaja is, as you would say my daughter, totally banana balls. Unhinged. A wild card, though she wasn't always cruel.

There's no answer for the information but to have her confirm my fears thickens the cold pool of dread in my gut. *Good-bye, Fire.*

Good-bye, my darling girl.

I pull Pax into a hug, pressing our bodies together just in case, because I can't bear the thought of having to come back to this place to get him. I imagine the ranger's station and the place we sat in front of the fire, Wolf stretched out beside us.

And then we're there. Brick dust and gray adhesive crumbles off my hands when I brush them together, trying to stop the trembling and get a grip before Pax asks me what's wrong. I don't want to talk about my mother, mostly because I don't know how to feel. Besides her, all of the people in my life fit into nice little molds. The Others are bad. Cadi and Ko are good. The humans aren't a threat. Lucas is who I depend on, Pax a buoyant strength.

Fire, though? I have no read on whether she's telling the truth about not leading the Prime and his children right to me with her silent orders and comfort over the past couple of years. The images of the Elements that hang in our Cells are cold, their eyes revealing nothing but revulsion for the population they rule, but now I know they fell in love with human beings. Fire loved a man, Ben, and together they made me, even though they both knew the Others would kill them if my existence was discovered. She took steps to hide me when the Others *did* find out, so why would she help them capture me now?

The truth burrows beneath my questions, perhaps kept hidden by my fear, by the fact that maybe I'm not ready to know. Whatever the truth is, it isn't simple. The Elements aren't good or bad. They're neither friend nor enemy. My soul aches to know my mother, to feel the warmth of her arms around me, to let her tell me how to harness my reactions to Pax and help me understand my feelings for Lucas. My brain urges caution, though, reminding me of the Others' level of control over their own. Fire is a prisoner, after all.

My heart can't decide which side to take, but no matter what else is true, I know I'd be stupid to trust her.

18.

It's early evening when we return from our successful covert mission in the hive. I have trouble believing it worked but, with Fire's warning about it not lasting forever ringing in my ears, I snuggle into the couch, head to toe with Pax. With my free hand dangling onto Wolf's back, my eyes slip closed with breathless anticipation of sleep for the first time in weeks.

My dreams are nonexistent, and I don't wake up in my walled-off sinum or anywhere else. In the morning, my eyes pop open to an empty room, which speeds my heartbeat for a moment until the sound of Pax in the wasteroom finds its way to my ears. The hours of uninterrupted rest make my body feel loose and fresh for the first time in weeks. I stretch my arms all the way above my head, squeaking a little as my joints pop and my toes dig into the arm of the couch.

When Pax walks into the room and smiles at me, I smile back, thinking that this is how life could be if things were different. Maybe this is how it was on Earth before the Others.

A shadow crosses Pax's face. "I only left you for, like, three minutes, I promise. I had to get a drink of water and brush my teeth."

· "It's okay. How long did I sleep?"

"A long time. It's almost dark again." He grins once more, confidence returned. "And guess what else?"

I sit up, propping my back against an arm of the couch and drawing my knees to my chest. His excitement infects the air and stretches my smile wider, even though I'm a little concerned that he let me sleep so long. We should have left this morning. Then again, we don't actually know where we're going. "What?"

"Wolf   caught   us   some   dinner."

Pax disappears into the kitchen for a few seconds, returning with an animal I've never seen before and don't recall learning about in any textbook. Kind of like a squirrel, but about four times as large, a darker brown, and with a flat tail.

"What is it?"

"No idea, but it's nice and fat."

My stomach rumbles in response. "Wolf's feeling better then, I guess?"

"Yeah. He scratched at the door this morning until I woke up and let him out. Instead of limping out and doing his business as usual, he took off. I was glad he came back, too, because you would have been pretty ticked off at me if he disappeared while you slept."

"Very true."

I slide to the floor and crawl to the fire, tossing on a few more soggy pieces of wood and coaxing the flames higher. Pax goes into the kitchen and the sound of him whacking at the dead animal makes me grateful all over again for his presence in my life. It's enough for me to *know* that I can skin and cook an animal. Not having to actually do it is preferable.

Wolf noses under my arm, earning some pets. Twigs and mud decorate his thick black-and-white coat, but by the time Pax brings in the skewered pieces of meat, the dog has cleaned himself up. I've considered washing him in the basin, but for one, he probably wouldn't like it, and two, he's going to get filthy again as soon as we leave anyway.

While the meat heats and sizzles, dripping juices into my crackling fire, the scent of food makes my hollow center throb. We've avoided the decision of what to do next long enough, so as we pick dinner from the animal's bones and listen to Wolf crunch his portion, I bring it up. "What are we going to do now that they know we're going to Portland?"

Pax chews for a couple of minutes; whether he's gathering his thoughts or simply doesn't want to talk with his mouth full, I can't say. He tosses Wolf a bone, then wipes his greasy hands on his pants. "I still want to go see what we can find out about Tommy, and maybe Deshi, too. You said you didn't see Desh in the hive, right?"

"Nope." To be honest, it hadn't crossed my mind to look for the real Deshi, our fourth, but he would have stuck out like a sore thumb in that room filled with blond-haired, black-eyed Others had he been there. "But the Others will be waiting for us, won't they?"

"Well, for one thing, they have to figure we're not stupid enough to go there now. For another, we might be able to convince them we're somewhere else." Pax's mischievous smile returns, flickering all the way into his eyes.

In spite of the situation, my own grin emerges without a second thought. That undeniable pull between us tugs hard when he looks at me like that, as though tackling me to the ground and kissing me in between laughs for hours might be all that's on his mind. It's confusing. Lucas made me feel something similar, but this is different. Without Lucas here, with everything Pax and I have been through now, my memory seems to be playing tricks on me, trying to convince me last autumn wasn't what I imagined, that it didn't feel like a promise of more to come.

In this moment, as my body urges me to throw myself into Pax's arms and give in, I miss Lucas so much I can't breathe. There's surely something really, really wrong with my head, not to mention the rest of me. Especially since Pax's smile distracts me from what he just said, which should be far more interesting in the midst of our current discussion.

"What do you mean convince them we're somewhere else?" I ask, trying to chase away the fog in my brain. "How—"

My confused and half-formed question is cut off by Wolf, who tenses like he did when the big brown cat appeared in the woods. The low, menacing growl threading the room is quiet, but throws me into a panic. His eyes are trained on the front door.

Pax gets to his knees. "Don't move."

He crawls over to the window, then peels back the tape at the bottom and raises his head enough to peer out the corner. Wolf goes with him, standing guard with his head and tail still pressing toward the ground. None of us make a move or a sound, and several minutes of silence threaten to shatter my trepidation into a million little shards. There must be someone or something out there for Wolf to react this way.

After my one-on-one time with the Others and then sleeping for the better part of an entire day, it's not all that crazy to assume they've come for us. Just because they didn't know exactly where we're holed up doesn't mean they can't trace a path from Iowa to Portland and figure it out.

"Pax."

He holds a hand up my direction, not tearing his eyes from the window.

I crawl to his side, trying to see around his big head. It doesn't work, but he does grace me with an exasperated look. Wolf growls again.

"What is it?"

"I don't know. There's a man in the trees, I think, but it's hard to make out his face."

"Move." I shove him aside and look for myself. At the tree line, the figure largely hidden by a huge fir tree is indeed a man. A black jacket covers his head and torso, making it impossible to tell if he's an Other. His legs aren't visible. He could be a Warden, or he could be anyone at all. Except he's in the Wilds.

The blanket falls back into place, blotting out the light from the full moon. Pax and I stare at each other for a few seconds, lost as to what to say.

"It could be an Other."

"Well, it's probably not a human," Pax mutters, a determined set to his jaw.

"Maybe it's Lucas. Or Deshi." The hope in my voice rings false.

We don't have enough information, but my gut says anyone lurking in the woods, staring at the cabin as though they know we're in here, can't be good. Lucas or Deshi would simply come inside if they're looking for shelter or for the two of us, because they'd have nothing to fear.

My hands tighten into fists. "Pax, it's an Other. We both know it. Now what are we going to do about it?"

Before he can answer, something slams into the front door. Wolf barks, a loud, warning sound, and scuttles backward as the ground trembles. Another look outside reveals the man has emerged from his hiding place and now stands directly in front of the ranger's station. His hood slips back, exposing a thick crop of shining blond hair. His black and blue eyes nearly glow in the evening and the moonlight glints off his perfect features.

I know who he is. He's Earth. Pamant. Deshi's father.

His hands jerk toward our safe haven and the ground shudders again, harder this time. It rattles the walls, and dishes crash to the floor in the kitchen. In the few seconds I watch, too stunned to pull away, the ground outside yawns open, three or four two-foot-wide cracks reaching from his feet toward the front door. He takes a step back and the trees nearest the station rip from the ground and topple, slamming into the roof so hard it caves in on the side over the fire.

Wolf scuttles to my side, shivering from fear. He spins in circles, his frantic stress jangling my own increasing anxiety. Outside, at least twenty Wardens appear behind Pamant, staying clear of the raining destruction but ready to apprehend us when the damage forces us outside.

The world quakes again, knocking me off balance and into a wall.

"Pax, we have to get out of here!"

A determined look darkens his olive complexion and he stumbles toward the couch, falling twice as pieces of the floor jut up in new patterns. The whole cabin is breaking apart at the seams. He grabs our bags and stuffs as many blankets and pieces of clothing inside as he can manage. It's not much, and tears fill my eyes at the thought of leaving everything we've accumulated behind, all the proof of our will to survive.

I shake it off, blinking back the tears and letting the anger heat me from the inside. Our *lives* are the proof that we're going to survive, I remind myself.

As Pax returns to my side, a familiar, soul-tearing voice shouts from outside the window.

"We know you're in there, son of Air, daughter of Fire. Come out and we promise not to harm you." Chief's words are smooth, calculated, but laden with so much hatred it drains the blood from my head. Before Pax and I can even form a thought, never mind a response, he continues. "If you won't come out for yourselves, do think about your friend Deshi. And poor Cadi, the only benefactor you have left."

His threat flips a switch in my head. I let Wolf get hurt. I pretended to be like everyone else while they disposed of Mrs. Morgan. I watched in silence while they tortured Ko until I wished they would kill him and end his misery.

It's time I accepted my role in this world, in this fight.

In a heartbeat, with Pax's protest barely registering, I've ripped the blanket off the window and shoved my hands out into the freezing cold night. Trees explode into balls of fire behind the Wardens, giving them no place to hide. Bile rises in my throat but I swallow it, setting the two Others on either side of the Prime's son on fire until their shrieks of outrage and pain scar my soul.

The line breaks as Chief stumbles away from the Wardens and the rest search in vain for a place to hide. The display does little but buy us time because the fire doesn't affect Pamant at all. In fact, the rumbling sound in the earth, as though a million wolves and bears and huge cats howl and screech together, clawing their way up to the surface, begins with renewed force.

This time it doesn't stop.

Trees fall in the forest, crashes deafening and shaking my brain inside my skull. The furniture in the living room and in the unused bedroom crashes into the walls, and Pax slams sideways into a door frame and then onto the floor. Blood spurts from a gash above his eyebrow. Wolf slides across a newly sloped floor, crashing into the table at the end of the couch and yelping in pain.

"Pax! Let's go!"

It's like he can't hear me. Maybe he can't. Getting across the shuddering floor gets more difficult by the second as the quaking increases, flopping me this way, then that. Cuts open up in my knees and along my arms each time I fall and struggle forward, ignoring the pain. By the time I get to his side, Pax's eyes are clearer and he's trying to stand, holding on to the wall for support. The light fixture in the center of the room tears loose and smashes to the floor, missing Wolf by mere inches. More items hurtle from the walls and shelves; chunks of ceiling splatter on the floor.

The shaking stops, but by the time we move for the door three Wardens are in the room. One grabs Pax and drags him toward the back door. He's not fighting. Instead, his body is completely limp and a dreamy look floats over his features. It's the connection to the hive; he's never experienced it until now.

Wolf launches himself at the second Warden, biting into his shoulder and ripping through clothing and flesh as the Other screams. The third advances on Wolf, grabbing him by the scruff and tossing him across the room. He hits the wall and slides down to the floor with a yelp, and the sight of the blood soaking his bandage again makes fury vibrate through my limbs.

The bitten Warden slumps on the floor, unconscious. I know from past experience that he won't stay wounded for long, but for now he's not my problem. All of my rage over Wolf's pain, at them trying to take Pax from me, too, flows into my palms. When I shove it forward, it hits the Warden who tossed my dog right in the face. The skin melts as he screams, clawing at his burning eyes, but all he does is set his arms on fire, too.

For the first time, it doesn't make me sick to my stomach to watch someone in pain. It doesn't make me happy, either, but I'm tired of the Others injuring people I love. Along with Pax, Wolf definitely qualifies as people.

He limps to my side, giving my hand a weak lick, and I rub between his ears.

Pax's scream splinters the night, filled with enough agony to explode the stars in the sky. Wolf and I race to the back door, stopping dead in the threshold. A Warden holds Pax upright with an arm around his neck while the Prime's son stares at him with wild, ecstatic pleasure on his face. Pax screams again, jerking against the pain I know is ripping through his head, as once again I stand by and watch. Blood trickles from Pax's nose when he goes limp and Chief drops him into the dirt. I feel as though his blood drips from my heart as well.

Chief turns toward me, a creepy, self-satisfied smile spreading his too-red lips. "I told you to come out and no one would get hurt. Now look what you've done." His eyes travel over my shoulder into the station, and I know he's wondering what happened to the Wardens he sent in to retrieve us.

I force down the loathing at playing his game. "Pax isn't the only one who got hurt."

"Yes, but whether or not the two of you retain our substantial healing abilities has not been tested. There

215

is so much you could learn about yourselves if you would simply let us study you more closely. You might find you are more like us than these humans." He spits out the last word as though the people he rules are nothing more than muck under his shiny boots. Something to be walked across and then scraped off.

"I am nothing like you. Neither is Pax, or Lucas."

"You can say whatever pretty words you like, but saying something does not make it so."

Movement catches my eye as Pax stirs, biting back a groan, and he slowly shifts his hands out from underneath him. Chief remains focused on me, so I move a few steps forward, Wolf at my side. His eyes turn wary at the sight of my animal, and I suspect their mind torture has no effect on the nonhumans of this planet. The Others might have many kinds of strength, but Wolf's teeth likely still make him nervous. If he could see his Warden's shoulder, they would for sure.

"Your animal is injured. You should really take better care of him."

Heat starts in my middle, in the place he poked with the insult, the one that's sensitive and guilt-ridden over the number of times Wolf has been hurt trying to protect us. I squash it for now; losing my temper doesn't seem wise at the moment. I wonder a little about why the Prime's son doesn't fear me more, since the last time he hurt one of my friends I lit him on fire.

"I told you before, you will not surprise me again. I'm ready for your tricks."

"Are you ready for mine?" Pax's voice rasps out the threat, and then a spinning cloud surrounds our torturer.

The wind is like nothing I've ever witnessed, knocking me to my knees and threatening to blow me backward into the ranger's station. Wolf hunkers low to the ground, crawling to my side on his belly. Two Wardens lose the battle and fly through the air, slamming into the ground several hundred yards away. Chief tries to fight his way toward Pax, but he is having trouble walking.

"Althea! Come here!" The howling wind swallows Pax's words, only impressions reaching me through the swirling gale.

I crawl to him on my hands and knees. Wolf keeps pace on his stomach. When we get there, Pax reaches out and grabs my hand in one of his, the other still raised toward the sky, whipping the world into a shrieking whirlwind. A tree rips from its roots and flies above our heads, smashing into the forest.

"We have to travel. There's too many of them, and I can't hold this for very long."

"But the last time Lucas and I did that we were separated!"

Already the storm is weakening. The Prime's son and the Wardens stop trying to stay upright and struggle to move toward us instead. I avoid their gazes, guessing they need eye or physical contact to attack with their mind powers.

Fatigue drags Pax's face down toward his chin, those telling purplish circles around his eyes saying the torture and drawing on so much power is taking a toll. I did what I could with fire earlier, but it barely slowed them down.

The ground explodes around us, opening a huge crevice a few yards away, yawning bigger by the second. One of the Wardens falls into it, screeching as he tumbles out of sight. The noise is deafening, the earth protesting being split apart.

All of a sudden I realize we forgot about Pamant.

The Element's eyes flash, a disturbingly cold exterior blocking emotions that I don't have time to decipher. I may not know how to feel about my mother, but this man terrifies me now more than ever. Pax is right. If we stay here, the planet will swallow us whole. Being apart is better than being dead.

I turn back to him and nod, crushing our hands together. With my free hand I pat the ground in between us. Wolf slithers into the tight space, his eyes frantic and frightened. Pax's gaze is sad, resigned, and I know he doesn't think Wolf will be able to go with us, but I have to at least try.

"It's going to be okay, Summer. Trust me."

Pax presses against Wolf's right side, and I push against his left. Our arms go around him, around each other, and I let the storm of heat boiling in my stomach, in my heart go. Pax's scent of apples and cinnamon tinged with smoldering autumn leaves fills my nose, burning my throat as it grows and slams into my cloying perfume of jasmine. Soon the wind surrounds only us and Wolf, who squirms against us in the moments before everything goes black.

19.

It's not like before, the traveling. Usually I don't notice it's happened until the crush of utter loneliness and heavy, empty blackness threaten to smudge me out of existence. This time I still feel too light, like a floating shadow or beam of light, but I am not alone. When my corporeal body gathers back around me, it's not accompanied by any fear. The thump of my bones into the earth is also a surprise; I've never woken up in unfamiliar surroundings.

Sunlight greets me. It's morning, as always, so at least a little bit of time's been lost—maybe. I may not be afraid of not existing, but the question of where and when I am grabs my heart in a squeeze.

White snow, as far as the eye can see, falls from huge oak and maple trees as squirrels prance through their branches. The day is new, with filmy sunshine and the morning songs of birds filling the air. Their chatter is joined by a groan, and I roll my head toward the sound. Tears fill my eyes at the sight of Pax, still looking pained and exhausted, but he's here. With me.

He offers a weak, slow smile at the stark relief I'm sure is on my face. "Hey, I told you to trust me."

220

A noise jerks my attention from Pax, from the brilliant news that we're alive and together. It's the sound of a stick cracking beneath a footstep. We're in the Wilds, so it's not a human. Maybe an animal, but Pax and I are in no condition to fight a rabbit, never mind anything more threatening.

Wolf limps out from behind a boulder at the edge of a stream a few feet away. The sight of him clogs my throat and shoves me to my knees so I can bury my face in his musky, thick fur when he drops to his haunches next to us.

Blood drips from the sagging bandages around his body. The battle in the ranger's station was too much for his barely healed wounds, and we didn't get away with any provisions. Even though the winter here is colder than where we came from, I shrug out of my coat and remove my sweatshirt. I still have a T-shirt on, but the icy wind chills my skin in an instant.

I try ripping the sweatshirt, but my hands are shaking. It's the cresting emotions racing through my bloodstream and lightening my brain. Love. Fear. Desperation. The mix overwhelms me until there's no strength in my arms or anywhere else. Pax struggles into a seated position and takes the smoldering shirt from me without a word, rubbing it in the snow to extinguish the evidence of my lost control. While he rips it, I unwind the bloodied shreds from Wolf's chest and leg, then clean the reopened wound with fresh snow. Pax covers the seeping gash again with expert fingers to finish our treatment.

Wolf studies us with an unamused gaze, as though he's asking what the heck we're going to do now that we've brought him here and bandaged him up again. I'd like to know the answer to that myself.

In fact, there are a couple of questions still outstanding.

"How did you know we'd stay together?" Somehow he knew; I know he did. It didn't scare him the way it did me, the idea of being apart.

"I lied about where I got the bracelets. Ko made them. The guy who delivered them said if we wore them they would keep us together. At first, I hoped that meant Desh would get away with me when I traveled, but he didn't."

I wonder why Ko didn't give any to Lucas and I. Maybe he had planned to but the Prime took him before he could do it. "Why did you lie?"

"I didn't want to get your hopes up."

And he didn't want to travel, my subconscious whispers. I should be mad that Pax lied about the bracelet, but I'm still too happy that they allowed us to escape together. The strange, not-quite-real beauty of the rainbow threads makes sense now. Ko must've made it with his spells or magic or whatever. Now that Pax has told the truth, I swear I can feel a different energy thrumming around the bones in my wrist.

"Are you mad?"

"Yes. You didn't have to lie. I know you never intended to travel until after we found out what happened to your summer family." Something he said registers, makes me stop. "Wait, what do you mean, *the guy who delivered* the bracelets for Ko? Who brought them to you?"

Pax's lips twist up as though he just sucked on a lemon. "Some kid. I never got his name. He was in the prison rooms sometimes with Deshi and me, but somehow he was able to come and go, claimed he ran errands for Cadi and Ko."

Worry dampens my happiness at our escape. "What if he's working for the Others? The bracelets could be a tracking device, or—"

"No, trust me. Whoever the guy is, he's not on *their* side. I can't explain it, and I don't know his reasons for helping, but he hates them." When I don't respond, he heaves a sigh of relief. Talking about the boy obviously irritates him, a fact he confirms by changing the subject. "Where do you think we are?"

I look around, noting the maple trees and the dense foliage. Not the fields of Iowa or the fir trees and mountains of Oregon. "Connecticut."

"Well, that's about the worst thing ever."

"What's wrong with Connecticut?" One place isn't any worse than another, as far as I can tell. We're away from the Others, my mind is temporarily walled off, and we're together. Where we are is the least of my concerns at the moment.

"Nothing, except we spent the last month killing ourselves trying to get to Portland, and then in the blink of an eye we're all the way on the farthest side of the planet." Pax balls some snow in his hand and tosses it toward a tree.

Wolf wanders over to inspect it, making me smile. At least he's not permanently damaged.

I picture the map shoved in my bag. We *are* farther away now. Much farther away. In fact, it doesn't seem possible to walk back to Portland.

"I said I'd go to Portland and help you find out what you want to know, and that's what we're going to do. We'll figure it out."

I'm thinking about suggesting we try traveling again, but the words stick. We're lucky to be together and in one piece; to try it again so soon feels like pushing our luck. Pax stands up, then pulls me to my feet beside him, familiar sparks flying between our fingertips.

"You mean traveling." It's not a question, and a thoughtful—not hopeful—look paints his handsome features. The intelligence in his blue eyes flickers, as though his mind is already working on the problem at hand, and he runs a hand through his messy hair.

When Pax walks off I follow, even though I have no idea where he's headed. It doesn't make any difference, so I don't even ask. We need to either build or find a place to stay while we decide what to do.

My own brain clicks through the limited information we have about how our season hopping works, but the more I consider it, the less likely it seems that we can control where we end up. I've traveled twice without Cadi or Ko helping, but both times it happened because my life was in danger. Not to mention I didn't get to pick my destination.

"I keep thinking about what Cadi told Lucas and me before the Others took her. That we travel because of the protective enchantment Ko created when the Prime found out we existed."

"What's an enchantment?"

Frustration yanks on my patience; there are so many concepts I don't fully understand and can't really explain. "When Ko informed our parents about what he did to keep us safe, that's what he called it—an enchantment. I think it's what makes the humans look through us, and then explain it away when we accidentally display emotion or, well, disappear."

"Enchantment." Pax tries out the strange word, rolling it around in his mouth. "And the way we travel is part of that protection somehow?"

"Right. And we've been assuming that the power to travel is inside us somewhere, and we just haven't figured out how to activate or control it, but what if that's wrong? What if the power doesn't belong to us and it belongs to the people who created the enchantment?"

"But if that's true, how did you and Lucas travel from autumn before? And what made us be able to pool our energy and do it again? We have to have *some* control over it, even if it's just an innate panic response or something."

"Maybe, but I still say they could have built the protection that way, to force us to travel when we freak out to that level, or something."

With Ko possibly dead and Cadi most likely operating under duress as well, the enchantment might not last forever. I've never thought of it like that, or considered what we would do once their protection sloughed completely off, revealing us for what we truly are—letting the humans see us, emotion, free will, and all. Just being around them could cause a panic.

For now, I suppose the enchantment's unbroken. We traveled; it must still be working.

Even as I try to convince myself of that truth, dread wraps slimy fingers around the back of my neck, oozing fear down my back in globs. "Ko can't help us anymore, Pax. If he's even alive. You should have seen him. And Chief took Cadi weeks ago, if not months. If something happens to them, what happens to our protection?"

"What are they protecting us from anyway, now that the Others know we exist?" Pax's eyebrows draw together, pinching above his nose.

The strange urge to kiss the wrinkle steals into my mind. I give myself a physical shake, ignoring the strange look Pax shoots my way. Probably because I'm smiling at a really serious conversation.

"The Others know about us, but the humans don't," I say. "I mean, what would happen if we walked into a Sanctioned City without the enchantment? Would it be mass chaos because no one would know what to make of us? They'd be terrified."

He doesn't have an answer for that, and after another ten minutes of kicking a path through the snow, a boundary fence looms above us. We look at it and then at each other.

"I think we should go inside." The idea pops out of nowhere, but once my brain has hold of it, that's really what it wants to do. "Maybe we can find out where Lucas is."

Pax's face has a war with itself, pity and irritation battling for space. It's hard to know if he doesn't like talking about Lucas because he's afraid something happened to him, because I promised to focus on getting back to Portland, or because of a more personal reason I'm not quite ready to face.

"It's still winter, though. He won't be here."

That's most likely true, but there are other things we could find out. "We could still use whatever information we can get. Like about whether or not the humans can really see us, and if the Others are still wasting Wardens looking for us in the Sanctioned Cities."

"What happens if they *can* see us and everything spins out of control?" Pax's eyes harden, and I know he's thinking about what happened to his Portland family when they saw him and Broke.

The memory of Mrs. Morgan makes me wary, too, and I start to think maybe going into town isn't worth the risk. But then I remember Leah. She could tell us what happened after Lucas and I left.

Now that she's in the forefront of my mind, an aching worry opens up about how she's coping with her veil down. Lucas and I didn't know what we were doing when we removed it and left her to face a life of pretending to be a contented automaton when she's the opposite.

We left her here alone.

I hope her mind will be in one piece when I find her.

"I think I know a way we can do it carefully." Taking a deep breath, I tell Pax about Leah. About how Lucas accidentally jabbed holes in her veil before we understood what our thoughts could do. How she acted strange after that day, being intentionally mean every chance she got. And how we—no, I—completely erased her veil before we left town. "She might be able to answer our questions. If she's still . . . okay."

"This girl knew the Others were controlling her mind?" Awe infuses Pax's voice at the knowledge, as though maybe he finally sees potential in humanity instead of viewing them as simply a heavy burden on the four of us.

"She begged me to 'take them out,' so yeah, Leah definitely knew her mind wasn't her own after Lucas messed with it. And then the Others refused to repair her veil so she must've been really confused. I still don't know why they left her that way, though, unless they thought she would lead them back to the person who damaged her." Another option occurs to me, one I've refused to examine too closely because of my feelings for Lucas. "It's strange, but maybe behind their veils, where their real feelings live, the human minds remember things."

"What do you mean?"

"Did you ever have a long period in one place? Like I lived in Portland for three years except summers once, in Intermediate Cell. Lucas lived those three years here, in Danbury."

"Yes. I stayed in Atlanta for three years, too, but without autumns, of course. Why?"

It continues to strike me as so desperately lonely, the way the four of us were kept apart, as though I've never truly been a whole person. Even after meeting Lucas and Pax, I still feel that way to an extent. Maybe it will never go away. I push the sadness away and refocus.

"Lucas stayed here, in Connecticut. He and Leah were friends, and when she could see through the veil, she remembered him. I don't think she had any specific memories, but it's more like she recalled the feeling of trusting him."

The explanation isn't very good, but it's the best I can do when it doesn't make total sense to me, either. But the idea that Monica and Val, the girlfriends I made in Portland, might have residual fond memories of our friendship warms my freezing blood a little.

"Okay. I do agree that the more information we have, the better." Pax's eyes are wary for the first time in days. "But after we learn what we can from Leah, we work on getting to Portland. Deal?"

He's worried I'll go back on my word, maybe, or that I've forgotten what it means to him to find Tommy, to right the perceived wrongs he committed last season. Those same feelings are part of the reason I want to see Leah, and it stings that he can't see that I understand. The insult shortens my words. "Yes. We're still going to Portland."

"Good. Then let's go find your friend."

20.

In spite of the fact that I may have destroyed Leah's brain, I have no idea where in Danbury she lives. This is a problem, but not the biggest one we're facing since we haven't found a way to get through the fence yet. Lucas and I escaped last autumn when we discovered a section of the boundary where electricity had stopped running, but Pax and I haven't had that kind of luck today. Cadi opened a hole in the boundary with a button, another option. I've told Pax about it, but he thinks we should try sneaking in first. I melted the nearest camera, but if we use the button, the Others still might have a way to monitor it.

Wolf ambles in and out of the trees, sniffing and peeing on what are apparently offensive patches of snow. He's carefree and not nervous at all, which relaxes the knots tightening my shoulders and the back of my neck. There's plenty of time to worry once I see Leah again. I refuse to even consider the possibility that she'll be gone. Disposed of or Broken.

"Once we get into town, we need to avoid being seen in case there are Wardens around. Maybe we can follow her home after Cell and then leave a note for her to find?"

Pax grunts, a little distracted by the search. "Why not just talk to her?"

"Because what if they fixed her veil or something? Or they're using her to get information? Or what if someone else sees us—"

He cuts me off with a quiet chuckle. "Okay, okay. You're going to have to calm down before you melt the snow out of the trees and make it rain."

"This could take all day, you know." I'm about to ask if we can eat breakfast, forgetting for a moment that we have no food. Wolf is still playing around, sticking his nose into snow drifts, so we won't be eating anytime soon. Another reason to sneak into town.

The sun has passed its crest and started to sink before we give up. Pax and I have stalked the entire boundary three times, but found no portion of the fence that's not electrified. We uncovered Cadi's little black button on the second loop after we started to brush the snow out of the way along the fence. Based on the time of day, I'd guess Cell releases within the next twenty minutes, so it's now or never. Pax isn't going to agree to stay in Danbury long, so if I want to get in to try to see Leah, we're going to have to use the button and hope nothing happens.

Besides, if last autumn taught me anything, it's that the Others are arrogant. They believe their race so superior, their ability to control not only the humans but their own kind so complete that they don't take precautions. Since the Others can wriggle into our minds when we're not paying attention, they might not think it's necessary to monitor every way in and out of the Sanctioned Cities. Of course, that way of thinking might have become a bit outdated after they learned the Elements managed to keep their half-breed children a secret for more than ten years.

Snow and mud crust the little back button and it resists under my foot for a couple of seconds. But then several paces to our left, just like it did when Cadi came to collect Mrs. Morgan's things, a gate slides open in the boundary. No alarms sound. No Wardens rush from the park to apprehend us. The day is as cold and quiet as it's been since we arrived. Wolf sits and stays when I tell him to, eyes full of betrayal and confusion. It pains me to leave him out here, even though the Wilds are his territory. The sinking fear that he'll decide being my dog is too dangerous or that he'll think we're abandoning him twists in my belly.

Being back in the Danbury park feels strange. Everywhere I look, shadows of Lucas glimmer and then flutter away, reminding me that he's not here anymore.

He can't be. Loss drags down my heart until it feels too heavy to beat. Lucas should be here with us. It's not that I'm sorry Pax and I found each other. It's not even that my feelings for Lucas are so much stronger than what's developing between Pax and I.

But I want Lucas back.

I don't feel right without him.

Pax doesn't comment on the extra distance I shove between us as we walk. Honestly, it's not only Lucas making me pull away. It's this place. Where I learned I'm not human. That my real father is dead.

Danbury's the place I accidentally destroyed my fake mother, and where my life changed forever when I found, then lost, my first true friend. Where I met a kind woman named Cadi who believes I'm one of only four beings alive with the ability to save this planet, who taught me there are people willing to go to any length to preserve my life, no matter what it costs them.

There are no kids around as we move through the park, which isn't a surprise since the wind shudders in an icy blast and dark clouds gather, threatening more snow accumulation. Lucas's father must be a busy guy these days, with winter at its peak. It means we'll find our Cellmates in town, either having pizza or bowling.

Pax and I huddle together for warmth along the back outside wall of the pizza place, waiting for the free hour to be up and for everyone to head home. No one is out in the streets. We don't see any Wardens or adults, and for a second it's almost like the entire past couple of months have been a dream. Everything in Danbury is just so . . . *normal*. With the exception of when kids walk to and from school, or during assigned Outings, the Sanctioned Cities always seem deserted.

Laughter fills the air as my former Cellmates spill onto the street. A lot of them were in the pizza parlor, but a fair number chose bowling, too, by the look of things. The thought of bowling brings back the teasing memory of the Autumn Mixer: my first official Partnering activity with Lucas.

The sight of Leah's inky curls bouncing as she listens to a conversation between a huddle of girls snaps me out of the past. "That's her."

I want to walk with them, to overhear their conversation, but concern that our presence alone will be enough to upset their fragile balance keeps me hidden. Instead we trail them at a distance, keeping to people's backyards, taking refuge in the lengthening shadows provided by twilight. Leah is one of the first kids to peel off and head a different direction, but she doesn't go alone. The girl with the thick corn-silk braid keeps pace with our quarry, not leaving until they enter identical houses next door to each other.

Her name eludes me at first, but then I remember—Brittany. She had been interested in Partnering with Greg before he fell and Broke during exercise block one day. Before the Other I still sometimes think of as Deshi killed him.

The street sits in cold silence, as though it's holding its breath. Night swarms in from the edges of the world until it swallows everything whole, oppressive and total.

Pax raises his eyebrows at me. "What now?"

It's obvious that leaving her a note won't work anymore, because that would require paper and something to write with, neither of which is readily available. Plus, she's already inside. We'll have to catch her alone. Easier said than done, really.

"We'll wait until after everyone retires then sneak into her room."

Pax's eyes widen, the expression inside them wavering between worry over my sanity and amusement at the idea, I'm guessing. "We're going to just walk into her bedroom after dark and hope she doesn't jump out the window at the sight of us?"

The image makes me flinch. "Yes. It's the best option. She's alone, so if she doesn't remember me and Lucas and what happened, then we can contain her reaction. And if she does remember, we might scare her for a minute but she'll get over it."

"I guess. I can't say I'm comfortable with the whole idea, but this is your operation." He pauses, letting the slow smile stretch its way across his face. "Now, remember how easily I went along with your harebrained ideas once we're back in Portland and *you're* following *my* lead."

He's got me on that one. If he trusts me to make decisions in Danbury, I'm going to feel guilty trying to talk him out of any crazy notions once it's Tommy we're after. Which is not to say I won't still do it. But I might feel bad.

A thought wiggles around the edges of my brain for a few seconds until I snag it in my hands and surprise flutters. I can't believe I didn't realize sooner. "Wait, have you never been to Danbury before?"

Pax has mentioned Atlanta and Portland. He never said anything about Iowa being new when we were there. It makes sense that Danbury would be the place he would miss out on. The autumns, with their bursts of colorful leaves, are vivid here, and we all seem to skip the location that offers the richest experience of our home season.

"Nope. First time. And I have to say, since I typically spend my winters in Atlanta, this is quite the change of scenery. So was Iowa, where it's usually spring for me."

All of the Sanctioned Cities are laid out exactly the same, so it's not like there's anything to show him, outside the trees and the weather. Still, we have hours to kill before Leah and her family will retire for the night. It would be okay to check on Mr. Morgan, maybe, if we're careful.

Before last season, before the Others learned kids like me existed and might be dangerous, no one roamed the streets at night. Adults never left their houses except on preapproved family Outings. Children hunkered indoors no later than 5 p.m. on Cell days. Wardens never showed their faces unless there'd been an accident, a Breaking, or when registering new babies.

Back then no one saw me. Pax and I could have strolled down the middle of the street, laughing at the top of our lungs, and not a single person would have noticed anything amiss.

This world, though, is unknown to me. We've been alone in the Wilds for weeks. Those facts might remain the same, or they might be different. Wardens might still patrol every hour, the way they did in the autumn. Our Spritan protection might be weakening along with the beings who designed it. There's no way for us to know any of those things.

So instead of taking the streets, I lead Pax through the backyards of Danbury, sticking close to the rears of the houses where we won't be easily seen. The fact that it's dark—and it's winter—aids our efforts, since families draw the curtains once night falls. The kitchen windows face the backyards, so we wouldn't be missed otherwise. My heart hurts when we pass the house where Lucas lived. As we approach the Morgans' back porch, it aches even deeper, filling my chest with throbbing memories.

Pax sinks down next to me on the Morgans' back porch, the red bricks cold but free of snow. Mr. Morgan must have cleaned the porch off after he finished his Career duties today. The thought of him in there all alone, with no one to talk to while he eats dinner or watches his Saturday movies, shoves a wet rag in my throat. It's impossible to swallow, and soon it pushes tears down my cheeks. I look away, hoping to hide them from Pax.

It's not that I don't think he'd understand how it makes me sad to think of a lonely Mr. Morgan. It's more that Pax has a strange way of making me feel like an equal—a girl strong enough to stand beside him, capable of handling anything the world can throw at

240

me. Even now, he doesn't mention my weakness, and we sit there in silence as the moon rises and stars wink into the clear black sky, the earlier clouds having dissipated. The temperature drops until my entire body quakes, especially since my sweatshirt is now wrapped around Wolf's injuries. When the Morgans' kitchen light winks out, I rub the water from my cheeks and take a few trembling breaths.

"You know, I can think of a really fun way to warm up, if you're interested." Pax's teasing smile makes clear his meaning, heating my cheeks. As we've become surer of each other's presence, he's been more apt to bring the unspoken attraction between us into the realm of acknowledgment, ensuring I can't forget about it, no matter how hard I try.

The mental image of kissing him again, of the spicy sweet taste of his mouth on mine, lights my entire body on fire. I try to hide my embarrassment, and also my reaction, but his stupid smile grows wider until it looks as though it's going to fall off his face.

To distract him, and also because my own body is annoying me, I stand up and rub my hands together as though that's preferable to his plan for warming up. "You are so irritating. Let's go."

"You like me."

Rolling my eyes, I retrace our steps from earlier toady. Pax traipses along side me, his self-assurance soaking the air around us. I do like him, despite the care we've taken to ensure that the attraction between us doesn't get out of hand. I don't know why it feels like such a betrayal of Lucas to admit it, but it doesn't feel like it's okay to like them both.

We're going to have to find a way to work together, and in this entire universe, there are only three people who can understand what's going on inside of me. It should make me happy that both Pax and Lucas are kind people who make me smile, who make me feel good about myself in different ways. And it does. It would be better if the two boys were attached to feelings of simple friendship, though. Instead, with their stupid kisses and scents and their ability to create safety in the circles of their arms, the emotions they stir inside me are more than that.

Needing to tread carefully, I consider my response. Now is not the time to get caught up in feelings, not when the fate of our lives and the planet hang in the balance. "Of course I like you. You're a good friend."

Pax snorts. "You like me a lot."

I can't help but smile. "Yes. I like you a lot. Now, be quiet."

21.

We walk the rest of the way to Leah's in companionable silence. All of the houses are dark, the yards still. There's no wind to hide the sound of our crunching footsteps but not a single person has been outside since the kids returned home after their free hour, so there's no reason to be concerned about being discovered.

Our destination looks exactly like every other house on the block. Pax and I lock eyes on the back porch, silently agreeing that this plan is still a go. Well, my eyes ask him the question but he only shrugs, like, *Your plan, crazy girl*, before grinning at me again.

The doorknob turns easily in my hand. Some of the Cell rooms are locked, but our houses usually aren't. I never thought about it before, but it makes sense. That way the Others have free access to us—their *property*—anytime, day or night.

We pause in the kitchen, listening for a moment. No sound penetrates the perfect blackness, so I take the lead, holding my breath as we tiptoe past the master bedroom. Up the stairs, I choose the room that's in the same place as mine always was, with a window that overlooks the street. The day Lucas was hurt I learned that his room was placed in the same position, so it stands to reason that Leah's would be, too.

That, at least, works in our favor. It takes a few seconds for my eyes to adjust, but the moonlight slipping through the part in the curtains helps. The shadows of furniture appear first, then Leah's still form in the bed. Up close, her midnight curls are exactly as I remember, and just as wild. The bed dwarfs her tiny frame, making her appear like a small child instead of a sixteen-year-old girl like me.

Pax stays back by the windows. A good idea, considering she's never seen him before. And in any case, having a boy looming over her bed would be the surest way to make her go banana balls. There's actually no way that I know of to wake someone that isn't startling.

I kneel on the floor and reach out a tentative hand, shaking her shoulder gently.

Leah's eyes pop open and fill with fear, and I slap my hand over her mouth before she can yell. It takes just a moment, even in the dark, before she recognizes me and her eyes fill up with tears. Those two reactions say she remembers everything and she's still free from Other control. Regular humans don't cry. Ever. They don't even know what tears are.

I remove my hand from her lips and try a smile.

Hers is a little wobbly but she manages one, too. "Althea?"

Her eyes find Pax as he moves to my side, his own disarming smile firmly in place. It doesn't seem to affect her as it does me; confusion and wariness sputter across her dainty features.

"Who's he?" Leah has the presence of mind to whisper, even though she doesn't look pleased.

"This is Pax. He's like me . . . and Lucas."

"Where's Lucas, though?" Her question is faintly accusatory, as though I lost him on purpose, and adds another million pounds to the guilt already in residence on my shoulders.

I try and fail to stop tears from flooding my eyes. "I don't know. He's not here, then? You haven't seen him since autumn?"

Dismay pulls her lips down into a frown and pinches a line at the bridge of her nose. "No. Not since you guys helped me and ran off."

"Oh." It takes a moment, but I shake off the sorrow. I knew he wouldn't be here. We came for answers, not to find Lucas. "Well, Pax and I ended up here kind of by accident, and I wanted to come and see if you were okay. So . . . are you okay?"

In perhaps the most surprising thing to happen to me all winter—which is saying a lot—Leah leans forward and throws her arms around my neck, tugging me into a hug. I wrap my arms around her in return, and it feels nice. Like maybe Leah and I could be friends. It's strange to think I could make friends by just being myself, emotions and all. Pax and Lucas are my friends, but because we've been forced together because of what we are, not because we chose one another. It doesn't mean we don't like one another, but this is different.

When she pulls back, her smile is shy. "Thanks. I'm okay. It's been easier than I imagined, honestly. Except for the fact that I'm really lonely most of the time."

The ache of loss in her voice speaks to that place inside me, the empty one that hollowed out over years of having not a single person with whom to share my life. I squeeze her hand. "I know. I understand, believe me. What's been going on with the Others since Lucas and I disappeared?"

"They left the same night and haven't been back. Except to collect a Broken baby. And our chemistry Monitor. She Broke, too, they said."

The woman with the quivery smile. She'd never been quite right. Content enough, but not like the rest of them.

We stay for hours, letting Leah talk and ask as many questions as we can answer. It's clear she's not satisfied with our responses from the pink in her cheeks and the way her voice continues to rise. But the night outside the window fades to gray, signaling that it's time to go.

Leah finally says what's on her mind. "I thought you guys were going to fix this."

The accusation drapes over the chilly space. I don't know what to tell her.

"Fix what?" Pax comes to my rescue. And while his question could be construed as belligerent or defensive, instead it's soft and heavy with trepidation.

He recognizes not only the sorrow in Leah but the implied expectation.

"Everything. All of us. The Others aren't going to let us live once they're done with our planet."

Her trust confirms that we are burdened with the survival of an entire planet, an entire race, and one that we don't even truly belong to. The saving grace is that Leah is the only person we're going to let down because no one else is aware of the dire situation they're living in.

"Leah . . ." I stop, gather my thoughts, then try again. "Leah, we don't know what we're doing. We only just learned why we're different, that we're not affected by the mind control."

"But you have powers. I saw them."

The last thing I want to do is dampen the hope burning in her smoky gray gaze. "We do have powers. We're figuring out how they might be able to help everyone, I promise. We're trying."

Pax surprises me by sitting on the edge of the bed. He takes a deep breath, then locks eyes with this poor girl who has no one to count on but us. "We can't promise anything. But we're not giving up, okay? We're going to try our best to fix it."

It's the first time he's admitted that he thinks the humans and their home might be worth saving. The doubt threaded into his words says he still doesn't believe we can win. Even I can't see a way out of this, and if anything, Pamant's display of horrible Element power has further convinced me that we don't stand a chance. We're probably going to die, our brains picked into a million pieces.

But we're going to fight.

Leah bites her bottom lip and does her best to smile, then wraps her curls up in a ponytail. She excuses herself to go to the wasteroom, leaving Pax and

I alone with this new awareness hovering between us. That he's going to care.

He smiles and shrugs, and I reach out and punch his shoulder affectionately. Something Leah said makes me think, and when she returns, dressed in jeans and a deep purple sweater, I decide to ask yet another favor. "You said something earlier about what's going to happen when the Others are 'done with our planet.' What did you mean by that?"

She gives me a weird look, as though I've gone daft, and it's so much like the old, sarcastic Leah. "What we realized in astronomy the day Greg Broke. All of the Others' host planets are extinct. Why would we be any different?"

An idea springs to mind. "Would you be willing to do something for us? A bit of information gathering?"

I kind of expected a fearful response from her, given that she's already hiding in plain sight. Every day, she could make a slip that could be reported and get her hauled away in a matter of minutes. Instead, excitement lights her eyes until they sparkle. She and Pax have a similar inclination for mischief, it seems.

"Sure. What do you want me to do?"

"Just keep your eyes and ears open. If we're going to get rid of the Others, we're going to have to find out

249

what it is they need to survive, what they need from Earth and the humans. So we can take it away."

"How is she going to find that out? Not even Cadi and Ko know the answer, and their planet was already destroyed." Skepticism creases the skin around Pax's eyes, along with what looks like concern that poking around could get Leah into trouble.

It warms my blood that he cares about what happens to a girl he's never met before today. "Maybe she can't learn anything, I don't know. But what's it going to hurt for her to be extra observant?"

"I have an idea," Leah interrupts, a genuine smile beaming from her face. "What if I do some research when I can? We have astronomy books, right? And the Monitors love when we're extra curious about planets and their specifics. Maybe if I learn everything I can about the Others' previous hosts, some commonality will emerge that could lead us to the answer."

It's smart. Whether or not it could be that simple to learn why the Others choose their hosts remains to be seen, but it's proactive, and the idea of being one step ahead fills me with excitement, too. We've been reacting to everything—knowledge, events, attacks— since last season. It's like protecting Wolf and shoving fire out the window yesterday. If we want to even have a chance at winning back this planet, the three of us have to find a way to go on the offensive instead of playing catch up all the time.

Neither of us responds right away, causing embarrassment and doubt to rise in Leah's eyes. "It's silly, I guess. I mean . . ."

"Leah, it's not silly at all. I think it's a really good idea. Just please be careful." I let the hope fizzing in my heart bubble out in my voice.

"Althea's right. We'd love it if you could help, but the last thing we want is for something to happen to you. This is our fight. So don't get hurt."

Leah levels one of her classic contemptuous gazes at my autumn friend. He jerks away as though it's a physical force and I stifle a snort.

"With all due respect, strange boy I just met, this is my fight, too. It's all of our fight because this planet belongs to *humanity*. I happen to be the only person who knows what's really going on, that's all."

Pax raises his hand and retreats from the bed, standing by my side. "Fair enough."

I let myself smile. It might be a long time before we can find our way back to Danbury, so I'm glad that Leah will have something to hold on to during the times it feels like she can't go on alone another day. I had Ko; Leah has us. And after we find Lucas, we'll find a way to come back to hear what Leah has found out.

At least we have some information already—the Wardens haven't come back since Lucas and I traveled.

I lean down and snag Leah into another quick hug. "We have to go before your parents wake up. But thank you, Leah. We'll be back to check on you again when we can."

"Wait. There's no Cell today; it's Saturday. Would you wait until free hour? I'll meet you in the park if you want. There's something I need to show you."

We shouldn't. Pax and I don't even know how we're going to leave or how we're going to get to Portland. But we owe this girl, and the ability to say no escapes me. "Sure. In a few hours, then?" My stomach grumbles. "And maybe sneak us a little food? We haven't eaten in a while."

"Yes. I won't be late."

"We'll be at the boundary outside the park."

***

Pax and I get back to the spot where we crossed through the fence within ten minutes, before the sun wakes up the town. Our breath still billows in frosty clouds before our faces, and I pick up a sturdy stick and poke it through the fence, using it to open the gate for the second time.

The sight of Wolf bounding up to greet us makes me grin, and a glance at Pax reveals he feels the same way about our furry pal.

"Hey, Wolf! Did you miss us, buddy?" I kneel in the snow, letting him lick my cheek, not worrying about my jeans getting wet and cold.

"Since we have to wait a couple of hours on your friend, let's find somewhere dry to sit and start figuring out how we're going to get out of here."

The two of us hardly speak for the next three hours except to toss out ideas that the other shoots down. The notion that we might have to be in mortal danger in order to travel on our own is discomfiting. I'd rather not get into a bad position just so we can get to Portland. Walking is a better option, even if it does take until spring. The sun breaks through the heavy gray clouds, warming the winter day to a tolerable temperature and melting some of the snow.

Come on, Cadi. If you're out there, now would be a great time for a magic message about how we can travel with our own powers.

She doesn't answer. Not that I expected her to, but sometimes it's still nice to pretend there are still loving Spritans looking out for us.

The sound of snow crunching under boots interrupts our frustration, and we make our way back toward the fence, staying under the cover of the trees until we see Leah. Only she's not alone.

I recognize the thick blond braid and stop in my tracks. Both Leah's and Brittany's faces pale at the sight of Wolf, but right now, I'm more concerned with the fact that Brittany also looks undone at the sight of Pax and I. We're getting to see a veiled human, to gauge her reaction to us. It looks as though our enchantment is holding, but not as completely as it once did. She doesn't go all mad, but she doesn't accept me as readily as she did a few months ago, either.

"Is that a . . . an animal? A *wolf*?" Leah's normally confident tone slips out in a shocked whisper.

I shoot Pax a triumphant look. "See, everyone but you thinks he's a wolf."

"He's a dog—"

A weird, gurgling noise issues from Brittany and cuts off our disagreement. Her light eyes flick from Wolf to Pax to me in a wild circle—a reaction I've seen before. "Pax, she's freaking out."

Leah's eyes widen, panic growing. "I'm sorry. I brought her because I hoped you'd fix her, too, so I wouldn't be alone. I'll help her, I promise. She won't be mean the way I was at first when they were still sort of inside me." Leah's babbling now, tears running down her cheeks.

As angry as I am that she's put us in this position, her words reach out and cling to the memories of my old life, to all of the days I would have given anything for a friend. I can't blame her for this.

Pax and I hold a silent conversation that ends with a shrug on his end. "We have to do something. It won't hurt, if your friend thinks she can keep Blondie under control."

I step forward, not unsure or scared the way I was with the Healer or even with Leah, and punch open the gate again. "You have to come out here with us so we can contain her."

"Outside the boundary?" Leah squeaks.

"Who are you people? What are you doing with an animal? We should tell a Monitor. You could be sick. We could all be sick!" Brittany's voice rises higher with every word.

"Leah. Now," I demand softly.

Pax reaches out quickly and wraps a firm arm around Brittany's waist. She struggles, wheezing as her breath comes in terrified gasps, so I press against her other side and we drag her into the Wilds. Leah keeps up, staying as far away from Wolf as possible.

We manage to get Brittany to the sun-warmed boulders we used earlier as a thinking spot. Pax turns her toward me and I grab her hands, forcing her to make eye contact. I try reaching out for her mind with mine, thinking perhaps if I can feel my way like I can in the Other tunnels, I can simply find the veil and take it down. Like building the wall.

It doesn't work, so I go back to the tactic we discovered by accident.

Brittany, there's no need to be scared. You know me. I'm Althea, we were Cellmates last autumn. She stops struggling as fear leaves, replaced by confusion at my voice in her head. *That's right. The Others aren't what they say. They've been controlling everything. Everyone. But not you. Not anymore.*

Brittany shakes her head, clouds rolling clear of her vision after several minutes. She still looks confused, and until she speaks I'm scared that it didn't work, that she's Broken for good. She stares at Wolf for a moment, then Leah, then Pax, and finally me. It's not frantic like before, though. It's more like she's trying to figure out what to say.

Her voice is shaking when she finds it. "How did this happen? How could I not have known? I feel different. Lighter. More free. But all these years, those pieces of my thoughts that escaped before I could catch them never felt important. Why?"

If only we knew why the human brains don't recognize the alien presence in their minds and rebel against it. They do, in a way, I guess, but the yearly Purging ceremony takes care of their lingering defiance by emptying the stored-up feelings. "We don't know. But Leah can fill you in on everything we *do* know."

"Like that animals aren't dangerous?" Her eyes are riveted to Wolf.

"Well, he's not exactly *not* dangerous, but he seems to like us okay." Pax is joking but I shoot him a look, shaking my head.

"What about your cat? Is it crawling with fleas?" Leah interjects.

"Cat?" I follow Leah's gaze, finding a yellow cat not unlike the one I glimpsed in that Iowa tree. It lazes in the sun several yards away, licking a slim paw while watching us with disinterested eyes. The thing isn't big enough to frighten me. It's not like the animal that attacked Wolf—this one is even smaller than a raccoon.

But it's unsettling, the way that I feel like I've seen it somewhere before. "That's not our cat."

"Can I touch the wolf dog?" Brittany's plaintive curiosity is a little bothersome, making me wonder if I hurt her somehow. She's always been kind of a bold girl, though.

Pax and I exchange a wary glance.

"Um, yeah. He likes it when you scratch his ears."

Wolf stands perfectly still as she approaches, her hand outstretched, palm facing the ground. Brittany's soft intake of breath at the touch of her skin on his fur delights me, in spite of my worry over her soundness of mind. Leah joins her a moment later, and their awed smiles make the entire trip to Danbury worth it. Not only have we told them the Others are liars, but with Wolf's presence, we've shown them, too.

"You girls should get back. Your hour is almost up." Regret deepens Pax's voice.

They step away from Wolf looking enthralled and sad to leave him behind.

Leah reaches into her backpack and hands me several cans of vegetables. "Thank you, Althea. I'll tell Brittany everything. You can count on us."

They turn to go, and it makes me sad and a little relieved at the same time. It's a nice feeling, there being more than two people who know what I am and don't care. But Leah and Brittany are our responsibility now. We follow and close the gate after they pass back through. Something occurs to me and I call out, causing Leah to turn around.

"Yeah?"

"If you see Lucas . . ." There are so many things I want Lucas to know, but not a lot that I want to say in front of Pax. Or Leah and Brittany, for that matter.

Instead I swallow and force a smile. "Tell him I'll find him."

She nods, and Pax and I watch until they disappear.

"Do you think they'll be okay?"

"I don't know." As usual, Pax's refusal to lie is a strange comfort.

Honestly, I want to figure out how to leave this place, to get to Portland and find out what happened to little Tommy. Because now, more than ever, I want to focus on finding Lucas.

We're headed back to the rock we've been using as a seat when the yellow cat with the purplish eyes plants itself in our path. Pax and I stop and stare at it. It stares back.

Then it flickers, shifts, stretches . . . and turns into a boy.

22.

I scream, stumbling back into Pax. We tangle and fall in a heap in the cold snow. Ringing laughter meets my ears, coming from the tall boy with shoulder-length yellow hair that used to be a cat. His impossibly purple eyes overflow with mirth, infuriating me.

"How did you do that?" I demand.

The boy tries to swallow his laughter, eyes twinkling. "What do you mean? Do what?"

"You were a cat! Right in midair, you changed into"—I gesture from his head to his toes—"*you*."

"Did I, now? That's a strange thing to see. Could be your eyes are playing tricks."

Pax untangles from me, standing and brushing off his clothes. Now that the initial shock has settled, fear grabs me in a firm grasp. This boy is a stranger, one with powerful abilities, and we shouldn't trust him. I slide a worried glance toward Pax, trying to communicate that we need to handle this situation carefully, but his face reflects a curious calm.

He nods at the boy, who grunts in response.

"Do you two know each other?" It finally dawns on me to ask.

A reluctant whoosh of air spills past Pax's lips. "He's the one I told you about. Who brought me the bracelet, who helps Ko sometimes with running errands."

As I study the stranger, no longer frightened but still curious, the memory of not only the cat in Iowa, but the golden bird in the cabin, the strange little lizard in Wyoming—all yellow with purple eyes—clicks into place. "You've been spying on us."

He doesn't admit to anything, just squints into the sun. "Do you want that help or not?"

"What on Earth are you talking about?"

He rolls his eyes as though I'm asking the dumbest questions in the history of questions. A heavy sigh follows. "About an hour ago? *Oh Cadi, help us please we can't figure this out,* wah, wah, wah, blah, blah, et cetera."

My mouth drops open. "I didn't say any of that out loud!"

"And you're not Cadi." Pax regains his powers of speech in time to save me from smacking the impertinent stranger across the face.

If I could even catch him, which I sense wouldn't be easy. There's something inhuman about the way he moves; it's like watching water in motion. As though he could collapse into droplets on a whim, rearrange his molecules into steam, and float away. Of course, maybe none of that is really that strange, considering he just changed from a cat into a person.

"No. I'm Griffin. Cadi is, shall we say, indisposed, but asked for my help."

Suspicion tickles my thoughts, scratching a bit like the wrong end of a feather sticking out of a pillow. "How do we know she sent you? You've been following us for weeks."

"Please. I wasn't following you. More like checking in to see if you'd managed to die yet. It will be a shame if the Spritans' efforts go to waste."

His word games make my head hurt, and the callous indifference toward our lives seeps pain into my heart. It's hard to tell if he really cares about Cadi or Ko, or about what they hope to accomplish. "I'm Althea. This is Pax. But maybe you already know all of that."

"I do."

"Can we cut the crap?" Pax snaps. "Tell us how you know about us. And Cadi."

"Strange, those questions. Here I thought all you wanted was to get to Portland in a hurry." Griffin acts as though it's perfectly normal to know what we've been discussing for weeks.

He leaps from where he's standing onto the top of the boulder, landing gracefully on one foot. The jump takes him several feet into the air, heightening my curiosity about what exactly he might be, because he's definitely not human.

"What are you?" Pax notices the boy's unusual qualities as well.

"It hurts that you don't appreciate my human qualities. Really, it does."

Pax and I creep toward where Griffin has taken a seat. Neither of us speaks, and I for one am determined to wait him out. We've only met two kinds of beings who know who we are without being told: Cadi and Ko, and the Others. Griffin resembles a little of both, but with an essence that's also completely unique.

My conversation with Cadi in the woods last autumn explodes in my memory. About how the Others took females from Sprita to breed with so they could steal their magic genes. And Cadi said the Others had taken species before and after them. Could Griffin be Something Else like us, an example of the Others' attempt to create the most effective version of themselves?

"Are you part Other?" I ask.

"Well, at least one of you has a brain between your ears. Okay. I'm going to give you a two-minute history lesson and answer three questions. Only three, no more. After that, if you want my help to get to Portland, I'll take you there. If not, you can continue to try to figure it out on your own. You might, eventually, although I daresay it could take you a while. Do we have a deal?"

It's not like I'm going to turn down the chance to learn more about this planet. I nod, and after a moment Pax does, too, even though it looks like it pains him to do so. Pax holds his entire body stiff, as though he's suddenly made out of metal. It won't surprise me if he creaks when he moves. He seemed unhappy detailing his previous interaction with Griffin, too, so I guess it makes sense that's he's not jumping for joy at this appearance.

"Okay. Baby history. I am descended from a race called the Sidhe. Over half of our people left home, a planet called Lionn, thousands of years ago. They made a new home here on Earth, living, well, more or less in harmony with the humans. When the Others arrived almost twenty years ago, we were not susceptible to their mind control and therefore presented the only legitimate threat on this planet. My people were driven to near extinction. Many died off, or reverted to simple life-forms. The Others murdered some, and the very unlucky were enslaved. Once the Others learned of our extraordinary talents, they began to manipulate our genetics." A self-satisfied, twisted smile flinches across his face. "It did not go as planned."

Cadi said that, too. That some species hadn't weathered the genetic probing as well as the Spritans. I wonder if I want to know what happened to the Sidhe. He falls silent, and I think that's the end of our lesson. It didn't last two minutes. He owes us more free information before we have to decide what three questions to ask.

"My twin sister and I are the only Sidhe that remain."

This time he is finished, evidenced by the way he spreads his hands toward us, inviting our questions. I want to ask what a twin sister is, but that seems like a silly thing to waste a question on. Perhaps we'll learn it another time.

Pax and I try conferring in silence, but there are too many variables and it doesn't work very well. I give up first. "Okay, we each get one question, then we'll agree on a third?"

He nods, then goes first without asking. "How did Cadi send you to help us?"

"She heard Red here asking for help. She and Ko have some extra connection to you four because of the protections you carry around, and to my sister and I through magic. Cadi is no longer authorized to go anywhere unescorted, and they've got both her and Ko locked in rooms that prevent physical manifestations of magic. She simply asked me to come and take you to Portland. I'm not typically inclined to be helpful, you understand, but I make exceptions when it suits me."

Griffin gave us more information with that answer than I expected, and it takes me a second to decide what else exactly I want to know. I'm curious what exception he sees in helping Pax and I, but the lure of Earth's history and the Others' invasion proves too much to deny, and I settle on my question. "What abilities did the Others hope to glean from your people?"

This time, the smile on Griffin's lips conveys undiluted pride. "The Sidhe are an ancient race. Far older than the Others and much more powerful. We can change shapes, as you saw, and magic is as natural to us as breathing. Our elders who chose to revert to simple forms became part of the universe's essence once again in the form of wind, or water, or trees. The Others saw only our magic, particularly the shape-shifting abilities, and wished it for themselves. They can take on alien forms, as they've done with their human bodies, but it's not innate as it is for us."

"Why didn't the genetic manipulation work?"

If Griffin notices I've asked a third question, he doesn't say a word. "Our magic is not light and malleable, as it is for the Spritans. The Sidhe are . . . what is a good word for you to understand? Troublemakers? Our magic is dark and old. Heavy. It cannot be tampered with, and the children born of Other and Sidhe mixtures retained none of the desired Other traits. Especially the ability to control our minds. The Prime Other killed everyone but Greer—that's my sister—and myself in a furious rage. I'm not sure why he kept us alive, to be honest, unless they wish to try again at some point. It's been years since they've been to see us. Perhaps they've forgotten we exist."

I wish they would forget Pax and Lucas and I exist. The difference is that the Others believe Griffin and Greer have nothing they want, and they're kept locked away where they can't pose any kind of threat. Perhaps if they caught us, we could make them believe we're not a threat and they would leave us to rot in a prison.

I think I'd rather be dead.

An endless supply of questions remains. I want to know how he's standing here talking to us if he and his sister are prisoners. What kind of favor does he owe Cadi? Are she and Ko okay? Does he know where we can find Deshi? How many more half-breeds exist in the Other tunnels besides the Sidhe, the Spritans, and the four of us?

But we only get one more question, and I have no idea which one is more important, or even if any of them matter at all. All of a sudden, I'm exhausted. Like Griffin's presence has sucked out all my energy.

"If the Others have you and your sister imprisoned, how can you be here?" Pax voices the next inquiry, sounding tired out by this interaction as well.

Griffin hops down, light as a feather. "You already asked your three."

He's right, of course. I realize now I'd been silly to think he hadn't noticed. This is not a boy who misses anything at all.

A couple of feet away, he raises both hands in front of him. He spreads them out wide, tearing a hole in the afternoon air that shimmers and ripples around the outer edge of his . . . I guess it's a portal. Griffin glances over his shoulder at us as though this is the most normal event ever, as though he yawned instead of pulling open a gap in the universe.

Pax's mouth is open, making me realize mine is, too. We don't get any more questions, though, so we stand and stare until Griffin rolls his eyes again.

"You're telling me you've wanted to get to Portland all this time and now you can't take the ten steps to get there? Let's move, kids."

"Wait." Pax turns to me, lowering his voice even though the way Griffin talks about his people they probably have superhearing, too, since they're the greatest things to ever grace the universe for a gabillion years or whatever.

"Remember what I was saying in Wyoming, about distracting the Others so we could at least be a little safer in Portland?"

"Vaguely." Pamant cracking the ground under our feet had put a rather hasty end to that conversation.

"Well, we need them to think we're still here. Set some stuff on fire, Summer."

Understanding dawns, and even though I'm not sure the Others are naïve enough to fall for the ploy, it's worth a try. Without checking with Griffin, I turn my palms toward the forest. It makes me sad to burn it, even for a good cause, but I swallow the sorrow and let it gather in my belly. It mixes with my irritation at Griffin and the huge expanse of knowledge we're missing, with my love for Wolf, my concern over Leah and Brittany. Soon it's too hot to hold in, and I push it hard, out through my skin.

Four trees burst into flames, sending birds screeching for the sky and squirrels searching for new stomping grounds. Pax lifts his own hands, closing his eyes and whipping up a storm that crashes some smaller branches to the earth. Two skip across the ground until they smash into the boundary, exploding into sparks. It might not be enough to get anyone's attention, although the smoke rising from our handiwork will be easily seen from the windows in town. We can only hope someone will report the anomaly to the Others and they'll come here and waste some time searching for us in Connecticut while we search for Tommy in Portland.

"Are we ready now, you destructive little fiends?" Griffin's jaw tightens, as though maybe he's pissed at us for hurting the nature from which his people apparently sprung.

It crosses my mind to tell him I don't like it either, but honestly don't feel like explaining myself since he's pretty much unwilling to return the favor. Instead, Pax and I walk forward together, and then take the small step over the shimmering threshold into another place.

Before Griffin closes the window I remember Wolf, and turn and pat my leg. He looks uncertain about both the hole and the boy holding it open, but when Griffin starts to let it slip closed, the dog decides he'd rather be with us. Having his warm body at my side provides an instant calm.

Griffin steps through the portal after us, then drops his hands to his side. Before we can thank him, or try to get him to tell us anything more about where we are or what we're supposed to do now, he leaps into the air, transforms into a huge, golden bird, and disappears into the sun.

23.

"Okay, did that really just happen?" I give my head a shake, trying to dislodge the surreal image of Griffin. "Did you know he could do that? Change into animals?"

"No. But he was just as big of a jerk when I met him before."

Pax is right about Griffin's attitude, but something about the boy makes me hopeful even though arrogance spills out of him like water. Perhaps it's that he's so relaxed about the life he leads, as though maybe it's not as bad as it seems to be under the Others' thumb. That's not true, but it is nice to believe it for a moment. "He's certainly interesting."

"What, you like him?" Pax's voice rises at the end, incredulous.

"I don't *like* him, exactly. But you have to admit his appearance is interesting. There might be even more people—er, beings—like us. It's just kind of nice, I suppose, to think we're not alone."

He purses his lips as though he tastes something sour. "I suppose. But I don't trust him. Once he loses whatever interest he has in us, he won't lift a finger to help anymore."

It's true we don't know why Griffin is helping, other than that Cadi asked him to, but there must be a real reason. I can tell he's not the type to do anything out of the goodness of his heart. If he has a heart in the first place. "Well, we're in Portland," I say, refocusing. "Time to make a plan for finding out what happened to Tommy."

It's been a while since I've been in this city, but this place does look familiar. I walk a little ways into the trees, Pax at my heels. A large, clear pond tells me Griffin left us in the park. There isn't a pond in any of the other Sanctioned Cities, a fact I always found curious, since they are otherwise identical.

Voices rise and fall, startling me from my reverie. There shouldn't be anyone here; we left Danbury after free hour ended on Saturday. Yet people *are* here, and Pax and I are going to have to make a snap decision on whether to hide or take our chances and try to just act "normal." Our experience in Connecticut left me confident the protection that keeps people from seeing us for what we are remains mostly in place, although how much longer it will hide us, or how well, is anyone's guess. We know the Wardens are no longer kicking around Connecticut, but since they learned while interrogating me that we were headed to Portland, they might be waiting for us nearby.

Our hope is that the fire and damage outside Danbury drew them to the east. They saw us disappear outside the ranger's station; who's to say we didn't travel to Connecticut? At the very least, the Others will no longer be positive they know where to find us.

"I say we try to blend in." Pax meets my eyes, exhibiting a confidence I don't feel.

"What if the Others haven't been alerted to what happened in Connecticut yet? They could be waiting for us to show our faces in town."

"Well, Leah said there haven't been Wardens in town this winter, and I doubt they'll risk confusing the humans unless they're sure we'd be dumb enough to walk straight into a Sanctioned City in the middle of the day. Also, once they *do* see what we did back there, they're not going to think we can get all the way to Portland this quickly. The Others know we were walking before and that we can't control our travels." They've seen us disappear in front of their faces twice, but as far as knowing where we'll appear, I don't see how they could know that. "They won't be certain where to look, but I would guess they'll think we'd stay in the Wilds, like we have been." He shrugs.

The reasoning makes some sense, but it still makes me nervous. Plus, we have Wolf.

The dog stares at us, cocking his head back and forth during our whispered discussion as though he can understand what we're saying. Perhaps he can, but if so, I sure wish he could talk. I bet Wolf would give excellent advice.

None of the kids venture all the way to the boundary, which isn't a surprise. I was nearly always alone, walking in a loop around the fence that kept us penned in. Only then I believed it was there to keep animals and terrors penned out. What a difference a few months and a mountain of truth have made in my life.

"What are we going to do with Wolf if we go into town? If we're going to be gone a day or more, I don't want to leave him."

Pax stares at Wolf, his lips pulled into a frown. "The thing is, I don't have anywhere to stay. You can probably still stay with your Portland family, but I don't have that option."

Because his family is dead.

Pax doesn't say the words, but they're there, hanging in between us like some horrible, unspoken monster. I take a deep breath, trying to puzzle out the best way to get into town and be able to ask questions about Tommy.

"Okay, so after free hour you want me to just go to the Hammonds' like nothing happened? Then what? Go to Cell on Monday? And you'll stay out here? With Wolf?"

"Well I want to go to Cell with you. Two pairs of ears are better than one, and if the humans still accept our presence then why not? They won't think anything of it if we join them. They never have before."

I consider for a moment, trying to free the thinking part of my brain from the wash of terror at the prospect of not *hiding*. We've been so concerned with no one seeing us, with running for so long that my body is automatically rejecting the idea of doing the opposite. I want more time to acclimate, to get my brain to accept this new direction.

"I'm not going today. We'll both stay here tonight, and I'll go back after free hour tomorrow." I swallow, urging my heart to slow down. "I don't want to stay any longer than I have to, and one day in their house, worrying the whole time they'll wake up and start screaming, is plenty."

"Summer, you're being silly. It's cold out, and we haven't eaten in a couple of days."

He's right, but it doesn't make sense for him to stay out here, starving and freezing, either. "We shouldn't split up, though. How about this? We can both sneak into the Hammonds' after they go to sleep, so I wake up there like normal. That way we'll be warm, Wolf can hide in my bedroom, and there'll be food in the kitchen." It's a good plan, I think, even if I am probably biased because it means not leaving Pax and Wolf and going into town alone.

Pax smiles, a slow one, but it's his eyes that catch my breath. "Okay."

He understands my reasons, which aren't only leaving them or fear of being discovered. It's being alone that scares me the most. If we're separated and something happens, if the Others come or Pax travels . . . terror quarters my heart at the thought.

The small, niggling fear that Pax's loyalty still lies with Tommy, and not me, whispers in my ear. The voice reminds me that he left Deshi alone, that he'll hide instead of fight, if there's a choice.

***

Later that night, an hour after the adults have retired and Pax and I have made sure there aren't Wardens pacing the streets, we venture into the city proper. There's no snow in Portland, and it's not nearly as cold as it was in Connecticut or on the path we trekked this direction for those two weeks. We could have stayed outside tonight and been fine with body and dog heat, but my stomach is hollow and grumbling, so this is better.

The Hammonds' house breathes silence around us, warm air welcoming and smelling faintly of onions and garlic. It intensifies the hunger burbling in my middle, eliciting a growl so loud the neighbors might have heard. Pax covers his mouth to staunch the flow of his laughter, and I have to look away to avoid catching it.

"Shh. Let's get Wolf upstairs, then we'll find some food."

He nods. Wolf hesitates at the foot of the stairs, making me realize he's never been in a real house before, but his trust in me wins out after a minute and he follows us past the closed door of my Portland parents' room into my old space. The comforter is clean and smooth, the blue and silver strangely comforting in its familiarity. Like always, the room looks like I could have left it this morning, even though this hasn't been mine for months.

The stairs presented a bit of a problem for Wolf, but the bed is apparently inviting. He leaps right onto it, mud-smeared paws leaving prints everywhere. He must have picked it up in the backyard. I squeak out a protest, but the damage is already done. I didn't notice him leaving tracks downstairs, but the carpet on the stairs is a mixture of silver and dark gray threads.

Pax shakes his head at the dog, then laughs quietly. "Guess we can add 'clean the comforter' to our list of things to do before we leave."

"You stupid dog." I scratch his ears and Wolf rolls over on his back, begging for a belly rub. I oblige, but stop when Pax's stomach rumbles this time. "Stay here with Wolf."

I wipe up the paw prints on the iron gray kitchen tile, erasing our presence from the kitchen. We scarf down the leftover spaghetti and meatballs from dinner, which I took against my better judgment, since they'll likely miss it. But it tastes good enough to validate the choice, and as long as things in town stay the same as they've always been, the Hammonds will find a way to explain it to themselves in the morning.

Pax and I change clothes, another bonus of staying at the Hammonds. I have drawers of pajamas, and he fits into a pair of gray sweatpants. Almost. They're too short, with the ankle elastic stretched around his calves. My own clothes hang loose on my frame. There have been too many days without proper nourishment on this journey. We'll have to find a way around that from here on out, because we need our strength to fight.

I check the door to make sure it's locked, then crawl into bed, pushing a too-comfortable Wolf out of the way. Pax and I keep the usual distance between our bodies, even though I'm hyperaware of his strong chest, spicy apple scent, and the invisible string trying to yank me against his side.

"So, how did you know Griffin had been following us?" Pax's baritone vibrates into my chest.

So much for getting some good rest. But honestly, Pax wanting to chat about our situation is a somewhat rare gift, and I snatch it up before he changes his mind. Griffin and his sister have been on my mind all afternoon, too.

"Before you came to the cabin in Iowa, there was a bird with feathers the exact color of his hair and it had those purple eyes. It made waste on me." My mouth twists at the disgusting memory.

I can tell by the way Pax holds his breath that he's trying not to laugh, and after a minute the humor is apparent, even though it would have been a lot funnier if Griffin had done that to someone else. "And then I saw a little cat the same color, with the same eyes, in a tree the night we stayed in the underground place in Iowa. Then the lizard in Wyoming, the one that seemed like it really enjoyed scaring me. Same colors. Same *attitude*."

"I wish we knew what he wants in return for helping us. Do you think he's keeping tabs on Winter, too?"

The desire to go back in time and use one of our questions to ask Griffin if Lucas is okay gnaws at my ability to breathe. Why didn't I think to ask him that? "I don't know," I say, hoping Pax can't hear the tremble in my words. "Maybe he's as curious as we are, even for all his talk about being superior. Like he thinks what Cadi and Ko believe— that we could expel the Others from Earth and help put things back together. From what he said, the Sidhe had a pretty good thing going here before the Others took over. He might be willing to help us if it meant reclaiming his spot at the top the food chain."

"Could be. He doesn't seem the type that enjoys being bossed around."

"Whatever the reason, I'm glad he showed up today." I change the subject, trying to steer us toward the immediate future. "Are we just going to ask about Tommy at Cell on Monday?" Pax's summer brother was a lot younger than us; he would have still been in Primer Cell, but everyone will know what happened. It was on the news, but part of me worries the Others changed people's memories the way they did after Mrs. Morgan disappeared. That whatever they tell us will be what the Others want us to know, not what actually became of the little boy.

"Yes. People are always gossipy when there's a Break and the Wardens show up. If they remember, they'll tell us, maybe at lunch." Pax's voice goes soft.

I know how he feels. It tore me apart, having to act as if it wasn't anything more than an interesting event after Mrs. Morgan Broke. "And then what are we going to do?"

"I don't know. I suppose it depends on what we find out."

Neither of us speaks for a few moments, but I'm not ready to stop talking yet. "You never told me how they explained the Sullivans having two children."

On Earth, Partners used to have more than one baby, but the Others determined the practice unnecessary, and the question has bothered me for weeks.

"Tommy isn't their real son, either. Mrs. Sullivan's sister Broke while she birthed Tommy and his father died from a heart condition a year later. The Others placed him with my parents before I ever started staying with them."

"Oh."

Pax doesn't seem to want to talk anymore, and after a few minutes my eyes drop closed. Our world might not be anything close to perfect, and we're likely the least safe beings on all of Earth, but tonight we're warm and indoors. It worries me what will happen if Pax finds out that Tommy Broke, that the Others took him away. He won't have anything pushing him forward anymore. I want to tell him that horrors lurk in all of our pasts, and there are people I wish I could go back and help, but that going back is impossible.

The only thing we can do is move forward.

Pax's breathing evens out while I hold my tongue, and comfort sits stubbornly outside my grasp. Contentment won't ever be mine as long as Lucas isn't beside me, as long as Leah and Brittany are in danger, and as long as we have no idea how to accomplish the impossible task set before us.

After we learn what we can in Portland, I'm moving on. I can only hope that Pax will want to come, too.

24.

The next morning, Mr. Hammond's voice telling me it's time to get up startles me out of what must have been a nice, deep sleep. I can't believe we slept through the rising of the sun, the dawn of a new day. Relief that we locked the bedroom door uncoils my tense muscles, poised to run if my fake father came in and found me in bed with a boy and a dog.

"Morning," Pax mumbles.

Pax's grin is even slower in the mornings. It's sleepy, too, I suppose. I smile back, trying not to breathe on him before I brush my teeth. My bare feet hit the thick carpeting as I head for the connected cleansing room. "I'm going to take a shower."

Just the idea of getting to take a hot shower fills my body with expectation, making me realize how much the Others provide and how easily I took it for granted my entire life. Hot water, a roof, parents, food three times a day—it would almost seem as though they care about what happens to us, except we know they don't. Not in the end.

Curiosity needles my skin along with the pinpricks of scalding water, shooting questions at my brain. Why do the Others need humans alive and cooperative? What do they take from our planet that sustains them? How much is there, and when will it run out?

In spite of how much we've learned so far, the number of facts we don't know remains larger by at least half. And all of the important questions are still waiting to be answered, with us clueless as to how to go about getting them.

A knock shakes me out of my spiraling hopelessness, and through the foggy shower door, I see Pax's head poke through the doorway.

"Hey! I'm in the shower."

"Yes, I realize that. I'm not looking, I promise."

His face is turned away from me, but he's not fooling anyone.

"I can see you looking in the mirror."

"Too bad for me you've got the water so hot. I can hardly breathe, never mind see through the steam."

"Yes, too bad," I say sarcastically. "Can I help you with something?"

"What? Oh, right. Don't turn the water off. I want to take a shower after you and that way they'll just think you were in there a long time. And hurry up."

He shuts the door, leaving me to shake my head. I pick up the pace, since a long shower is one thing, but a half-hour one would be hard to explain. Pax and I trade places, and while he's in the shower I get dressed and ready for the day. It's tempting to invade his personal space with an excuse to use the sink, but I avoid it. We've gotten a little too comfortable, spending every hour of every day together for at least three weeks now. It's not going to be an easy habit to break once we're not alone anymore.

Or once we go our separate ways.

That line of reasoning flies straight out of my mind, along with every other thought, when he strides out of the bathroom in nothing but a towel tied around his waist. Water droplets glisten across his shoulders, fall between the hard muscles of his back. His olive skin, so very different from my pale freckles, contrasts with the dark hair on his chest and I think he's maybe the most beautiful thing I've ever seen.

His eyebrows are raised when my perusal finally reaches his face, heating my cheeks and pretty much the rest of me.

"I, um. I'm going to go down to breakfast. You should get dressed and sneak out the front door while we're eating."

Pax doesn't respond, eyes locked on mine, chest rising and falling too rapidly. I flee the bedroom and the half-naked boy that makes me forget all of the things that I shouldn't.

I escape from one anxiety-ridden situation into another, remembering as I clamor down the stairs that the Hammonds might not react as they have in the past. It's hard to know what to expect, seeing them again after all this time, but it comforts me a little that out of all of my parents, they're the ones who knew me best. I try to have faith, recalling how Leah seemed to instinctively know she could trust Lucas, even though all the specifics of their friendship had been erased.

Not for the first time, the idea that perhaps the human brains operate on a more complex level than even the Others understand winks in my mind. Maybe even though they purge specific feelings and memories, there are impressions that linger. I doubt there's any way I'll ever know if I'm right, but it's nice to believe in something stronger than the Others' control. To believe that one day, if the humans do all wake up, they'll still feel a little bit the same about the people they care about.

The Hammonds barely look up when I slide into the kitchen and take my usual seat. The rich, warm smell of cinnamon rolls makes me want to cry, and the pan of gooey buns on the table are the most wonderful thing about being here in Portland.

"Good morning, Althea." Mr. Hammond meets my eyes, a normal, pleasant smile on his face. Until it wobbles and something that looks like confusion flickers in his muddy gaze.

He called me Althea. That's what they called me after I spent months training them, when I lived here. Otherwise, they've always called me Allie. The Morgans call me Thea. The Clarks prefer AllyCat, which always irked me the most, being compared to a dirty animal. Well, at least before I had one for a pet.

It should please me that even though Pax and I are not planning to be here more than a day or two, I won't have to endure the whole nickname thing again. Instead of relief, though, it causes worry because the behavior is slightly different than expected, making me nervous. There's nothing to do except try to act normal.

Since it's Sunday, the hour after breakfast is free, so I use it to my advantage and meet Pax in the park. He and Wolf snuck out during breakfast so the dog could make waste. There was no reason to assume every family on the street wasn't also at the table, that no one could see them, but still, we can't keep doing this. Wolf doesn't belong here, and I doubt the enchantment that hides us from people's common sense extends to him. If even one person sees that dog we are in big, fat trouble.

"We need to leave Wolf in the Wilds today. It's too risky." I look around, taking in our empty surroundings. "Wait, no one's here."

"Yeah. Is that bad?" Pax sounds like he doesn't think so, but I'm not so sure.

"The Hammonds make me nervous."

He perks up. "I thought you said they were normal."

"They were, mostly. It's little things, the stuff that no one besides me would notice, but they're not exactly the same. I just have a feeling that we don't have much time, that's all. And if we can find some of our Cellmates today, we can start investigating. It might even be easier, without blocks and Monitors and lessons taking up our time."

"You're right. No matter how nice the food and the shower and the warm bed are, we don't belong here anymore," Pax says, looking gloomy.

Sadness sinks so deep into my bones they ache from the strain of holding it all in. We never belonged here, not really, but the thought of living without the simple comforts of the Sanctioned Cities, of always being on the run, spills fatigue through me. "We should enjoy them while we can, I think."

After we let Wolf into the Wilds, Pax walks at my side into town, leaving a safe distance between us. We don't want to act too familiar and draw attention. With the fear of our protective invisibility weakening, it would be better if people didn't think twice about us. It hasn't escaped my attention that any contact with humans could put them in danger. Who knows what the Others might do if they found out—take them all out of town in their riders, hook them up to brain-reading machines, and pick out the information about us—and then dispose of them all afterward. And that's the nice scenario.

The thought sends shivers down my limbs, quickening my steps. We have to get out of here soon. I promised Pax we'd find out what happened to Tommy, but as soon as we do, first on my to do list is staying as far away as possible from the content human population.

***

A good number of our Cellmates loiter in the bowling alley during free hour, but the faces I'm looking for crowd around a table in the pizzeria. Val's long, straight black hair is tied back in a ponytail, and her head bends close to Monica's. Monica's ebony skin shines in the morning sunlight streaming through the windows, and the two of them laugh and smile over a private joke that once would have included me as well. There's no food at this hour, only an indoor establishment in which to hang out with friends, though there are drinks available.

When Monica looks up and meets my eyes, breath catches in my chest. The same brief confusion I saw in Mr. Hammond's face registers, followed quickly by recognition, and finally pleasure.

Then she waves at me. "Althea! Come sit with us!"

My heart stops. Val and Monica haven't recognized me, or asked me to sit with them, for over three years. Since I left after the three years and stayed only a season, they forgot they knew me. Like everyone else

But now they're acting like they do.

There's no way to understand exactly what's going on, or how things have changed, but the fact that they're different at all speeds my heart into a gallop.

Instead of running, which is what my legs are begging for, I force a smile and lead Pax over to where the girls sit side by side. There's a boy at their table, too, something that just now registers, hunched close enough to Val for me to think they're probably courting. That's at least one thing in our favor.

"Hi!" Monica's white teeth flash.

"Morning." Neither of them ask who Pax is, or for an introduction, as we slide into the last free spaces of the booth. That is a good sign at least. Even though he and I have never been in Portland at the same time, we've both lived here. They remember him, too.

The boy next to Val isn't handsome, at least not to my taste. His hair is a dirty shade of blond, not pretty like the Others' hair or shiny the way Griffin's was, and his eyes are a washed-out, faded brown. He smiles at me but it doesn't reach his eyes; it's the creepy, empty smile I've come to associate with someone without any control over their own emotions. I don't recognize him or recall his name, but asking isn't an option, so instead I ignore him and fumble for a way to start a conversation with these girls who I haven't seen in months and haven't talked to in far longer.

Nothing enters my mind, no way to try to learn about Tommy or even broach the subject. They save me, continuing their conversation as though we've been here the entire time.

"There should be a Winter Mixer or Gathering, too. It's forever until the spring one!" Val, always the more social of the two girls, sticks out her lower lip in a pout.

Because she's not really upset or discontent, it looks strange on her face, as though she's more amused than annoyed. The Term class is always eager for the next event. The last year represents the only time in our lives in which exciting affairs dot our landscape, and the conversation presents a perfect segue.

"I know, right? Then again, it's hard to imagine anything being more exciting than the whole incident with the Sullivans last autumn." I take a sip of the lemonade Pax grabbed off the conveyor belt and sat in front of me, watching my sort-of friends for their response.

Along with the bittersweet liquid, I swallow self-loathing at making light of what happened to Pax's family. Hopefully he understands. That's how humans respond to Breaking, to anything out of the ordinary. With a disturbing amount of curiosity and an equally horrifying lack of empathy. Still, Pax's presence intensifies the distaste coating my tongue at having to mimic the typical reaction.

"True. It just about overshadowed both last year events!" Monica's black eyes sparkle with good humor.

"I know. I mean, Partners dying and their kid Breaking gets everyone's attention normally, but the way he *killed* her? All the blood on the television news?" Val's response is hushed, and the boy at her side watches her lips move the entire time.

So Tommy *is* Broken. I don't dare look at Pax, unsure that I'll be able to contain my emotions if I watch him trying to harness his own.

"Well, they told us it wasn't anything to worry about. Like we couldn't catch it or anything." Monica's always been a bit more fearful of diseases than everyone else. We used to take turns counting how many times a day she ducked into a wasteroom to wash her hands.

All of the sudden, even though they're sitting here discussing what happened to Pax's family like they would talk about the weather, I miss them so much it hurts. Pax's presence eases my isolation, like Lucas's did, but my relationships with them also contain certain pressures.

The pressure to keep one another alive, to figure out what we are and how to stop the Others from leaving the Earth a burning pit when they leave. Then there are the romantic expectations that rose out of nowhere with Lucas's and Pax's respective arrivals, like the way ivy crawls over the side of a house. It's beautiful, and desirable, but sometimes it's cloying and too much to handle. Pax and Lucas are my friends, but they can never be only my friends. That's what I miss the most, having these girls to hang out with without any expectations or complications.

I realize my silence has gone on a while when Pax nudges my knee with his. He hasn't spoken at all, whether he doesn't trust himself because of the subject or he's afraid they'll realize something's amiss if he calls attention to himself, I'm not sure, but I've got to keep going. "Poor Tommy."

Breath stales in my chest as I wait for one of them to take the bait. To my surprise, it's the previously silent boy who responds. His limpid gaze reflects more suspicion than expected. "Poor Tommy?"

I recognize my mistake right away, the empathetic statement of loss, but it's too late to turn back now. "He was a little boy. It must have been interesting, to see what happened."

"That's why he Broke. The Others took him right away, and people can't feel anything after they Break." The boy squints at me, the defensiveness in his gaze making me squirm.

Pax grabs my leg this time and squeezes, a silent signal to sit still.

"She's just saying it's too bad that he won't grow up, Vincent. Even if Tommy didn't know what happened." Monica, full of loyalty as always, comes to my rescue.

Vincent shrugs, sucking the last of the cola from his glass and making slurping sounds with the straw that set my teeth on edge.

"I remember being surprised to hear he Broke; when we saw him on television, he looked fine. I mean, a little shocked, which is to be expected, but not

Broken." They probably don't know anything else, but we have some more time so it's worth trying to dig deeper.

Val squinches up her face, trying to recall the television broadcast that burned a permanent memory into my brain the moment it flashed across the screen. "They took him to a Healer that night, right after. He wasn't declared Broken for a couple of days." She shrugs. "Maybe he couldn't stop remembering it all and finally . . ." She bangs the heel of her hand against her forehead, as though that's how a person's mind Breaks into pieces.

The motion brings a sick image of Greg, his head cracked open like an egg in a skillet, but it's not always that way. Mrs. Morgan's frantic desperation, Leah's turn to twisted pranks. Human beings can shatter from the inside out, as well as the outside in.

I'm grateful when some of the kids start to look down at their watches, an action that signals the end of free hour. Everyone stands, stretching their arms and legs as they shuffle toward the door. Val, Monica, and Vincent bid us polite farewells and leave Pax and me to trail down the street after them. We don't speak, and I wonder how Pax holds up after hearing all of that. He learned his loss of control not only made his fake parents die in a horrible murder-suicide, and not only did his unintentional actions leave Tommy an orphan again—but he Broke, too.

I wonder for a moment, though, if Tommy truly Broke. Emmy and Reese, two girls in our chemistry class last autumn, were taken away and called Broken, too, but they weren't, not that I saw. The Others took them because they suspected they had frozen some beakers and acted erratically. Lucas actually did it, and guilt over what happened to them weighs permanently on my heart. The Wardens also whisked away several Terminals with nosebleeds during a family Outing, but they didn't seem Broken, either. Those moments planted the idea that perhaps they don't kill the Broken, and it's never been far from my mind.

Not that the Others wouldn't kill perfectly healthy, normal people if they felt threatened—I'm sure they would. But the Others need the humans for some purpose, the same way they need this planet. What if the ones they call Broken are part of that plan somehow?

We pause a block from the Hammonds' house, Pax coming to a dead stop as though he simply can't make his feet go another step. His eyes are far away, looking perhaps into a past he wants to forget, or into poor little Tommy's uncertain future. When Emmy and Reese were taken, Lucas said that we couldn't help them until we figure out why the Others want us so badly. The destiny of humanity might lie in our hands, but as of now, the three of us have hurt far more people than we've helped.

"You go in, the Hammonds will be waiting to do Sunday Sharing with you."

Like Saturday afternoon movies, Sunday Sharing is a required family activity. I have no idea what I'm going to share, but it doesn't matter.

"What are you going to do?" My tongue itches with the need to tell him we need to move on, but now isn't the time.

"I'll go hang out with Wolf for a little while. I'll be back tonight, after they go to bed." He won't look at me.

"Pax, it's not—"

"My fault? You keep saying that, Summer, but it doesn't make it true."

25.

Pax returns well after the Hammonds are in bed, and long after I start worrying he won't come back at all. His clothes are dirty and he stinks of the outdoors, but once he changes and slides into bed, the familiar cinnamon and apple smell of him wafts around me. He doesn't talk, and after what happened earlier, I'm not sure that trying to push it is the best course of action.

With the lights off, the sound of his quiet breathing drags down my eyelids. It creates a transparent blanket, because even though it can't protect me, the familiar sound and smells in this room warm me. Part of me wishes we could hide here forever, forget about the Broken people and the Others and beings like Cadi and Griffin, tortured and locked up somewhere in the Others' control.

Even if those things could be ignored, I could never forget Lucas.

The longer we lounge in Portland, snuggled in a cozy bed with hot showers and a pantry full of food, the less satisfied I feel. I've done what Pax asked, and come to Portland to learn what became of the Sullivans' son.

We learned he's Broken, and now it's time to find Lucas, to move forward and figure out what to do next.

I don't say any of this aloud, no matter how the words fight for a place on my tongue. Pax is in pain. It won't hurt anything to wait until morning.

"What do you think happens to them? The Broken?" His voice scrapes out the words, hoarse as though he's spent the day yelling instead of walking alone in the Wilds.

"I don't know."

I relay the story of Emmy and Reese, which Pax hasn't heard until now, and he's quiet for a few minutes afterward. When I tell him about the Wardens' offering at the Outing, how the pink dust made my Cellmates bleed and be taken away, he tells me the kids in Atlanta had experienced the same thing.

"And you said with Mrs. Morgan, the Others used a different word? *Disposed*?"

"Yes. But they also told the humans she was Broken—they just used that word between themselves. So that doesn't really tell us much." I itch to reach out for him, to try to offer comfort, but Pax and I don't work that way.

A heavy sigh wheezes from deep within him, whooshing out like he's trying to expel all of the bad feelings eating him alive. I know because I've sighed like that before, as though getting rid of the air in my lungs could somehow cleanse my entire life.

"I know we don't have any proof, or reason to believe they don't kill the Broken, Summer, but I need to believe it's possible, at least for now."

"I think it's possible they keep them alive." I would never lie to him, even if he begged.

The truth is we don't know, and there are enough questions surrounding all of the Others' actions on Earth and the planets they destroyed before this one to make me question everything.

***

Pax leaves the house before me in the morning, sneaking out to go check on Wolf again while I endure breakfast with the Hammonds. I'm supposed to meet him in the park after Cell to decide what to do next, but it's time to insist we figure out how to find Lucas. There's no reason to go to Cell, really, since we found out about Tommy yesterday, but Pax still wants to. I'm not sure if he's thinking about more clues, or craving something resembling normal, no matter how scary and ugly it can be.

Halfway down the front walk, a yellow mouse darts across my path. I yelp and nearly fall, tripping over my tennis shoes as I stumble onto the grass before it dawns on me that it's probably not, in fact, a mouse.

Not that I'm particularly familiar with mice, but they're likely not yellow. And shouldn't be inside the boundary.

"Griffin," I hiss, realizing I sound like an idiot talking to the yard. "Get back here and tell me why you're spying, or so help me, I'm going to stomp on your little mouse tail."

He runs from behind a bush, clambering up my pant leg and clinging before I can make a move or shake it off. I bite back the squeal threatening to erupt and manage to grab him by the tail. In my palm, the abnormal yellow mouse with huge purple eyes smiles at me, I swear, the second before he pees on my hand.

This time I do squeak, probably sounding a bit like an actual mouse myself, before flinging him away from me into the yard. After a quick glance around to confirm no one is going to report a Broken girl prancing about and talking to herself—no one would believe there's a mouse inside the boundary, not that a person would speak to one if it were—I glare in the direction he scampered off.

"Stay away from us, Griffin, unless you want to help. We're not goofing around. And if you make waste on me again, in *any* form, I'll eat you for dinner."

He doesn't reappear on my way to school. I wiped my sticky palm on the grass, but still go straight to the wasteroom to wash it clean before heading to opening block. It's strange, after all these weeks, to sit in Cell blocks. Nothing has changed: the Monitors give the same lessons, the kids talk about the same useless things, lunch is the identical chicken and fruit salads I've eaten every weekday for over ten years. The whole day feels as though I'm trying to breathe underwater but have forgotten how. The life I had before last autumn doesn't seem real, like a dream that was stolen by morning sunlight.

My stress level builds slowly all day, but it's not until lunch that I realize I haven't overheated once. It's like my ability to control my fire hands has emerged without my noticing. Now that I think about it, I haven't had a major loss of control of the heat inside me in weeks; the only times it's even threatened to escape is when Pax looks at me like he wants to kiss me. Which, in spite of the distance he keeps between us, happens far more often than I want to admit.

We join Val, Monica, and Vincent in the eatery, but it's a struggle to put food into my belly, even after weeks of not having enough to eat. We shouldn't be wasting time here; Lucas has waited long enough. Not that I have any idea where or how to find him, but we've got to start figuring it out soon. As we're leaving the eatery, Pax and I hang back, taking our first opportunity to be alone since this morning.

He smiles, which should make me feel better after his reaction to yesterday's news, but it doesn't. It makes him look like everyone else, and the sight sends a shudder straight down my spine.

"How's your day?"

"It's fine, I guess. I don't like being here. It's creepy now that I know it's all controlled. Like they're hollow people being marched around by imaginary strings." I grimace. "I saw Griffin this morning, by the way. He was a mouse. He peed on my hand."

"What? Where?"

"Outside the Hammonds'."

A light twitches on in Pax's eyes. "What did he want?"

It twists a worry in my gut, though I'm not sure what or why. "To irritate me, I think." I pause, thinking a minute and wondering how to get Pax to tell me what he's thinking. "For someone who acts disinterested in us and our whole situation, he sure is around an awful lot."

"We're going to need a lot more than three questions to figure that guy out," Pax grumbles.

"Like a lifetime or four, most likely. I don't know, I told him to stay away unless he wants to help us."

304

Pax's jaw clenches. "We need answers, and he has them. I know it."

After Cell, we go to the park for free hour to check on Wolf. A steady drizzle keeps the kids indoors, and the clearing is deserted. A light breeze spreads ripples across the pond's surface, swirling the faint combination of jasmine and cinnamon apples around us.

"Summer, I'm going to suggest something that's going to sound insane, and you're going to say no without thinking, but I'm asking you to consider what it could mean before you do."

His statement catches me off guard. He's obviously been thinking about whatever it is for a while, since he's had enough time to decide the idea won't appeal to me. Curiosity swells and I nod, trying to prepare my face for not reacting like he expects.

"I want answers, and we're never going to get them running and hiding."

The extended pause frays my nerve endings. "Pax, please. Spit it out."

"I think we should kidnap an Other and question him."

My attempt at controlling my expression fails as my chin drops toward my collarbone.   "Pax . . ." I trail off and take a deep breath, remembering that he's my friend and I should take the time to think about what he's saying. A good five minutes later, nothing but the word *impossible* has crossed my mind. Pax waits the entire time with his hands clasped in front of him, eyes on Wolf, who pees on every tree and bush in the vicinity.

"Even if we could get our hands on an Other—which we can't, since we don't know where to find them and they're never alone—have you missed the part where their minds are connected? If we snagged one, I seriously doubt he'd answer any questions for us, to start with. For another, his mind would be a beacon, telling every single Other on Earth exactly where to find us. Not to mention, one wrong move, one accidental look in his eyes, and a single Other could cause so much pain he'd be the one capturing us."

"You're not even considering it."

"Not considering it? Pax, did you hear anything I just said? Those aren't just reasons I invented because I'm afraid! The worst possible thing that could happen is for one or both of us to get caught before we find Lucas and Deshi, before we can pool our power and find out what kind of threat we pose."

"This from the girl who's been desperate to convince me for months that we're the ones who can save this planet. Now you want to cower in the corners, looking for your boyfriend instead of making a move. We need information, knowledge. We're never going to get anywhere without it."

I take a deep breath, trying to ignore the million cuts his contemptuous tone just sliced in my heart. He's hurting and desperate. I've been there, and I lashed out at people being kind to me, too. Once I've calmed down and am sure my voice won't wobble, I try again.

"I don't disagree that we need to know more, but Cadi said we'd be more powerful with all of us. And if we're going up against them, we're going to need every last bit of power we can get. We *need* Lucas and the real Deshi."

The wind picks up, howling through the trees and turning the late afternoon colder. The sun drops toward the horizon as we sit in disagreement, both unwilling to budge.

Free hour is almost up, and I trudge back to the Hammonds' alone, Pax staying in the park until we can sneak him into the house. When Mr. Hammond goes into the kitchen for dinner, I let Pax in the front door. He creeps upstairs while I eat roast beef with peas and applesauce with a family that, because of an unfathomable protective spell dropped over me by a half-breed from another planet, thinks I'm their daughter.

Pax and I get ready for bed in silence until finally, I can't take it anymore. "I'm sorry about Tommy, I am. I'm sorry about Mrs. Morgan, too, and the Sullivans. And Emmy and Reese, and the kids who inhaled that pink dust on accident. But getting ourselves locked up or killed isn't going to help any of them."

Pax sinks onto the edge of the bed, dropping his face into his hands and massaging the bridge of his nose. His dark brown hair falls over his forehead in a tousle that begs to be brushed back. Instead I crawl up on the window seat, drawing my knees up and hugging them to my chest. He doesn't look at me for a long time.

"It makes sense. We have to take care of ourselves first." He sounds like a robot saying programmed words he thinks I want to hear.

"It's not only that. Those events already happened. They're done and in the past and we can't fix them. The only way we can, I don't know, honor their deaths or disappearances is to fix the future. We need a real plan, Pax. Not some half-baked idea of catching an Other and making him talk."

He smiles at me, but it's not slow or teasing. It's worn thin. "You said when they had you tied up, you wondered for a minute if you couldn't get inside their heads, too—cause pain, find things out. What about that?"

The very idea makes my limbs tingle. Fear and anticipation fight for prominence in my blood. "I *do* think that might be the answer, or at least part of it. Or it could have been, before they realized we have our own places in their tunnels. They're probably already figuring out a way to combat us, and honestly, they've had years of practice guarding their secrets. We haven't. And even if I wanted to try, my alcove is bricked off. Which means I can't even get into the rest of the hive."

"Or you don't want to try." He spits out the words as though they're poison.

Heat boils in my belly, begging to burst through my chest and mouth and out of my hands. He is making it very, *very* hard not to be angry. In his attempt to assuage his own guilt, he's trying to force me to share it, not realizing I'm already stooped under almost more than I can carry. I see all of this objectively; I know he's upset about the situation, not with me. But I'm still getting mad.

Without answering, I turn away from him. Pax perches on the edge of the bed, hands curled tight around the comforter, as stiff as a tree. Minutes pass before my conflicted core settles down enough to allow sleep to wash over me.

In the morning, Pax is gone.

26.

At first, I'm only a tiny bit worried, figuring Pax cured his restless angst by going to check on Wolf before the day began. We didn't decide what to do today, but I'm not attending Cell. Even if we're just going to sit in the Wilds and not talk, we're leaving the boundary. The longer we spend here, the tighter my nerves wind. After yesterday, they're about to snap.

I go down for breakfast because stirring up trouble in the final couple of hours doesn't seem like a good idea, but when the Hammonds shoo me out the front door I wait ten minutes, then sneak back up to my room while Mr. Hammond is shut in his office and Mrs. Hammond cleans the kitchen from breakfast.

I try to ease my anxiety by packing for the next leg of our journey, stowing extra clothes for both of us, blankets, and some toiletries until there's no room left. Then I flip the comforter so the navy blue faces up, hiding the evidence of Wolf's presence. Still, Pax doesn't return. The idea that he would leave me here alone frays my confidence, but I can't believe it's possible. He knows our best chance is together, even if we don't agree on how to go about things.

After a couple hours of pacing and stomach cramps, I've had enough of waiting. My anger returns, aimed at my supposed friend who would leave me here to stress and worry all day without an explanation. It's one thing to need some time or space, but it's quite another to leave without a word.

Hot from the inside out, and closer to losing control than I've been in weeks, I grab the bag off the bed and sling it over my shoulder. It knocks a pillow to the ground, and even though it seems like a silly thing to rectify, I'd rather not give the Hammonds anything to wonder about if they look in this room tomorrow. They probably won't think anything of it, since somehow it's always okay when I'm here and also when I'm not, but things are changing. We've hurt enough people with our carelessness.

Sighing, I drop the bag and fall to my knees to retrieve the silver pillow. A piece of paper catches my eye under the bed, out of place and strange in this place. I must have knocked it off in my sleep:

Summer –

I understand your side of things, I do. But I can't leave Portland or move on without knowing for sure whether Tommy is alive or dead. Without that knowledge, there's nothing for me to fight for. You can't

help, and I'm not mad. I think I know someone who can,
though. Don't worry. I'll be back soon.

Panic roars in my ears like gallons of water rushing over rocks. He could be out there looking for an Other, or maybe finding one and getting captured. He could be injured. And he probably has Wolf with him; maybe he's hurt, too.

When I calm down enough to form an actual thought, my brain settles on the question of who on Earth he believed might help him with his stupid, reckless plan.

The options are seriously limited. There's no one who would help who *could* help.

Except Griffin.

Once the name hits me in the face, I know it must be him. The thoughtful spark in Pax's eyes yesterday when I mentioned that Griffin was still keeping tabs on us. The Sidhe's natural inclination toward mischief and his endless amusement at watching our escapes and near failures suggest he would help Pax find an Other just so he could delight in the aftermath. He might have his own reasons for wanting to see us challenge the Others, but we can't depend on that. We can't depend on him.

We can only depend on ourselves, and now Pax and Wolf are out there, in danger, and I don't know where they've gone.

All I know is that I can't just sit here.

Taking care to not get caught, I steal through the Sanctioned City of Portland to the boundary in the park. There's no time to waste looking for a place to cross, so I ignore my instincts and reach a stick through the fence, pressing the button to open the gate. It's amazing how easy it is to find now that I know they're in the same place in every city. Or at least in Danbury and Portland, but the Others do have a penchant for uniformity.

On the other side of the boundary, my eyes scan the Wilds as the opening clicks shut behind me. It looks pretty much like every other part of the Wilds, and in spite of the fact that Pax and Wolf are missing, being back out here feels right. It feels like I can breathe again.

The bag drags my shoulder down, but switching sides every once in a while helps. Unlike when I left Des Moines laden with supplies earlier this winter, I have two good legs and it's not snowing. Plus, walking for hours a day, weeks on end, has turned my legs into ropy muscle. Still the problem remains, I'm walking to nowhere.

When the sun reaches a high point, even though its rays are too weak to warm the afternoon, it makes me slow to a stop. Half the day has passed with no results to show for it, but I don't know what else to do. A scream borne of helplessness gathers in my throat, begs for release, but even alone in the Wilds I don't dare let it loose. The Others could be anywhere.

Pax's story about where the Wardens took him last summer, where they imprisoned him and Deshi, makes me realize I *do* have a destination. They ferried him to a building that sounded exactly like the one where they took the Morgans and me outside of Danbury. Maybe there are buildings like those outside each Sanctioned City.

I bite my lip, trying to remember how long the rider sped through the Wilds that night, but it's no use. My mind was not on my surroundings at the time. But a black glass building waits in the Wilds outside of Portland, and if I was looking to ambush an Other, that's where I would look. That's where Pax went, I'm sure of it.

Now that the sun has crested and begun to fall, at least I know I'm stomping in one direction and not in circles. The thought of Lucas and me, of our inexperience with navigating that first night we went looking for Cadi, almost makes me smile. We walked in a huge loop before we realized all of the hours spent memorizing star charts could help us stay on a straight path. The memory burns, and for a second I stop, tempted to leave and go after Lucas on my own. But I don't know how to travel out of winter without help, be it from Pax, the Spritans, or the Sidhe. None of who seem able or willing to assist in reuniting me with Lucas.

When Wolf bounds toward me through a clump of bushes, panting and wild-eyed, I can't help the relieved smile that takes over my face. Tears gather, revealing how much terror is pent up inside me. It's not the time to give in to them, but for a moment, with my arms around Wolf's neck, I admit to myself how scared today has made me.

Of finding Pax. And of not finding Pax. About what I might have to do to get him out of a situation he foolishly let Griffin lead him into—for there is no doubt in my mind that Griffin was instrumental in taking my friend away from me.

"Good boy, Wolf. Good boy. Do you know where Pax is? I know you do."

I stand back, keeping my eyes trained on my dog, who looks as though he'd rather not go back the way he came. There's no telling what he's witnessed today, but if it frightened him, then that's all the more reason we need to hurry.

"C'mon, Wolf. Find Pax."

His mismatched eyes regard me for several minutes, flicking from my gaze into the Wilds and back. Finally he makes that agreeable chuffing noise and turns. Every few steps he stops, checking behind him to make sure he hasn't lost me or to sniff the underbrush. It's not long before he slows, pressing closer to the ground. Then Wolf stops, emitting a long, soft whine. His gaze shines with what would be concern if he were a person, making me wish again that he could talk. His eyes slide from me to a spot up ahead, perhaps through the next clump of trees.

This time, he lets me take the lead, pressing close to my side as I take hesitant steps forward until voices melt from the silence.

"Please, just tell me what I want to know. I don't want to do this anymore."

"You should have considered that before luring me out here."

The first voice, pinched and edged with trepidation and impatience, belongs to Pax. The second, honey-coated and pleasing, is the unmistakable voice of an Other.

The clearing comes into view as I crouch down and peer through some evergreen branches. The scene steals the breath from my lungs and sinks a boulder into my hollow stomach.

Pax has really done it. He's found an Other.

The alien leech sits at the base of a tree, arms tied behind him and a blindfold hiding his penetrating black eyes. His Warden uniform is torn and what is probably blood—it looks black from here—is dried on his mouth and forehead.

Bile froths into my throat at the sight of the damaged captive. Unless it's Griffin's doing, then Pax injured him trying to get the answers he craves. And Griffin is nowhere to be seen.

I reconsider that thought when a bright yellow snake catches my eye. It watches Pax and the Other with violet eyes, tongue flicking between its lips. If Griffin didn't have his snake body wound tight around a tree branch, I would have pulled him down and crushed his head beneath my boot. He's an observer now, nothing more, leaving Pax to deal with a situation he can't hope to control on his own. Which also means Griffin's actions—or lack thereof—are going to force me into that clearing.

At least Pax covered the Other's eyes. My mind is safe, at least for now. That is, if we're right that they have to see or touch us to cause pain.

Pax looks up, relief easing his defensive posture when I step out of the bushes, telling Wolf to stay. Wolf must have had enough violence for one day, because my dog remains on his belly.

"What are you doing here?"

In spite of my anger, or perhaps because of it, tears fill my eyes. Pax is okay. We're still together. All we have to do is undo what he's done. "You've been gone all day. I thought something had happened to you, so I came looking and then Wolf found me."

"You shouldn't be here."

"*You* shouldn't have gone to you-know-who for help." I shoot a pointed glare at the golden snake, which stares back without a trace of guilt. Some misguided sense of loyalty stops me from saying his name, in case the Warden doesn't know about Griffin's role in his capture. I lower my voice to a whisper. "We can't trust him."

The Warden smiles widely, the motion capturing my attention, and his smooth, water-spilling-over-rocks voice turns my head. "It's curious you would think to protect Griffin, but it's not necessary. I know he engineered my confinement, and he knows I won't do anything to earn him any attention for it."

The puffiness of his mouth causes a lisp that's almost funny. His statement flicks question after question through my mind, and even though I'm dying to know how he knows about Griffin helping us and why he won't rat the arrogant boy out, I won't give the Warden the satisfaction of engaging.

Instead I drag Pax a little ways away, still whispering even though there's no chance the Other won't overhear. "Have you lost your mind? Did you Break when I wasn't looking?"

"I wanted answers, that's all—"

"Really? It seems like what you want is to get us both killed." My assessment is harsh. Pax is grieving and full of guilt, but that doesn't mean he's not being selfish. This entire winter, I've done what he's asked, I've followed him thinking that once he found out the truth he would accept it and then we could move on. I didn't realize Pax never had any intention of moving past this moment.

Perhaps I've been stupid to trust that he ever planned to help me find Lucas or help us devise a way to rescue the people of Earth from their overlords. But then memories struggle forward—ones of Pax's heat-filled eyes locked onto mine, that slow smile, the way he pushed me to believe in my own ability to survive. I sigh, unsure of which person he is or if it's okay if he turns out to be a little bit of both. "Did he tell you anything?"

He shakes his head. "No. Nothing."

"So you hurt him."

To my relief, embarrassment floods his cheeks. At least some part of him knows this isn't right. To torture someone—even an Other—who is defenseless makes us no better than them.

And we are. No matter if half of our genes came from them, we *are* better. We have to believe that, or at least I do, otherwise the question of whose side we belong on rears its ugly head and I have no good answer.

"I had to, and I'm not sorry. They hurt you. They took away Tommy . . ." Pax trails off. Maybe he knows the excuses remedy nothing.

"We have to let him go, and we have to get out of here before he alerts the Others."

"He hasn't yet," Pax rushes to assure me. "If he had, they'd be here by now."

"Maybe not, but all they have to do is realize he's missing and they can locate him in minutes, Pax. Minutes." I narrow my eyes. "How far are we from the black building?"

He tries to hide his surprise that I figured it out.

"You mean the Observatory Pod," the Warden interrupts, still lisping.

When we look back toward him, he grins. Black hate wells up inside me like a fountain of ink, even though this particular Other has never done anything to me. I swallow hard, ignoring him, and wait for Pax to give me an answer.

"Not far," Pax admits.

"Which means when he does decide to ask for help, they'll be here in what? Ten minutes? We need to get out of here."

"She's right, you know. It's not that I do not desire to answer your questions—although I admit I have no reason to do so—but the Prime's controls in my mind would make it difficult at best. We are the perfect open books to our commanders, and the perfect vaults to those who would try to learn our secrets." The Warden's voice softens, laced with sorrow or something very like it.

He appears to be a teenager, perhaps a few years older, and every bit as handsome as they always are, even with black blood crusted against his chin. I wonder, not for the first time, what they actually look like inside these humanlike shells. The Others who tried to refresh me in Danbury referenced not being able to enhance hearing in human bodies, and Chief proved their ability to shape-shift, if only for a limited amount of time.

I cross the clearing to the Other, watching his breath catch when he hears my footsteps. Like he's afraid.

"Althea, who smells of jasmine. Pax here gave me quite a beating, but I had to allow it. Chief wants you in particular." A sorrowful smile ghosts his lips again, then he draws a deep breath of chilly air and leans his head back against the rough bark.

What he's saying dawns on me in that instant. He's been stalling all day, taking Pax's abuse and refusing to answer questions, biding his time.

Waiting for me.

27.

The second I realize he's told them where we are, I step forward and wrap my warm hands around his forearm. The Other jerks backward, trying desperately to twist out of my grasp. He must have heard the tale of what my hands did to his friends back in Danbury, and the beat of his heart pounds wildly against my palms.

It's not my intention to burn him, or melt his arm the way I did those Wardens before. Instead, I close my eyes and open my mind, waiting for the instant connection that happened when I touched the Other in the Cell last autumn.

This experience feels different, mostly because there's nothing to see. Before there were images, I could see everything that happened in the hive, but now only words filter through the blackness. They're soft, hard to make out at first but grow louder by the moment. It takes a second to realize it's because I walled off my alcove. It's blocking my ability to see what's going on, but not to hear.

"Natej has found them. The girl, too. Close. Send everyone—*everyone*." The voice belongs to the Prime, and it trickles dread down the back of my neck, leaving chills in its wake.

Cool hands cover my upper arms, shaking me, knocking me loose from inside the tunnels. My eyes feel ready to pop as they refocus on this world and find Pax's worried gaze.

"What happened?"

"Never mind. They know where we are and they're coming right now."

"The Broken are not dead. Not all of them." The Warden—Natej—utters the two sentences in a quick whisper, and at first I think I haven't heard him correctly.

Pax whirls, striding back and hauling the unruffled Other to his feet. "What did you say?"

Natej grimaces in pain, gritting his teeth. "I thought since your trip to Portland is going to end in your deaths, you might as well have one of the answers you've been searching for."

The words stop Pax and me in our tracks, and before they can rearrange into something resembling coherence in my brain, the rest of the Others are here.

They fill the Wilds, denser than the trees. They circle the clearing, muscles taut as they wait for instruction on how to bring us in. I'm not sure there's even any point in fighting, but Pax raises his hands and starts an impressive windstorm before I can move.

Leaves and branches whirl through the air, a big limb knocking at least four Others backward in a heap. They're on their feet again before I can blink, racing at Pax, ready to tear him limb from limb with their bare hands.

I raise my own palms without thinking, push the heat rising into them with all my might. Fire lands on three of the four Others heading for Pax, igniting their clothes and hair. They drop to the ground screaming, but the rest of the Others don't pause, even when some are taken out by flying debris.

Dirt rains on the burning trio out of nowhere, putting out the flames and allowing them to heal. At the edge of the clearing, Pamant stands with a grim smile on his perfect, evil face.

They've brought an Element to the fight; the only answer is to run. We can't stand against him, not with only the two of us. It doesn't even matter, because two against more than two hundred isn't a fight, anyway. Our only chance might be to travel. The bracelets would keep us together, but there's no way I can get to Pax in time, not the way they're rushing toward us.

Three Others land on Pax, and the storm sweeping around the clearing like a twister stills in an instant. My will to fight dissipates, and when I reach into my center to find the heat, there's nothing there but defeat. Wolf leaps on the pile of men struggling to keep Pax down and his hands out of commission, but one of the Others flings him away into the trees.

A sob catches in my throat as four or five pairs of hands pin my arms behind my back. In the distance, behind the circle of hard, beautiful, exquisitely painful Other faces, a shaggy yellow wolf jumps on my Wolf, and they tumble into the foliage. When they don't come back, I am thankful to Griffin for doing this one nice thing, luring my dog away to safety.

The Others slam me down onto my butt in the dirt. They secure some slippery, clear mittens over my hands, then do the same to Pax. Our backs press against each other's, and the solid reality of him makes me feel better, but also worse. Whatever they've slid over my hands feels thick and cool, like mud or glue, and a familiar energy thrums against my palms. It's Spritan, and the realization further batters my hope. The Others must have figured out how I escaped their clutches before and had Cadi construct bonds that trap our powers.

To test the theory I look for the heat, and with the last of my energy, try to push it into the gloves to melt them away. A strange sensation meets my attempt; it feels like the slick restraints grow colder, open jaws made of ice and swallow the fire whole.

The Prime emerges from the cluster of Wardens, unharmed but looking slightly ruffled. Dirt smudges his cheeks and pieces of torn leaves stick in his thick blond hair. Anger flashes in his black eyes, and I look away, determined not to give him easy access to my mind, but that quick glance tells me he's run out of patience.

"I've decided that, even though you are two mere half-breed children, it is unwise to continue to underestimate you. That is why I've brought every available asset to ensure you will not escape." The Prime's voice caresses me, soft and intimate despite the anger boiling inside it. The effect makes me want to scream. "We have plans for the two of you. This has been an interesting exercise, but the time has come to learn what you can do, and then put an end to this annoyance."

He walks over and pats me on the head, smiling when I jerk to the side to avoid his touch.

"We'll be with the two of you shortly. Sit tight." He turns away and strides toward a group of Wardens, ordering them around the clearing.

Some Wardens come over to double check the security of our bonds then leave us alone while they tend to their wounded. The worst affected have fallen unconscious while they heal—the ones I burned and at least a couple Pax hit with a tree branch.

The scene in front of us, the fact that I'm tied and bound inside some kind of gloves that prevent me from using my power, all appears a little like a dream. It can't be happening, not after all we've been through; we can't have been subdued with such ease. The Others wander about, dragging injured comrades onto those floating cots and sending them flying back through the Wilds, probably to the black building—the Observatory Pod, as the Warden called it. They murmur quietly among themselves, with the largest cluster of bodies surrounding Natej, the Other Griffin and Pax kidnapped.

"Are you okay, Summer?"

Okay? The Others caught us. They're going to poke around in our minds until they learn what we can do with human veils. Then they're going to kill us.

It's over. I am definitely not *okay*.

"I'm not hurt, if that's what you mean." None of this is what Pax wanted, I know, but at this moment it's hard not to blame him for our predicament.

"If you're waiting for me to apologize, I'm not going to do it. I did what I had to do."

"Fine. Could you just shut up, then?"

"I didn't want you to get hurt, though. I never wanted that," Pax whispers, defeated. "But at least we found out about the Broken. That's something."

With the heat trapped in my core, steam builds up, ready to pour out of my ears. Fighting with Pax isn't going to help anything, but I'm as pissed as I've ever been, apology or no, knowledge or no. What good does knowing about the Broken do if we're dead?

I breathe in and out, concentrating on calming down. A small worry that I'm going to overheat and melt from the inside out without a way to release the boiling anger pushes against my attempt to quell the panic swirling like a whirlpool in my gut.

An unnatural, purple-eyed rat scurries from the underbrush and over to us. Griffin. The sight of him brews a dual reaction of hope and irritation. He's part of the reason we're in this mess, and after everything he made clear when he led us to Portland and his actions since, I don't trust his motives. His little rodent feet scurry over my wrists, sending the immediate response to my brain to jerk away. I grit my teeth and stay still, willing to accept his help, if that's what he's offering.

Nothing happens at first, but then Pax's arms relax and his hands pull away from mine.

And the Others notice what's happening.

Pax yanks away from me and stumbles to his feet as Griffin the rat scurries out of the clearing. A sudden resurgence of will to escape, to run, to be free jolts me out of my stupor. Lucas is out there waiting, and Deshi has endured Other captivity for months. Our secrets are their secrets, too, and we can't give up. I want out of here. We have to get away.

Except my hands are still bound. My powers remain trapped under the slippery mittens, slick with my sweat on the inside but perfectly undamaged.

The Others run in a pack toward us, and Pax bends at my back. A sob catches in my throat. There's not enough time; we're not going to make it. "Hurry and let me loose. Get these gloves off!" Alarms ring in my ears, warning that the small opening provided by Griffin's unexpected help grows smaller by the second.

I feel a tug at my wrist and hear the snap of threads. My bracelet.

"I'm sorry, Summer."

Pax springs after Griffin, who's now a golden bird with unhurried purple eyes gazing down at the fracas as though he's viewing a family Outing to the park on a special weekend. Nothing out of the ordinary.

Pax left me. And he took my bracelet.

At least fifty Others stay, surrounding me in a circle, while the rest crash through the underbrush in search of Pax. I don't know if they're aware of Griffin's involvement. Natej certainly knows but claimed he wouldn't tell.

Anguish tightens my chest, making it hard to breathe. The return of crushing loneliness, the utter despair at being abandoned, washes through me, stabbing grief into every pore until my eyes don't work. My muscles ache.

The mass of Others who went into the Wilds after Pax return empty-handed.

Two of them grab me by the armpits and hoist me to my feet. My body, limp with defeat and dejection, drags between them. In the Wilds, surrounded by hundreds of Others, I have never, ever felt more alone.

28.

They sit me on a giant chair made of smooth, black granite. The mittens that covered my hands in the clearing have grown, molded up my forearms and over my elbows. Those two factors combined ensure I won't be melting myself out of this situation anytime soon, no matter how soaked my clothes get from the uncontrollable sweat.

I've been alone for hours, it seems. Enough time to struggle with staying calm, not enough to prepare myself for what's coming. Long enough to go over what happened again and again, but not to find a way to exonerate Pax. He could have stayed, but he didn't.

He left me. Like he left Deshi, and Tommy.

It's my fault for believing that because he regretted those things he'd be made of stronger stuff when things got bad again. But he chose Griffin instead of me. Pax ran away, and if the past is any indication, he's not coming back until it's too late.

So I've used the time to prepare myself for the inevitable. As much as anyone can ever prepare themselves for torture and death. One thing being with Pax has taught me, the thing that remains true after everything, is that I am strong. The last miniscule chance I have is to somehow prevent them from getting the answers they seek. Without the knowledge of what exact kind of threat we Dissidents present, I don't think they'll kill me. Or they might.

The memory of the searing pain, the unbelievable surety that my brain was bring ripped into pieces, lands in my stomach like a bag full of scrabbling bugs. Ko and Cadi have endured this for months. *Months*. And they haven't given up our most dangerous secrets. They're stronger than me—there's no doubt about that. But I can hold out for a while. I can give Lucas a little more time. Time for what, I have no idea. To stay alive, I guess.

When we left autumn, Lucas and I agreed that we didn't think we could hide forever. That running wouldn't buy us anything but time, and it hasn't. We agreed to do it because we wanted those hours, those days, to maybe figure out a new plan. Only the time we earned wasn't spent together, and now I can see it was wasted altogether.

The missing him is so horrible right now, it's almost worse than the knowledge of what's coming. Maybe it is worse because it's always with me, and when the Others step out of my mind, they allow moments of relief, no matter how brief.

They dragged me through a room identical to the one the Others used in Danbury to refresh Mr. Morgan's and the Healer's memories. We went through a door at the back, exactly like the one Mrs. Morgan disappeared into, the one she never came back out of.

I'll probably never come out, either.

A quick inventory of our abilities reminds me what the Prime knows, what he doesn't, and what he can't. Most important—maybe the one single thing that cannot be revealed—is our ability to wake up the humans to what happened on their planet. We can't control it yet, but if the Others learn what we can do, we'll never get the chance to free humanity and bring them into the fight for their planet.

The door bangs open, slamming against the cold, stainless steel wall and admitting what appears to be my torture team for the evening: the Prime and his two children, three Wardens, and a slumped but conscious Ko, whose navy blue eyes spill love and sorrow into my heart. I use my mind to put my veil knowledge into a trunk inside my walled-off alcove, lock it, and swallow the key.

The Prime sits in the only available seat besides mine. The Wardens block the door, holding Ko's arms, while the Prime's still nameless son and Kendaja flank their father. With the exception of Kendaja, their faces

335

are taut, stoic masks, but experience has taught me it's possible to rattle both the Prime and his erratic son. I spare a glance at Kendaja's beautiful, glee-contorted face and a hot poker of fear stabs my heart. Her unpredictability makes me fear her more than the rest, and when I meet her glittering gaze, she pants harder.

"You could save yourself the pain and trouble, and tell us what we'd like to know." The Prime's eyes are flat, not flashing and angry the way they were earlier. Like he's determined to not let me wrangle emotion from him.

"What is that exactly?"

"I would like to know what abilities you and the boys have inherited from your Elemental parents, nothing more."

Just everything. Nothing more. "Haven't you had Deshi here for months? Why don't you already know?" I'm stalling, but this has been a nagging curiosity. They've been able to study Deshi, so why is the Prime still so curious about the rest of us?

He narrows his eyes, seeming to consider his answer.

"Answer the question," Chief butts in, unable to control his irritation with me another moment.

I seem to be able to get under his skin with relative ease, though I've never been able to figure out why. "What's your name?"

He doesn't answer. In the silence, Kendaja giggles again then clicks her tongue against the roof of her mouth until my nerves can no longer bear it.

"If you tell me your name, I'll tell you what we can do." It's a lie. I want nothing more than a few extra moments, although I admit the longer he refuses to tell me, the more curious I am.

His eyebrows shoot up, but nothing comes out of his mouth.

The Prime's lips twitch into a snarl. "This is ridiculous. Your playing games with this girl is going to get us nowhere, Zakej. His name is Zakej. Now, tell us."

Zakej. Somehow I expected it to be embarrassing, or for there to be an obvious reason he doesn't want to tell me, but now it seems to have been nothing more than a piece of information to hold out of my grasp just because he can. There must be a reason the Prime's son hates me in particular, and I would give just about anything to know what it is. Perhaps it is simply spilling over from Fire to me, since she rejected him in favor of my human father.

He strides forward, and when I close my eyes to avoid his gaze and the pain it will bring, he wraps rough hands around my neck. Zakej's fingers tighten around my throat, choking off my air supply, but he doesn't go into my head. There's no imagined pain, only real pain as he crushes my windpipe and my body panics without my permission.

As black spots dance closer and closer to the center of my vision, he drops his hand. My ragged gasping fills the small room, but it feels detached and far away, as though it's not coming from me at all.

"Talk. That was me being kind." Zakej's voice is similar to the rest of the Others', smooth and coated, but it's always held an edge of bitter rage. He leans down, bracing his hands on his knees so he can peer directly into my face. "It is not the same, in the physical world, when I enter your mind. It will hurt more. And the damage will be permanent," he whispers, like it's a secret between the two of us. He reaches out and runs his fingers through my hair, leaning close and inhaling. "It will be a shame to damage such beauty. Necessary. But a shame. I would like to put it to much more enjoyable use."

A new kind of fear trips through my blood, slams my heart into my rib cage. The implications of the statement suck all the moisture from my mouth, and the hard glint in his eyes say my terror-filled reaction is thrilling him in some way.

I clear my throat, coaxing sound from my scorched windpipe, and return his conspiratorial whisper with as much haughty confidence as I can muster. "We can control the elements with our emotions. I can light things on fire, Pax can kick up a heck of a windstorm, and—" Zakej's hand whips across my cheek, snapping my head back into the chair and exploding sparks in front of my eyes.

"We are already aware. Tell me what else."

"We can't do anything else. Except your mind control doesn't work on us, but you've surely figured that one out on your own."

With my lie, he reaches out and gently picks up my hand. Zakej runs his fingers over my knuckles the way Lucas used to, making me sick and hurt and full of longing all at once.

Then he's in my mind.

He laughs. "Oh, such feelings for two boys who both abandoned you instead of fighting to save your life. Those are a product of your weak human half, I assure you."

I grit my teeth, resentful of the prodding, windy presence in my head, but open everything except what's in the trunk. He can't get all the way in, because of my wall, and the feeling of him bumping into it rattles my teeth. The first few minutes help me understand a little more about how this works—he heard the thought about Lucas as it happened, but the trunk rests safe in my sinum, protected by the brick wall built of sheer determination.

Zakej pushes harder, toppling a few bricks inward as dust flies in my mind. When they hit the ground, it's as if someone slammed a fist into my jaw three times in a row. My head snaps back, pounding hard into the back of the chair. When the rolling black clouds clear from my sight, the Prime's son gives me a grim smile.

"Taking down that wall is going to hurt, I'm afraid."

The next two bricks that fall smash into my collarbone, and the crack reverberates off the metal walls. The third smashes my cheek. The fourth and fifth fall into my ribs, snapping them until they feel as though they're trying to stab through my skin. Screams of pain tear from my throat until it's raw, and I swallow a rusty tasting liquid that can only be blood. This can't be happening. The wall I built is made of mental strength, not real bricks.

But it is happening. Zakej is in my mind, battering the organ that created the barrier, slamming destruction through the rest of me.

The line between my brain and my body, between the realm of the hive and the physical plane, blurs and then dissolves until I am in both places at once. Inside my head. In the Observatory Pod. And there is nothing except pain.

It's hard to know whether the imaginary bricks crash through my body or Zakej beats me with his fists. It could be either. It might be both. It doesn't matter. Either way, the experience is not like before when we were in the tunnels. My bones are snapping, my face throbs, and one eye is swollen shut.

I can't sit up, but sagging only pokes what feels like a hundred knives into my lungs. I think I'm going to pass out, but I can't. I want to. I've never wanted anything more.

Zakej steps back after he's knocked down a big enough hole to walk through, nodding at his father. "Her sinum is open."

"We can find out whatever we want, Althea. I take no pleasure in hurting you, and I promise, if you cooperate, I will kill you quickly." The Prime's voice sounds slurred, probably a result of my damaged mind.

My ravaged body rejects the idea of enduring this kind of pain for days or weeks on end, but the sight of that tiny trunk in my mind, locked and safe, gives me a mental strength that should be impossible. Zakej snapped my bones, he pummeled bricks into my face, but he will not Break me. I raise my eyes to the Prime's and let him see my determination.

The act of defiance sparks the loss of control always lurking near his surface, and he is out of his chair and across the room in an instant. His strong, cold hands land on my left shoulder, ripping it out of place. The resulting shriek emerges without my permission but doesn't placate the Prime at all, and he rushes into my mind, ripping off pieces of my sanity as he goes.

Chunks of my brain shred under his clawing hands as he reaches deeper and deeper into my personal space. He tears memories of Val into snowflakes until they're so thin they'll never be the same. They feel false now, as though they were never real, that she was never my friend. The Prime has spotted my memory of the first time Lucas kissed me, and races for its happy glow, and even though I clutch at it and stumble backward, I know he's going to get it.

"Father!"

Zakej's voice reaches me like a bolt of lighting through a haze of clouds. I must have blacked out for a moment, but his command stopped the Prime from annihilating my memories completely. He's no longer touching me, but his chest heaves while he attempts to regain his composure. Fire more deadly than anything

I've ever created burns in his gaze, and although the hatred isn't personal the way it is with Zakej, it's powerful all the same.

He turns slowly, walking in deliberate steps back to his chair, where Kendaja pants and twitches, excited by the commotion. Once he's seated, the Prime reaches out to pat his agitated daughter on the hand. She smiles, a crazed, twisted expression that reminds me of Leah when Lucas first punctured her veil.

Kendaja is a violent, bloodthirsty animal on a chain. What will happen when the Prime allows her tether to slip from his fingers?

"She hasn't told us anything useful. You were going to render her useless." Zakej explains himself to his father, licking his lips nervously.

Render me useless. A snort escapes my nose. It shouldn't be funny considering the amount of pain it causes on the way out, but still I feel like laughing. Zakej doesn't care that I'm in pain or that his father almost destroyed my sanity. He intervened because he didn't want me to become useless.

"Quite right," the Prime agrees, straightening into a calmer posture.

"And there are different means at our disposal. To encourage her cooperation." Zakej's eyes flick to the doorway, to the Wardens and Ko.

343

My stomach sinks to the floor. All of the pain in my body—in fact, there exists barely anything besides pain in my body—goes numb as the Prime flicks his finger and the Wardens drag Ko over to where Kendaja hops excitedly from foot to foot, twirling in circles like a small child.

Ko's eyes lock onto mine at the last possible moment, before they turn him to face her. He'll have to endure her pain again. I have no way to know how many times he's gone through this before, for me. For all of us. It isn't fair, and I have the power to put a stop to it right now. He must see the conflict in my expression because he gives a tiny shake of his head. His lips don't move but his voice, kind and gentle, like a soothing caress, flows past my tumbled wall and into my mind like sunlight refracted on water.

I am not what's important any longer. My life means nothing, was for nothing, if you do not survive to fight another battle. This must happen.

Love coats the words until it drips from them, until the sheer force of their power squeezes my heart until it wants to burst open. Ko has never done anything but love, and the Others will punish him for it. Still, like Lucas and I did in the Wilds with Cadi, I will sit here and watch. Because the Spritans have made it clear

344

their sacrifice is a willing one, and they understand so much more about this fight than we do.

Kendaja wraps her spindly arms around his neck, holding him in place as she peers into his face. She coos, a strange sound usually reserved for women holding a new baby, and presses her cheek against his.

"A little kiss, magic man. Need, I need it. You'll be tasty, like love, I'll eat it. A last taste, one more kiss." She croons the words against his ear, holding him tight and swaying their bodies in an erratic rhythm. A shudder rolls through him at her words.

Kendaja leans forward and gently presses her full, rosy lips against Ko's. He screams, the sound muted because his mouth melds to hers, and his lower body flops and twitches for what seems like an eternity. Her arms squeeze him around the neck, tight enough that his head remains still as he convulses and moans.

She doesn't stop when he goes still, his frame limp, or when the light leaves his eyes. Her mouth doesn't lift from his until what can only be his brains leak from his ears in gray-gold lumps, sliding down the sides of his head and onto his shoulders, smacking the floor with sickening wet splats.

Once they stop oozing, she gently kisses the corner of his mouth. "That was nice," she whispers, and drops her arms to her sides.

Ko's body collapses into the mess on the floor, but screams still fill the room, bouncing off the walls and pounding in my head.

It takes a long time to realize that I'm the one screaming.

29.

I wake up in what feels like a tomb. Dark walls surround me on four sides, except for a door made of the same granite as the chair the Others tied me to during their interrogation. I'm assuming it's a substance that won't burn or melt, even though they still aren't comfortable enough to have removed the shiny, power-trapping sleeves on my arms. It gives me a small amount of satisfaction that my abilities still worry them even when half of my bones are broken and I'm unconscious from pain and horror.

Agony returns within minutes, and not just the stabbing ache in my chest and shoulder or the throbbing pulse in my face. Ravaging grief tears into me so deeply it feels as though my very essence is ripping in half. This must be what it's like to Break . . . they Broke me after all.

The thought sparks fear and I crawl inside my mind, inside my invaded alcove, and sob with relief when I find the trunk with our secret still locked. Back in my prison, the tears don't stop, even though every shuddering breath washes a fresh wave of pain through my shattered body.

347

"Would you stop that, please? It's annoying."

A girl's voice wriggles out of the darkness. Even though my eyes have adjusted well enough to make out the nearest walls and the door, my roommate's form soaks into the shadows, remaining hidden.

Her voice intrudes on a moment that should be private, sparking a kind of indignant anger that helps me forget everything else, if only for a moment. "Who are you?"

"Someone used to the peace and quiet of being alone."

I spent years and years alone and found very little peace in it. Quiet holds plenty of truth, though after my experience it's hard to believe anyone would choose it. Her tone annoys me, but it takes several moments to stir my scarred, debilitated brain into action.

"Well, I'm sorry. I'll put in a request for a new roommate first thing in the morning. I'm sure there's good service down here, right? Perhaps a daily debriefing where I can voice my concerns?"

Even though I intended sarcasm, the girl chuckles, and the sound rings familiar in my ears. I've heard it somewhere before—and recently—but my brain struggles to work properly after the beating I took. My fatigue almost tells me to forget it, that it doesn't matter. Nothing matters besides the trunk. I need to save my energy for that, not sparring with an invisible, smart-mouthed girl.

"You're funny."

"Thanks," I reply dryly. "I'll try to keep you entertained, since you're stuck with me. I doubt it will be for very long, though." My eyes slip closed and my voice slurs, ruining my attempt at a comeback.

"That's true. You don't seem likely to hold out very long. Then again, your friend surprised me with his stamina. At first. Perhaps you will do the same."

Curiosity wiggles past my pain, through my desire to be finished talking to this strange girl making light of my situation. "My friend?"

"The Asian guy? Deshi?"

"What's Asian?"

"Oh, for heaven's sake. You know nothing, daughter of Fire."

I don't ask her what heaven means or how she knows who I am because I don't want to annoy her with a million superfluous questions and have her ignore the important ones. Still, the word finds its place in my memory—*heaven*. It's in Lucas's note holder, in that little booklet of words.

"I'm talking about Deshi," she relents, sounding exasperated with my denseness. "Come here and I'll tell

349

you about it, *and* try to help with that horrid whimpering wheeze thing you're doing. It's annoying."

Crawling across the filthy floor toward her voice takes agonizing minutes, and when the girl's face emerges from the shadows, it strikes me. I should have recognized her laugh, and if not that, her careless attitude. In my current deteriorated state, it isn't until the female version of Griffin peers at me that it becomes clear.

"You're Griffin's sister."

She purses her lips. "His twin. Greer."

The girl introduces herself but doesn't extend her hand or seem all that happy to have someone to talk to, for that matter. "What's a twin?"

"You really *don't* know anything, do you? It means we were born at the same time."

The possibility of such a thing has never occurred to me, but the novelty wears off in an instant, replaced by the many problems crowding my life. There's no time for idle questions.

"Please, tell me about Deshi." It's almost too much to hope for, that he's alive and hasn't been tortured or tricked into divulging our secrets.

All at once, I know why he hasn't told the Others about what we can do. He doesn't know anything.

The Others got to him and Pax before they had time to meet, to brainstorm, and Pax didn't accidentally hurt the Sullivans until after he escaped from the Others. Deshi probably knows as much as I did before last autumn—that he smells different, that people don't see him for what he is, and that he can control the element of earth—but *not* that we can unveil the humans. Or perhaps he never guessed veils exist in the first place.

It's an odd realization, that a boy so like me remains so completely unaware. But the Prime must have run experiments on his brain, tried to map its abnormalities. Then again, the Others in Danbury tried mapping my mind to erase what happened to Mrs. Morgan, and it didn't work. Those abilities don't work on us, but even if they did, they can't get information out of his head that was never there to begin with. He's been held captive and hurt this entire time for nothing.

Greer's cool, soft hands surprise me out of my thoughts. She sets them on the bare skin of my neck, and even though her touch brushes my skin softer than flower petals, it causes me to wince.

"Hold still."

I wish turning to stone was an option, to stop both the pain and the immediate desire to flinch away from another being's touch. It's not, so I simply hold as still as possible, biting the inside of my cheek until I taste blood.

"Deshi has been here several months, but they can't seem to find what they need in his mind, even though he's cooperated. They gave up trying to force answers from him almost immediately." Greer's voice changes, pitching to a gentle tenor that matches the strokes of her fingers, which continue to smooth my skin as she talks. Underneath them, my bones shift and pull, causing pain before settling into a dull ache.

She's healing me.

A gasp escapes my control as she sweeps across my ribs, which hurt the worst, and I try to think of something to say, anything to take my mind off the pain. I manage to grind out a question through gritted teeth. "So, he's alive? And he's okay? What are they going to do with him?"

"I don't know. The only reason they haven't killed him yet is because Zakej convinced his father that he might be useful bait for you and the boys, but once they have all of you, that will be the end of it." She lifts her hands off of me and sighs, wiping a bit of perspiration from her brow. "There. I can't fix your face. They'd notice. And if they come back for you tomorrow—and they will—you'd better act good and hurt still."

No problem. Greer gives off the distinct impression she'd be happy to hurt me again for real if my acting doesn't live up to her expectations. "Why are you being nice to me?"

She shoots an exasperated look my direction, looking very much like Griffin. "I told you, the silence soothes me. You were making an awful racket, trying to breathe through those broken ribs."

Like Griffin, it feels as though she's not being entirely truthful about her reasons. Her attitude reminds me of my anger toward her brother for encouraging Pax instead of talking him out of the crazy scheme, and I scoot a little ways away. "I'll try to be less of a bother."

"That seems unlikely, given that your presence here has already affected me negatively."

"I just met you five minutes ago! How is that even possible?" Her flippant disregard for my pain should give rise to anger, but the plastic sleeves still trap the ability to let it loose, and honestly, I'm too tired to think about the energy it would take to get upset.

With everything that's happening, another Sidhe slipping offhand insults into normal conversation doesn't rate very high on my annoyance scale. Greer's face might be a copy of her brother's, but something kinder softens her cheeks and mouth, like maybe once she knew how to be happy, even if she isn't now.

Despite her claim that my presence bothers her, she continues talking. "Aren't you curious why Griffin suddenly decided to involve himself in your affairs?"

"Not really." I'm lying and she likely knows it. "Although if he'd kept his nose out of our business, I wouldn't be sitting here right now. And Ko wouldn't be . . ." I can't bring myself to say the word *dead,* even though not saying it won't change anything.

At the mention of his name, Greer recoils, purple eyes darkening to the color of grapes. "They killed him?"

Her voice cradles a strange mixture of sorrow and relief, a clash of sentiments, but an understandable one. It's horrible that Ko is gone, but after all he's been through, it's hard to imagine he's not better off.

"Yes." I'm suddenly scared she'll blame me, or think I'm horrible for sitting by and doing nothing. Why I should care what she thinks of me I haven't any idea, but even though I've only just met her, I do kind of care. I let it happen. She *should* blame me.

"Oh." Greer meets my eyes. "It's not your fault. I can tell you think it is, but this is the way he would have wanted it."

Silence rolls over our shared space, a welcome respite from talking about the thing I'd most like to not think about, and I pay quiet respects to the man—the Spritan—who saved my life more than once. When Greer speaks, her eyes are violet again and her voice holds more distaste than anything, as though speaking to me soils her tongue somehow. "What have you done with my brother, anyway?"

"*I* haven't done anything with *him*. Your brother is a menace. Whatever happens to him is well deserved, since he engineered this entire situation so he could sit in a tree and get a good laugh." I spit the words at her, venom at Griffin warring with the last image of him in my mind, when he saved Wolf, freed Pax, and got them both to safety.

And left me behind.

It's hard to know how to feel about the Sidhe boy. Which is how he likes it, I imagine.

"He didn't do it for a laugh." She pauses, seeming to reconsider. "Well, maybe he did, but not for the reasons you think. Griffin will return soon, and you can yell at him instead of me. We try not to leave for more than five or six hours at a time."

It seems impossible that I've been here for less than six hours. A lifetime has passed since the Others dragged me through the front doors. The building must come equipped with some sort of device that slows time.

I slump against the cool, granite wall, letting exhaustion and misery swish through me. "Why do you come back at all? I mean, you can get out, so why not just escape?"

Greer doesn't answer for a long time, so long my eyelids slip closed and the soft buzzing of sleep steals into my mind.

"We don't leave because of me."

Her soft answer startles me awake. "What?"

"Because I don't want to leave, and Griffin won't go without me. So we stay."

"Why don't you want to leave?" The idea strikes me as nonsensical. Who would want to stay with the Others when they could go? "How long have you been here?"

"Forever. Griffin and I were born here. Well, not in this particular Observatory Pod, though we've been held here since we were six."

"You've been in this holding cell since you were six?"

She nods, as though nothing about that statement should bother me. Or her. Which is crazy. I think of all the things the Others have done to me since they learned of my existence a couple of months ago, the terrible acts they've committed just today. How could she and Griffin endure that since they were children?

Greer smiles knowingly, as though she reads my thoughts, but there's no presence in my mind other than my own incredulity. "It's not bad, really. Griffin and I were the Others' first attempt at manipulating Sidhe genes into something usable when matched with their own makeup. It didn't work, which I'm sure my brother expounded on at some length—it's his favorite subject, after all—and they kind of forgot about us, I guess. The last time I saw one of them was our tenth birthday."

"How old are you now?"

"Eighteen."

"So why did he do it? Help Pax grab an Other?"

"He didn't help Pax grab just any Other. He helped him grab Nat." She closes her eyes for a moment, sucking in a deep breath as though she's steadying herself on a thin wire. "Did you . . . did you hurt him?"

"Griffin? No. I mean, if I could catch him I wouldn't hesitate, but—"

"Not Griffin. Nat."

Her question stops my mouth from running further down the wrong path, but it doesn't make sense right away. Then I remember when I grabbed the Other and heard the Prime's plan to ambush us. He'd called the Warden Pax kidnapped Natej. Nat?

"You mean Griffin wanted Pax to take that Warden specifically? Natej? Why?"

It's hard for me to wrap my mind around the idea that the Others have individual personalities. They've always seemed like identical copies of one another, each interchangeable with the next. The Others look alike, they act alike, they have no discernible interest in anything beyond their own agenda, whatever that might be. The sudden realization that they might actually be individuals stops my overwrought brain.

"Because he's the reason we don't leave . . . because I love him."

30.

"Excuse me?" I must have heard Greer wrong. She can't seriously love an Other.

A sad smile paints her lovely features, and she toys with a chunk of her golden hair, pressing it against her upper lip like a silky mustache. "It's stupid, right? I know."

"And does he . . . does he love you, too?" Breath builds in my lungs waiting for her response. It's important, the answer, though I'm not sure exactly why.

"He does, and he doesn't. Nat loves me, but not enough to break his bond to his species."

How does one break a bond with their species? If that's what Greer wants, she'll be waiting a long time, because it's not possible. Natej lives in the Other tunnels, or hive, or whatever it is. Cadi told us last autumn that they control every Other child's brain from the time they're born, and from what I've witnessed, Others don't question their loyalty.

Actually, until this moment, it never occurred to me that Others might have wants and desires that have nothing to do with the greater good of the whole. It's interesting—it presents at least the possibility that they could be divided. Except if Nat loves Greer—beautiful, alluring, sassy Greer—and the prospect of Partnering with her isn't enough to pull him free, then I'm not sure what would.

Then again, he did make that comment about not telling on Griffin for helping us. Did he do that because harming Griffin would sadden Greer?

She doesn't seem particularly upset as it is; she's more resigned than anything.

I heave a sigh, unsure of how to comfort her, or if she'd even want me to. "Boys make life harder."

A pretty laugh spills from her lips, surprise lighting her violet gaze. "Tell me about your boy troubles, Althea. I've always wanted a girlfriend to talk with, and Kendaja was never quite right, even before they encouraged her cruel streak."

I'm too tired to even shudder at the thought of the damaged girl as a child, and I'm sure I don't want to know what kind of encouragement they gave her to make her into the horrid specimen she is today. It's hard to imagine that insane murderer befriending Greer, even as children. Instead, my mind wanders to the autumn with Lucas. "Lucas was the first person I could ever talk to about how I'm different. He understood, because he's different, too, and . . ." I trail off, unsure how to explain what happened between Lucas and I, or if I even want to.

"And then something happened, and you were more than friends. This is an old tale. And what about the boy Griffin helped?"

"Pax. He's harder to like than Lucas, and he pushes me instead of trying to protect me, but I like that about him. It's like we're magnets, pulled together even though we try to fight it."

She grins in the dim room. "Those are the ones that get you. The hard cases. The ones you're not supposed to want but do anyway."

"How do you know anything about men, Greer? You've been locked in a granite prison for over half of your life."

"I like you, Althea. You're funny." She giggles again, reaching over to wipe a smudge of something off my chin. Probably blood. "My mother told us wonderful stories. Tales of true love and princes and dragons. And then there's Nat."

Her voice softens across his name, and no matter how it happened or the likely horrible end their affair has in store, she truly loves him. It shines in her eyes and under her skin. The bare truth of it makes me uncomfortable and sorry for her.

"Pax abandoned me. We were together, then Griffin got Pax loose, and the Others were running at us, and he just left." Tears fill my eyes but I swallow them, letting anger push them away. "He left me to face all of this alone."

"You can love people, and you can befriend them, but the only person you can ever one hundred percent depend on is yourself. It sounds like your Pax tried to teach you that by letting you stand on your own feet. And now you have to." Greer takes a deep breath and lays her head back against the wall. "That's the truth. But Ko and Cadi gave up everything for your four lives. They did it because they believed you guys might be able to save this planet. *Might.* But in order to even have that chance, you have to do it together. So chin up. He'll be back. Unless you die."

I could ask Greer how she knows that's the truth, but she doesn't open her eyes again or indicate any desire to continue the conversation.

Instead of asking any more questions, I copy her pose, letting my pounding head rest against the cool surface of the wall. Our breath fills the silence, and after a few minutes, she stretches her legs out in front of her. One foot falls against my boot, and even though it's silly, I swear warmth passes through the contact. Despite the fact that her brother used Pax to try to exact revenge on Natej for keeping his sister locked in this depressing place, I like Greer. She's forthright in a way her brother isn't, and a kindness hovers behind her sharp-edged wit. I think maybe she and I could be friends, if this world were different.

The knowledge she's passed on in this short amount of time is priceless, and her healing my snapped bones is a precious gift. They'll most likely kill me in the morning, so tonight I'll be thankful to have spent time with someone not intent on hurting me.

The last thing she said, about Pax coming back, sits in my palm like a promise I'm terrified to believe. Maybe not believing in it, giving up, is worse. Maybe it's better.

I close my fingers around the tiny scrap of hope, holding on tight.

***

The Others undo all of Greer's healing handiwork before noon the next day.

I actually have no idea of the time; black clouds have stolen hours or minutes, there's no way to tell. My ribs are splintered shivs in my chest; a second crack has joined the first in my collarbone. When the last bricks lining my alcove toppled, they smashed into my pelvis. Zakej wailed on my jaw again, at which point I passed out for a while, since that pain had never fully subsided.

The moment arrives, the one I've been expecting and dreading since I met Kendaja in my mind. She steps closer to me until her gleeful, frenzied face fills my field of vision. Drool trickles around the finger in her mouth, and I can't tear my eyes from her lips, wondering what it will feel like when the Prime orders her to press her mouth against mine, when she sucks the life from me.

Her father's voice flies over her shoulder, decimating the last of my resolve not to cry. My vision blurs and I swallow hard, unable to stop.

"While we work on unlocking that trunk, maybe we can start with a simpler question. Perhaps just tell us where your friends are. We will find them, young Lucas and Pax, and the length and brutality of their experience is in your hands, Althea. Tell us where to find them, and it will be easy. Continue to hold out, and your friends will continue to pay the price long after your body rots in the Wilds."

His threat hits me where it hurts, but lacks punch considering he's going to do what he wants with all of us, whether I cooperate or not. In response to my silence, Kendaja pops her finger free, then reaches out and grazes the skin at my hairline. Her touch burns hotter than any fire that's ever come from inside me, raising blisters as I bite down on my lip to keep from screaming.

Her nail slides down along the outside of my eye, pausing at my cheekbone. I can't see my own face, but the pain can only come from a cut like the one she gave Ko in the hive. Imagining my face split open gets easier as hot liquid runs down my cheek, into my mouth, and over my neck. She's not pressing buttons of agony inside my head, not now, but the exterior wound creates more than enough pain to cripple my faculties.

Kendaja twists, pinning her father with a beseeching look while she pants in expectation, spit dropping onto her chin.

He shakes his head at his daughter, whose shoulders slump. "In addition, we would like to know who has been helping you since Cadi and Ko have been made unavailable. Cooperate, and I promise to ask my daughter to lift that finger off your face as gentle as can be. That scar will be ugly enough as it is."

I refuse to betray Griffin on principle, and Greer because she was nice to me.

The rest of the afternoon passes in much the same manner. Much of it disappears into blessed unconsciousness. I have trouble talking through the shreds of the left side of my face. They brought Cadi in a while ago and had her mend the cut enough to stop the bleeding. It would, after all, be most inconvenient for me to die so soon.

She said nothing while she bent over me, blinking back continual tears. I know she would have removed the pain if she could, because everything in her body language said she would take away all of this if she had the power to do so. Those navy eyes held mine in a final, locked gaze, trying to communicate a message that never transmitted in full.

The gist of it seems to be that I should hold on. For what or who remains firmly in her mind. There's no room in my head for anything but hurt and a slip or two of loss and regret, so as she finishes I pretend to pass out again, letting my chin bob against my chest. Even if the ploy buys me only five minutes, it's a little bit of time to prepare for the next round. The trunk in my mind, where I stashed the one secret I can't let them have, has taken a beating. Zakej has been prying into that piece of my mind with pliers and hot pokers and anything else he can devise.

I'm jealous of how Griffin and Greer have been forgotten by the Others. Maybe Pax's plan would have worked. If we'd left the Others alone, lived in the Wilds with no intention of manipulating our genetics into a weapon, perhaps they might have forgotten about us, too, in time.

The fact that they don't have a clue who's helping us travel interests me. How many half-breed species live as part of the Other hive now, after their years spent hopping through space? The Others have a talent for mind manipulation, obviously, but they don't possess natural abilities to control or exploit the elements, work magic, or change perception or form. They desire to use the best qualities from the races they conquer and enslave to create some sort of super-Other, able to command a planet with the flick of a finger. To not only control a population, but to put down any resistance without having to fight.

That's how it seems to me, at least.

So it stands to reason that if there are half-Spritans such as Cadi and Ko, half-Sidhe such as Greer and Griffin, half-humans such as me—although granted, the humans don't have powers the Others want to steal, and Pax, Deshi, Lucas, and I were created without authorization—there must be more out there. Whether they survived is the question, I suppose, since Cadi did say many of the experiments failed.

"Wake her up. I'm done with this battle of wills. She's as stubborn as her mother, and it appears whatever powers they've inherited includes the Elements' ability to hold safe places inside them—a talent they're likely not aware even exists. She needs a different kind of convincing. We know what made Pamant cooperate, and the threat will work on her as well." The Prime's tight, angry voice makes fear writhe underneath my eyelids and into my heart.

"It didn't work yesterday." Zakej's irritated impatience attacks my bowels.

Yesterday they killed Ko. If they're going to attempt the same sort of torture a second time, there's only one person they could use. My heart stops as the Prime confirms the knowledge.

"She cares for the woman more. Cadi is the one who told them who they are. The bond is stronger. It will work." The Prime doesn't sound confident, despite his words.

"And if it doesn't?" Zakej snaps, his impatience evident.

"She will die in my mouth, I'll eat it, the fire it tastes good, like life, like strength," his sister responds, her voice lilting and soft and thick with thrill. "Like chicken."

Her maniacal giggles bounce off the walls, echoing, magnifying her madness.

"We do not know what will happen to the children's enchantments without a Spritan to control them." The Prime puts forward this offhand concern, ignoring Kendaja's erratic and horrible statement. It sounds more like morbid curiosity than anything, and Zakej's response confirms it.

"It doesn't matter. It would be better if their deaths do dissolve the protection. Nothing but good will come from their inability to hide among the humans, and if they can't travel, they can't escape. I say we kill the bitch no matter what happens."

"Wake her, Zakej. And you"—he points to two of the Others—"bring me the Spritan woman."

I open my eyes before Zakej can devise an evil plan to wake me. His look of surprise, followed quickly by narrowed eyes, amuses me and I smile. Which is almost worth it, even when he slaps me so hard my throbbing head smacks into the chair.

The sight of Cadi being walked in between two Wardens, so similar to the way Ko came to meet his doom yesterday, squashes any glint of pleasure from irritating Zakej. No tears fill her clear, dark blue eyes. They say, *Be strong Althea. Don't give in.*

I don't know if I can do this again. Watch Cadi suffer and die when all it would take to make it stop is to cough up that key and let them open the trunk in my sinum. They're going to find out what we can do eventually. Is Cadi's life worth postponing the inevitable?

369

There should be a way to protect the information *and* save Cadi's life. What makes her believe the humans, this planet, deserve to be saved? Why should we fight so hard for them? With all of the things I've learned about Earth over the winter, about war, all the facts gleaned from the stories they write and the way characters see this world, the answer remains hazy and uncertain.

Perhaps Cadi's worth ten times as much as all of the people on this planet put together. Maybe Pax and Lucas and I have been wrong, and our destinies lie with the Others, traveling from place to place, learning from our parents how to keep atmospheres happy and livable while our race destroys worlds.

But Cadi doesn't think so. Ko didn't either.

And it's not my call. Lucas and Pax have a say, and Deshi, if he wants one. I shouldn't make this decision alone, except alone is what I am. It's what I've always been, in spite of all of the nice notions of Cadi and Ko watching out for me, watching over me.

Alone, I've survived almost seventeen years. I've kept the Others away from our secret without any help.

"I think you remember how this works, Althea," the Prime taunts as Kendaja snakes her arms around Cadi's neck, licking her youthful red lips as her frantic eyes wait for her father's permission. The scene's pattern, identical to yesterday's, chokes off my air. "Answer my questions—all of them—or my daughter will turn the brain of the Spritan to mush. The very. Last. One."

Now, alone, I decide. I won't let Cadi die.

31.

"Stop."

The entire room freezes at my rasped plea. Kendaja's lips hover centimeters from Cadi's, stopped in midair at my word and a quick snap of the fingers from her father. The Prime cocks an eyebrow, a gesture that says he needs more than a single word if he's going to stay his daughter's gleeful, sadistic hand for much longer.

"I'll . . . I'll tell you what you want to know. About us. And who's helping. But I don't know where Pax went, and I haven't seen Lucas in months." Despair lodges a wad of wet paper in my throat, making it impossible to swallow.

"Yes, the boys did abandon you here. Is that what changed your mind?" Zakej asks the question.

The taunt turns his father's lips down in a distasteful frown. "It doesn't matter what changed her mind, and I am sick and tired of waiting for answers."

A flash of anger, replaced by a properly chastised expression, coats Zakej's face. For Kendaja's part, she sags with disappointment. My stomach unclenches when she loosens her grip on Cadi.

Their eyes turn to me like spotlights as they wait for me to follow through. I intend to, honestly, but now that it's time, the words are stuck between my heart and my mouth. It's as if that key, the one I swallowed to keep our secret safe, lodges in my esophagus. I'm so scared my arms are soaking wet with sweat inside the magic sleeves.

My eyes meet Cadi's. I find strength there, and draw a deep breath. "We—"

The door to the interrogation room bangs open, metal slamming against metal, interrupting my confession. It jerks me forward and elicits an immediate groan of pain when the motion wrenches the shoulder Greer snapped back into place last night.

It's a group of five Wardens, and there's something off about them. It takes a minute to put my finger on what's different, but then it hits me. Their faces squeeze tight; genuine horror snaps in their normally impassive obsidian eyes.

The Prime puts out a hand to stop them. "What is the meaning of this?"

The one in front, hard to distinguish in any way from his peers, swallows and shoots a glance around the room. He pauses on Cadi, then me, and licks his lips. "We should talk outside."

The Prime nods, beckoning Zakej with him out into the hallway. The Wardens exit in front of the two men. Kendaja and Cadi remain with me but both go silent, their faces slack. I realize they're listening to the conversation outside the door at the same instant I remember I can do the same, now that Zakej and his sister knocked down my wall.

Inside my mind, the faces and voices in the next room ring as clear as if they spoke right in front of me.

"What is it?" the Prime barks.

"Something's happening in Portland. We started getting reports from the Monitors, then the Administrators, then they came from everywhere."

"What is happening? Specifics!" The Prime's eyes bulge as blood rushes into his cheeks.

"They're shedding their veils. Many of them, and it's chaos. People are Breaking, they're confused. Some are dead, some are running. We need everyone. Now." The Warden gasps out his report. I'm not sure if he's panicking about what's happening or about having to report it to the Prime. Probably both.

How could this happen? I've only seen four people shed their veils, and I did it to three of them. Lucas did the fourth. The memories of Mrs. Morgan's desperate face, Leah's instinctive anger, and Pax's summer father snapping and killing his mother sliver my heart. If whatever's happening isn't isolated, things are going to spiral out of control, and fast. People could get hurt. Too many people.

Anger bubbles into my stomach, pushing heat into my limbs and toward my hands before I can remember the sleeves.

Except the sleeves are sloughing off, sliding past my elbows and wrists and onto the floor, like the pictures of snake skins in the biology textbooks. Regular bonds still trap my hands together and behind the chair, but my heat flows under my skin. A glance at Cadi reveals how it's possible; she winks at me even though she looks like she could dissolve into pieces any second.

I give her a forced smile then quickly melt the ties around my wrists, though I don't move from my seat. Kendaja stays within arm's reach of Cadi, not to mention the fact that the Wardens, the Prime, and Zakej stand just outside the door. It's not as though I'm free, but access to the only power I have to defend myself relieves some of the stress squeezing my lungs.

"Sound the alarm." The Prime and his son follow the Wardens away.

A bell peals in my head and echoes through the building, the same one they sounded the night Lucas and I escaped Danbury. I withdraw from the hive mind, focusing on this room and what can be done about my imprisonment here.

Not much. Kendaja makes no move to follow her father to Portland. Instead she leaves Cadi cross-legged on the floor and paces the room like a trapped animal might, back and forth between Cadi and her father's chair, over to me, to the door. Between that and her nervous tongue clicking, it isn't going to take long for me to lose my cool.

Cadi and I can't talk candidly with Kendaja here, even though it's not clear what she understands, but there's zero chance of reasoning with her. I sit still and try to figure out what could have happened in Portland, to figure out what to do now.

The same answer keeps blinking at me in loud, huge letters.

It has to be Pax. Or Lucas. Only the three of us have the capability to remove the Others' veils in human minds, but for so many to have happened at once is something new.

"Kill the magic lady, swallow the pain, drink, slurp. No answers, Fire girl, nothing told no quarter." Kendaja surprises me by breaking the silence.

Maybe I underestimated her autonomy.

No answer will placate her thirst for blood, or satisfy her desire to cause pain, so I simply stare at her.

376

She goes back to clicking and pacing, going nearer to Cadi with each turn about the room. Without the Prime or Zakej here to control her, Kendaja will eventually lose the battle with her self-control. It's only a matter of how long it takes.

It doesn't make much sense to not make a move when it's two against one. Cadi's pretty depleted, but she got rid of my plastic sleeves so her magic spell mojo still works. Kendaja might kill us both before we can get one foot out the door, but there's a pretty good chance she's going to kill us both the first chance she gets anyway.

I wait until Cadi looks my way again, then communicate my desire to take action as best as I can without words. I'm scared to use the tunnels with the Prime's daughter so close. Silent eye conversations will have to suffice, and Cadi's quick enough to follow my lead.

She doesn't disappoint me, tucking into a ball and rolling toward my chair the second I raise my hands and shoot fire toward Kendaja. It's stronger than I anticipated, the heat exploding across the small space and warming it to an unbearable temperature.

Kendaja's reflexes are excellent. She spins away from the blazes licking from me to her, though they do catch the hem of her black dress and crawl upward. She quickly falls to the ground and rolls, no longer aflame when she springs back to her feet.

She's fast. Too fast.

I avoid her gaze, grabbing Cadi by the back of her shirt, hauling the smaller woman to her feet, and shoving her behind me. Kendaja and I face off, except it's hard to stare down a woman you're afraid to look at. She flutters around the perimeter of the room, keeping as much space between us as possible but trying to get into a position to block us from the door.

A fight with a thing like Kendaja won't come out in my favor. No matter the horrible things she's done, or would delight in doing, I can't turn off that part inside of me that gets sick at the thought of turning the tables on her. She doesn't have to know that I won't, though.

She's heard the same stories as Natej and the rest about how Lucas and I damaged the Wardens in Danbury, how I burned her brother so badly he fell unconscious and Lucas entombed him, however temporarily, in a stream. It assuages my guilt that their wounds heal. It also makes it hard to believe we could ever beat them.

I ball the nausea over causing pain along with the sickening feeling of being left, the brutal torture, and everything else, then shove. Our enemy doesn't move fast enough this time, her hair catching fire along with her clothes. She falls to the ground and rolls clear of the flames, still calm and collected, from what I can tell. Cadi and I run past the fire and through the door.

In the next chamber, one filled with floating beds and refreshing equipment, air free of smoke and heat washes over us. Cadi coughs, the rattling noise shaking worry beneath my panic, but we'll have to take care of it later. The Others deserted the place when they left to figure out what's going on in Portland. I'm sure Kendaja won't be distracted for long, so I light everything on fire in this room, too, and haul Cadi one chamber closer to the outside.

"Althea, I can't go with you."

I stop and turn, my mouth dropping open to argue. Cadi's face, haggard and bruised, tells me she's tired. "I know it's hard, Cadi, but once we get out of here . . ."

I trail off because, once we get out of here, I have no idea what to do. Pax took my bracelet; I don't know where he went or how to get there. Griffin hasn't shown his face since last night, and Lucas could be across the planet. Tears fill my eyes, even though freedom waits inches away, but without anyone to share it with, the thought of it frightens me.

If Cadi won't come, I'm not sure I want to go out there. "Pax took my bracelet. The one Ko made."

My voice chokes on the words, which make no sense given our conversation, but for some reason that one act feels like a bigger betrayal than his leaving. I avert my eyes from Cadi, embarrassed to be crumbling emotionally at this ridiculous time, when strength should be flowing through me.

She takes two halting steps toward me then folds her sturdy arms around my waist. Only for a second, though, and then she pulls back and lifts my chin with a finger. "Here."

Cadi presses her palms together. When she pulls them apart, rainbow strands of thread—or something like it—twine together, braiding as they hover between her fingers. She secures it around my wrist, then sways back and forth, as though the effort has completely drained her. "Althea, I told you before I cannot leave for long. Because of their direct line into my mind, the Others would find me, and therefore you, too quickly. You need to go on your own."

"No. Not without you. I can show you how to build a wall, how to block their mind control at least for a little while."

"There are two things you must understand, child, so listen carefully. First, the ability to resist the mind

380

control of the Others is unique to you four and your Elemental parents. As you said, it is flawed, but no member of any species that I've known has been able to resist, even for a time. Second, you Dissidents need one another. Without Lucas, Pax, Deshi, and you together—all physically together—nothing can be accomplished. You cannot save Earth yourself, or with two or three. Time is running out. Reclaiming Deshi is already going to be difficult, considering—"

Cadi's face twists, mouth open in an O but no sound emerges. Her dark eyes stare over my shoulder, wide and filled with sorrow. Tears stream down her cheeks and drip off her chin like a river. I whirl around and stumble backward as Kendaja's finger stabs through Cadi's chest from behind, the nail poking through her thin shirt. A fountain of golden blood spurts from beneath it, and Cadi drops as though all of the bones in her body have suddenly dissolved at once. She doesn't move.

Kendaja's ravaged, blistered face and neck twist to me, and her smile raises the hair along my arms. "Fire is hot but I am not scared not scared, not scared of it," she coos. "I'll kiss the hot, Fire daughter."

It's the first time she's spoken directly to me without permission from her father, and the honeyed, happy voice spits nails into my ears. I look to the side of her, so she remains in my field of vision but can't lock on to my eyes and start chewing on my mind.

"Pretty girl, but not too smart, no, no not pretty smart." She takes a step my direction, then another.

"Althea!"

The voice spins me around, its familiar tone and warmth not changed by the stress weighing it down. At first, it's hard to believe the damage done over the last couple of days isn't causing my brain to play tricks on me, but then Pax appears, too.

He and Lucas stand inside the door of the black building, their faces grim, hands locked, eyes on me. And then they blow the place to pieces.

32.

Glass rains down as all of the windows explode simultaneously, from ones at the top of the building that reach into the clouds to the ones at the same level as my face. I fall flat on my belly and cover the back of my head with my hands, which end up cut and bleeding by the time the deadly shower passes. Scents of pine and apples, cinnamon and fresh snow, infuse the endless room.

Hands drag me to my feet, four of them, and I'm propelled toward the door, dragged between Pax and Lucas. Kendaja shrieks behind us, a sound more enraged than injured, and rushing feet crunch across the glass carpet.

We burst out into the early evening, surrounded by Wilds.

"Did you miss me?" Pax's hand squeezes tight on my arm, his eyes guarded despite his teasing tone.

"Took you long enough."

For now, we can tease. My feelings jumble into a hopeless knot at the sight of him. Lucas's hand freezes mine, the sensation so familiar and like home that it weakens my knees. It's as if I never let myself admit how much I've missed his steady presence until this moment, but now that I have, I want to curl up into a ball and cry for all of the days I've stayed strong.

"Sorry. Winter here was hard to find."

"Shut up." Lucas issues the hoarse command.

He turns, putting one hand out toward our pursuer and leaving the other wrapped around mine. A strange sensation washes through me, like nothing I've ever felt before in my life. My power leaves, flowing from my core and out through my hand, like always, but this time it goes into Lucas. Instead of feeling drained, it's doubled as more swishes back in the same way, into my center and back out, like a current in a river.

The hand held toward Kendaja fills with a jagged piece of ice, which Lucas flings at her. She dodges the projectile, but then the evening fills with them, winging at her like arrows loosed from a bow, and she dives behind a boulder to avoid them. The frozen daggers of ice smash against the rock, shattering into pieces on the dead, brown grass.

Lucas isn't done.

The sound of rushing water climbs into the air. A river emerges from the Wilds, wide and deep, running left to right through the clearing and right over Kendaja's hiding place. The rock must be smooth on the back side, and with nothing to hold on to, the coursing river carries her lithe frame from the clearing. She chirps shrill laughter, trying to twist her face to us and make eye contact until she disappears from sight.

Lucas doesn't lower his hand or turn my power loose for at least five minutes, until Kendaja has been ferried far enough to ensure us time to escape before she can find her way back. He drops his hand, turns to me, and crushes me in his arms.

They're cold, I'm hot, and his cool breath and pine scent swells my heart until it might burst open with the happiness of having him here. My arms heat up and squeeze tight around his neck, trying to merge our bodies into one being so we never have to be apart again.

"Ahem." Pax clears his throat, reminding me that he's here, too.

Lucas and I break apart, grinning like fools. Then his smile slips away, and he reaches out a finger to explore what is likely a horrific scar slicing down the side of my face. He starts to say something but I shake my head, biting my lip and holding his cool hand against my cheek.

I turn so we're both facing Pax, whose expressions march across his face too quickly to capture. Relief that we're okay. Anger at the damage I've suffered.

Irritation, perhaps at having brought Lucas. Worry that I'm not going to forgive him for leaving, even though it does seem now that Greer's suggestion that he had a plan might turn out to be right.

"What happened? The short version, because we need to leave."

"I took your bracelet and Griffin helped me travel to Atlanta, where I figured Lucas was since he wasn't in Danbury or Iowa or here. It took me longer than I thought to find him, since he was hiding, and then we came back. We couldn't take on a building full of Others, so we created a distraction."

"Created a distraction? By unveiling and probably Breaking half a city of human beings?! What were you two thinking? My life isn't worth that!" It's too much to believe, that more people will die to save me. Us.

"It was Griffin's idea." If Pax thinks that's any kind of defense, he's wrong.

"You mean you still haven't learned your lesson about listening to Griffin? After he started all of this by helping you grab Nat?"

"Who in the universe is Nat?"

"Could you two stop arguing for two seconds?" Lucas snaps. "This isn't helping anything. Althea, we didn't mean for things to get so out of hand. We were going to stir up a windstorm, maybe bust open the water filtration system, cause some trouble like Pax said you two did outside of Danbury." Lucas pauses, his calmness in the face of catastrophe working to slow my breathing, too. "But it didn't work. And then people seemed to really see us, so we wondered if Ko and Cadi were still alive. The humans got all agitated about our presence, and then Pax and I tried telling them to calm down, then I tried the talking in their heads thing, but there were too many to control. It didn't work." He runs his hands through his blond curls, poking my heart with memories.

Then something he said pushes through my muddled emotions. "Cadi!"

I limp into the Observatory Pod, the boys on my heels. When I get to the place where Kendaja dropped Cadi, she isn't there. The entire room is full only of echoes. In fact, the whole building could be deserted for the lack of noise.

"Althea, we've got to go." Lucas says softly, as though not to upset me.

"Cadi . . . she was here. Kendaja stabbed her in the chest. And . . . and they killed Ko yesterday. Because I wouldn't talk." My voice sounds faraway and flat, even to my own ears.

The boys exchange a glance, but I don't care. Cadi's gone. Even though she said she couldn't come with us, I was going to make her. It takes a minute, but I bury my grief for the millionth time in the past three days, take a deep breath, and face Lucas and Pax. Lucas looks worried, like I might fall apart any second. Pax is more wary, as though his main concern is that I don't blow up at him for his part in all of this.

Lucas takes a step toward me. "Griffin has a place we can hide while we figure out what to do next. We're supposed to meet him."

"No. We're not taking any more help from him. And we're not leaving until we fix what happened in the city. We *can* fix it."

"There are too many of them," Pax argues. "It won't work, and the place is teeming with Others. They'll catch us. We're stronger together, yes, but they took the Elements with them, too, and there's no way we can fight them, Summer."

There's a look on Lucas's face as though someone struck him. I grab his hand, begging him to understand. "Lucas, we can. You know we can. We fixed Leah, and earlier this winter I unveiled Brittany, remember her?"

He shakes his head slowly. "I agree with Pax, as much as it pains me. We have to leave, now, if we want to escape."

Anger hammers me like a dozen stones all at once. I jerk my hand from his, glaring at them both. "You two can do whatever you want. I've been here fighting to keep our secret from these people. I watched Ko die yesterday, and do you know why? So we could do what they think we can—help save this planet. I will not hurt it instead!"

The last sentence tears from my lips in a shriek, backing the boys up a few steps, and I march around them and outdoors. My feet find the direction I came from when looking for Pax, and the sound of the boys following me weakens my limbs with relief. Because we need one another, but also because I want to believe that deep down they agree that our job is to protect the humans, not to make their lives worse.

The trek back to Portland takes over an hour with Pax leading the way and me trying to hide how much walking hurts my ribs and collarbone. The gate into the park slides open at the push of the black button. Lucas grabs my hand again, forcing me to look at him. My jaw aches from clenching it so hard.

"Althea, think about it. If we go in there and start messing with people's minds, they're going to know what we're capable of. And everything you went through these past couple of days will be for nothing."

He's right. He's so right, but leaving them all confused and Broken and being sent off wherever people like that go strikes me as opposite of right. The weight of the decision of whether to save a few people or save them all on my shoulders—on our shoulders—sags me to my knees. It's too much responsibility. An entire planet, a race of people. I can't do it. Because of my silence, a race called Spritans was eliminated today. I don't want to be the cause of any more deaths, even if it means the Others know our secret. "I don't care. We have to try to help, no matter what it means for us."

Lucas nods, and after a moment, so does Pax. Something that might be love for them both warms me from the inside, like slurping hot soup on a cold winter afternoon.

In the end, our bravery means nothing. We skirt the edges of Portland, staying under the cover of trees or using buildings to block our presence, but there's nothing to see with the exception of a few riders and maybe three patrols of Wardens. They've contained whatever happened, carted off the Broken, or reset everyone's veils.

"We're too late." I can barely hear my own words.

"Let's just go meet Griffin and get out of here, Summer. We need to regroup."

"No. No Griffin." I hold out my arm and touch Lucas's wrist, adorned by my old bracelet. "We can travel on our own and stay together."

Lucas catches my fingers in his before I can pull away. "Griffin showed us a place that will be safe, at least for a while. And your dog is waiting there."

Wolf. I can't leave him alone because of my pride. If I really loved him I would, because the dog would certainly be better off without me, but my selfish need to let his fierce loyalty and soft, sweet face offer me comfort makes up my mind. I nod. "Fine. But we are done with him after this. We can't trust him. And he's infuriating."

They don't say anything, which I'm not stupid enough to assume means they agree, but sudden fatigue keeps my lips sealed. Fighting with them both takes too much energy, and to be honest, having a place to rest for a few days sounds better by the minute.

In the park, we find the gate into the Wilds standing open.

And our parents, all four Elements, stand guard.

33.

P ax, Lucas, and I stop in our tracks. We're silent, and so are the Elements.

The Prime steps around his most valuable assets, a grim smile stretching his face into a ghoulish mask. "You injured my daughter. That angers me."

It's on the tip of my tongue to mention that the damage done to Kendaja amounts to a fraction of what they've inflicted on me over the past twenty-four hours, but I bite back the commentary.

"Did you have anything to do with what happened in this City?"

The boys look away from the Prime, a smart move that I don't copy, though I do keep my eyes from meeting his. We can still protect our secret.

"It's *your* fault, what happened in Portland. Pax and Lucas came to rescue me, but ended up in town instead of in the Wilds. Since you had Ko killed, our invisibility was weakened. People realized they didn't belong and started to panic." My explanation has holes, but he's never dealt with a situation like this before, not on this planet, so what I'm proposing has to at least be considered.

"We will decide what happened later. In the meantime, the three of you will come with us."

I step back, sliding my right hand into Pax's as my left joins with Lucas. Power, strangely hot and cold, heady, flows between us. A maelstrom of pine, jasmine, apples, snow, cinnamon, and burned leaves lifts my hair into my face and coats my tongue.

The Prime's smile slips from his face. "Have it your way."

He nods at the Elements, who also join hands. They turn their heads simultaneously to face us, and I hold my breath.

Nothing happens.

"I said get them!" The Prime's shrill command sounds like a child not getting his way.

Pamant turns to his brethren. "You dare defy him?"

Are they not working together?

My mother shakes her head, frowning. "Do not do this, Pamant. I know what happened with your boy has changed your outlook, but—"

Pamant shoves a hand into her chest and Fire flies backward toward the electrified fence. She somersaults in the air, landing hard on the soles of her feet instead of crashing and getting zapped, but it still looks as though she's having trouble catching her breath. Before we can figure out what's happening, or who we should be fighting, Deshi's father pushes both hands our direction.

What feels like a solid granite wall slams into my chest, lifting me off my feet, sending me flying backward through the air. With none of my mother's grace, my back slams into a giant redwood trunk, knocking the oxygen from my lungs. The ground feels almost soft when my legs smash into it. Through my blurry eyes, Lucas appears, rocking on his hands and knees. I finally suck in a full breath as the earth quakes and rolls beneath my body.

Lucas and I crawl toward each other as the rumbling grows louder, until it sounds like a hundred riders race toward us at high speed.

"Where's Pax?" I shout over the din.

He looks around wildly, and when I follow suit it feels as if my spine twists into ten separate pieces. When I spot him, the pain from the torture and the tree fade into the background. "Oh, no."

The wall threw Pax farther than us, all the way to the center of the park and into some of the playground equipment. His body lies crumpled beneath a seesaw, and red blood pumps from a gash on his forehead.

Lucas grabs my hand and we stand, but another rocking quake knocks us back to our knees. Nearly screaming at the pain in my back, I swivel my head. A scene that can only be described as madness greets me.

Pamant continues to hold out his hands toward us, sending waves into the earth, commanding it to break into cracks. He's having a hard time keeping steady contact with his element, though, because the rest of the Elements obstruct his path. Fire, Air, and Water block his attempts successfully about every third push, even though when his power hits them they shudder and groan. Their hands are at their sides, like they're unwilling to use their abilities against one of their own, who they must love in spite of this current disagreement. Our parents haven't chosen our side, are not actively assisting us, but they *are* giving us the chance to escape.

The Wardens stand agape, watching the scene with the same horrified fascination coursing through my blood. Until the Prime yells something incomprehensible at them, forcing them into action. Our parents have no aversion to using their powers against the Others' enforcers, it seems, because the first ones to join the fray turn into fireballs. Clouds blot out the clear sky, accompanied by misty rain, the beginnings of a storm.

I turn away, unwilling to watch them destroy one another, and continue inching toward Pax. He still isn't moving, but I have to believe he's alive. Everything will be fine. When Lucas and I are about ten feet away, a huge shudder, one that lasts for minutes and rips trees up by their roots, thunders through the earth. Lucas and I curl around each other on the ground, holding on for dear life. The wrenching sound of tearing metal shoots adrenaline into my heart.

The jungle gym, at least eight feet tall, rips free from the dirt and topples, upset by a huge new crest pushing up beneath one side. It falls hard, smashing onto Pax's prone form.

I scream, finding strength from nowhere, and race toward him. It kills me that I can't reach him, can't touch him through the metal bars, and there's blood everywhere. A jagged arm of metal stabs into Pax's side, another through the meaty part of his shoulder.

Lucas lands next to me, the horror stamped on his face sending me into a spiral of dread so deep it's drowning me. A gasping fills my ears, and black swamps my vision until another round of shaking causes so much pain from my back that I wake up.

"Althea, stop. Stop! Get up. Help me lift this off him."

But we can't. No matter how hard we try, the jungle gym won't budge. It weighs too much, and the fact that it's putting pressure on Pax's body terrifies me that we're making it worse.

A fierce wind blows up from behind us, pushing me into the twisted metal at first. It reminds me of Pax, and sudden hope that he's okay, that he's using his power, springs tears to my eyes. Except he's not. His eyes are closed, and Pax hasn't moved a muscle since he landed here a few minutes ago. A lifetime ago.

The wind changes, swirling around my ankles and straight up from the ground. My loose, tangled hair reaches toward the sky, and Lucas and I have to fall to our knees and hold on to the metal toys to anchor ourselves to the ground.

The jungle gym lifts a few feet into the air.

I don't have to look to know what's going on, but I can't help it. The bright blue pinpoints in the center of Air's eyes meet my helpless gaze, the accompanying ache in the back of my head nothing more than a flicker after everything I've endured. Words infiltrate my mind, the reminder of my mental vulnerability rattling me.

Get him and go.

I nod, then turn back to my friends. Lucas and I lie flat on our bellies, both of us reaching as far as we can and wrapping our hands around an ankle. We pull Pax free, and the jungle gym slams back into the ground.

He doesn't groan. He doesn't move at all, but his chest rises and falls in a shallow motion.

"Where are we supposed to meet Griffin?"

"It's far, too far. We can't make it with Pax like this."

The frantic alarm on Lucas's calm demeanor scares me more than anything else that's happened today. We have to do something; our parents are fighting, but it's three instead of four. According to Cadi, only with all of them together are they more powerful than the rest of the Others, which means eventually they will be subdued. And they will be punished.

Now's not the time to worry about them. They know what they're doing, and we all know they're too valuable to be killed.

"Yes, we can, Lucas. We can make it. We *will* make it."

Without waiting for him to agree, I bend down and grab one of Pax's limp hands in both of mine. I tug hard, barely budging him. Then Lucas is beside me, his strong hands pulling on Pax's opposite arm, and we manage to move him.

Wind and rain slash through the park. Thunderclouds, courtesy of Lucas's father, darken the evening into a black night, interrupted by violent flashes of lightning. The rain increases until it's hard to see, and I think maybe the Others won't be able to guess which way we've gone.

Rain sluices down Lucas's face, flying off his lips like spit when he talks. "This way!"

He jerks his head backward, then strengthens his hold on Pax. Together we drag him across the engorged grass, water soaking my jeans up to my knees. It's over ten minutes before we see the pond, and Lucas stops at the edge. I can't hear anything over the pounding rain and cracking thunder, and barely register what's happening as Lucas bends and struggles to lift Pax over his shoulder then flings him into the pond, where he lands facedown with a splash.

"What are you doing?" I push at Lucas, trying to get his attention.

He shrugs me off and wades into the water, pulling Pax farther out. "Althea! Come here!"

I jump into the water, struggling to reach Lucas's side, and am grateful the water is shallow enough that I can touch the bottom. When I reach the boys, I can see a glinting circle in the water, barely visible underneath the raindrops dappling the surface.

Lucas shoves Pax down through the middle of the ring, then grabs my hand and pulls me under, too.

34.

On the opposite end of the portal, my head emerges from a much smaller pond, almost completely covered in ice. Pax floats nearby, faceup, still breathing.

Lucas bobs up beside me, spitting out water and gasping for air. "That was weird."

Wolf barks at the edge of the pond, then splashes in and grabs Pax by the collar of his shirt, dragging him out onto the shore. Lucas and I join him. Wolf licks my face, so clearly delighted to see me it takes some of the sting out of the disaster of this day. I push him gently away, and he eyes Lucas suspiciously while I bend over Pax.

"Althea, let's get him inside first. I'm sure you and he are freezing out here."

Of course, Lucas would be perfectly comfortable. But now that he mentions it, my numb, purple fingers register, along with Pax's blue lips and the water frozen in his dark brown hair. His face is gray, and it looks like his eyelashes are frozen to his face.

"Go inside where, Lucas?"

"Come on." He hooks his hands under Pax's armpits, looking at me expectantly.

My back screams at me as I crawl to my feet, joining the cacophony of aches and pains collected over the last day or so. Being slammed into that tree knocked something wonky, and I'll be lucky if my back isn't permanently damaged. For the first time, a house made out of logs catches my attention. The flickering of a fire glows through the windows, and a curl of smoke puffs from the brick column rising from one side. It looks impossible, so intact and functional. As though it couldn't exist in this devastated world.

Lucas follows my gaze. "Griffin says this place is safe, although now that the Others know someone is helping us that might not be true for very long. I get the feeling that guy will sell us out if a better deal comes along."

I think about Greer, about the way we sort of bonded in that prison, about how we might actually respect each other. What she said about her brother having his reasons for helping the three of us. "We'll have to hope he doesn't. Pax needs time to heal."

I bend down and grab Pax's legs, and Lucas and I walk slowly inside through ankle-deep snow, trying not to jostle him more than necessary. If only Griffin had found a perfect little hideaway where it's *warm*.

The inside of the place is as ideal as the outside. Furniture, rugs, what looks like a clean kitchen. If there's food in the cabinets, I'll sit down and cry.

We lay Pax on the couch. His ragged breathing worms anxiety into my stomach, and the fact that a freezing plunge and being dragged through snow hasn't woken him doesn't help. I put a hand on his forehead, smoothing the wet hair back. Lucas clears his throat, then offers some blankets he found in the bedroom.

"We should take these wet clothes off him first, get a look at his wounds."

"Okay." I pause, trying to hide the red warmth in my face.

"I can do it, Althea."

"No." Pax wouldn't want Lucas to take care of him. He wouldn't want me to, either, but we've been through so much together.

This is serious. Getting embarrassed over seeing his naked chest shouldn't factor in, especially since I've seen it before. I gingerly remove his shirt, biting my lip when I slip it over his shoulder and he groans. Lucas helps with his soaked jeans, which we have to peel down his legs. We cover him from the waist down since there aren't any injuries down there, and focus on his torso.

The wound in his shoulder goes clean through, but the blood weeps instead of gushing, and the edges are clean. It doesn't worry me, not the way the gouge in his side does. The hole opens below his rib cage, above his hip, and is still bleeding freely. I have no idea if the metal tore muscles or something more important. An organ, maybe. I don't like the way the skin is turning black around the wound, as though it's bleeding from the inside.

Lucas leaves again as I stare and fret, chewing a hole in the side of my cheek.

He returns with a kit filled with bandages and a bottle of the same antiseptic Pax and I found in the ranger's station in Wyoming. I dress the wound the same way Pax did Wolf's injuries, then cover his clammy, shivering body with more blankets.

The silence overcomes me; it's too complete. Lucas is here. Pax is alive. We're safe, even if it's only for a little while. We should be happier about the things that are going right.

In an attempt to do that, I smile at Lucas. "It's good to see you."

The heart-stopping smile that changed my life last autumn lights up his tired, lined face. "You have no idea. I've been so worried."

My hand goes to my locket, hoping for a vibration, for proof that Cadi survived Kendaja's attack and can tell Lucas and me what to do next. When nothing happens, certainty that the three of us are well and truly alone loosens my strength, drops me to the floor beside Pax.

The last thing Cadi said, might ever say, rings in my memory.

"Time is running out. Reclaiming Deshi is already going to be difficult, considering—"

Considering what, I may never know. But it doesn't matter. After everything that's happened this season, all that we've learned and seen, she's undoubtedly right about one thing.

Time is running out.

ACKNOWLEDGEMENTS

As always, a heap of people came together to make this novel so much better than it could ever have been with only me at the helm. My editor, Danielle Poiesz, who not only gently guides my stories in the best direction, but who calms my (frequent) bouts of authorly insecurity. Lauren Hougen, my copy editor, who asks the questions that never would have entered my mind, and by doing so, saves me piles of embarrassment later on. Nathalia Suellen, my brilliant cover designer, whose creativity and spirit are a constant source of inspiration. If you love *Winter Omens*, each of these ladies are as responsible as I am.

Again, I have to thank my family. Each and every one of you are beautiful people, and I feel blessed to share not only your DNA, but your lives. Particular thanks to Katie Martin, Kerstin Heinrich, and Kim Heinrich, who push my book into the hands of their friends and followers, and to my mother and my Aunt Cheryl, whose proofreading skills are invaluable.

I have some of the best beta readers and critique partners in all the land—a million thanks to Trieb, Kari, Diana, and Jen (the Amazing), along with of course Denise Grover Swank, who continues to amaze and inspire me with her stories and head for business. Also her ability to consume coffee and parent six children with little to no sleep.

Life would be decidedly less interesting and more isolated without my Twitter friends, who brighten my days, laugh with me, and are quick with support if that's what I need. It might seem strange to some people, but I truly wouldn't be where I am without you all.

Thanks, Mom and Dad, for your support not only in this endeavor, but in life.

ABOUT THE AUTHOR

Raised by a family of ex-farmers and/or almost rocks stars from Southeastern Iowa, Trisha Leigh has a film degree from Texas Christian University. She currently lives in Kansas City, MO, where she's hard at work on the remainder of the series. Her spare time is spent reviewing television and movies, relaxing with her loud, loving family, reading, and being dragged into the fresh air by her dogs Yoda and Jilly.

To learn more about Trisha Leigh, please visit her at trishaleigh.com.

Made in the USA
San Bernardino, CA
18 November 2015